# GOLD-SEEKING
## ON
# THE DALTON TRAIL

SLEDDING UP THE CHILKAT VALLEY

# GOLD-SEEKING ON THE DALTON TRAIL

## ARTHUR R. THOMPSON

**WOLF CREEK
CLASSICS**

ISBN 0-9687091-4-1

COPYRIGHT, 1900, BY LITTLE, BROWN AND COMPANY
ALL RIGHTS RESERVED
PRINTED IN CANADA

WOLF CREEK CLASSICS IS AN IMPRINT OF:

**WOLF CREEK BOOKS INC.**
BOX 31275, 211 MAIN STREET,
WHITEHORSE, YUKON
Y1A 5P7
WWW.WOLFCREEK.CA

ORIGINALLY PUBLISHED BY
UNIVERSITY PRESS • JOHN WILSON AND SON.
1900

TO

My Comrade of Many Camp-Fires

DEXTER WADLEIGH LEWIS

# PREFACE

AMONG my first passions was that for exploration. The Unknown — that region of mysteries lying upon the outskirts of commonplace environment — drew me with a mighty attraction. My earliest recollections are of wanderings into the domains of the neighbors, and of excursions — not infrequently in direct contravention to parental warnings — over fences, stone-walls, and roofs, and into cobwebbed attics, fragrant hay-lofts, and swaying tree-tops. Of my favorite tree, a sugar maple, I remember that, so thoroughly did I come to know every one of its branches, I could climb up or down unhesitatingly with eyes shut. At that advanced stage of acquaintance, however, it followed naturally that the mysteriousness, and hence the subtle attractiveness, of my friend the maple was considerably lessened.

By degrees the boundary line of the unknown was pushed back into surrounding fields. Wonderful caves were hollowed in sandy banks. Small pools, to the imaginative eyes of the six-year-old, became lakes abounding with delightful adventures. The wintry alternations of freezing and thawing were processes to be observed with closest attention and never-failing interest. Nature displayed some new charm with every mood.

There came a day when I looked beyond the fields, when even the river, sluggish and muddy in summer, a broad, clear torrent in spring, was known from end to end. Then it was that the range of low mountains — to me sublime in loftiness — at the western horizon held my fascinated gaze. To journey thither on foot became ambition's end and aim. This feat, at first regarded as undoubtedly beyond the powers of man unaided by horse and carry-all (the thing had once been done in that manner on the occasion of a picnic), was at length proved possible.

What next? Like Alexander, I sought new worlds. Nothing less than real camping out could satisfy that hitherto unappeasable longing. This dream was realized in due season among the mountains of New Hampshire; but the craving, far from losing its keenness, was whetted. Of late it has been fed, but never satiated, by wider rovings on land and sea. Perhaps it is in the blood and can never be eliminated.

Believing that this restlessness, accompanied by the love of adventure and out-of-door life, is natural to every boy, I have had in mind particularly in the writing of this narrative those thousands of boys in our cities who are bound within a restricted, and it may be unromantic, sphere of activity. To them I have wished to give a glimpse of trail life, not with a view to increasing their restlessness, — for I have not veiled discomforts and discouragements in relating enjoyments, — but to enlarge their horizon, — to give them, in imagination at least, mountain air and appetites, journeys by lake and river, and an acquaintance with men and conditions as they now exist in the great Northwest.

The Dalton trail, last year but little known, may soon become a much travelled highway. With a United States garrison at Pyramid, and the village of Klukwan a bone of contention between the governments of this country and Canada, the region which it traverses is coming more and more into notice. I would only add that natural features, scenery, and people, have been described faithfully, however inadequately, and the story throughout is based upon real happenings. Should any of my young readers pass over the trail to-day in the footsteps of David and Roly, they would find, save for possible vandalism of Indians or whites, the cabins on the North Alsek and in the Kah Sha gorge just as they are pictured, and they could be sure of a welcome from Lucky, Long Peter, and Coffee Jack.

# CONTENTS

| Chapter | | Page |
|---|---|---|
| I. | A Letter from Alaska | 1 |
| II. | Buying an Outfit | 7 |
| III. | From Seattle to Pyramid Harbor | 18 |
| IV. | The First Camp | 28 |
| V. | The Great Nugget, and how Uncle Will heard of it | 38 |
| VI. | Roly is Hurt | 47 |
| VII. | Camp at the Cave | 54 |
| VIII. | Sledding | 60 |
| IX. | Klukwan and the Fords | 69 |
| X. | A Porcupine-Hunt at Pleasant Camp | 77 |
| XI. | The Mysterious Thirty-six | 88 |
| XII. | The Summit of Chilkat Pass | 101 |
| XIII. | Dalton's Post | 112 |
| XIV. | From the Stik Village to Lake Dasar-Dee-Ash | 120 |
| XV. | Staking Claims | 127 |
| XVI. | A Conflagration | 135 |
| XVII. | Through the Ice | 142 |
| XVIII. | Building the Cabin | 149 |
| XIX. | The First Prospect-Hole | 157 |
| XX. | Roly goes Duck-Hunting | 166 |
| XXI. | Last Days at Pennock's Post | 175 |
| XXII. | A Hard Journey | 182 |

## CONTENTS

| CHAPTER | | PAGE |
|---|---|---|
| XXIII. | THE LAKE AFFORDS TWO MEALS AND A PERILOUS CROSSING | 192 |
| XXIV. | DAVID GETS HIS BEAR-SKIN | 201 |
| XXV. | MORAN'S CAMP | 210 |
| XXVI. | HOW THE GREAT NUGGET NEARLY COST THE BRADFORDS DEAR | 216 |
| XXVII. | AN INDIAN CREMATION | 223 |
| XXVIII. | THE PLAGUE OF MOSQUITOES | 231 |
| XXIX. | LOST IN THE MOUNTAINS | 238 |
| XXX. | WASHING OUT THE GOLD | 248 |
| XXXI. | DAVID MAKES A BOAT-JOURNEY | 256 |
| XXXII. | CHAMPLAIN'S LANDING | 264 |
| XXXIII. | ALONE IN THE WILDERNESS | 272 |
| XXXIV. | RAIDED BY A WOLF | 279 |
| XXXV. | A LONG MARCH, WITH A SURPRISE AT THE END OF IT | 289 |
| XXXVI. | HOW DAVID MET THE OFFENDER AND WAS PREVENTED FROM SPEAKING HIS MIND | 297 |
| XXXVII. | HOMEWARD BOUND | 306 |
| XXXVIII. | A CARIBOU, AND HOW IT WAS KILLED | 314 |
| XXXIX. | DANGERS OF THE SUMMER FORDS | 321 |
| XL. | SUNDAY IN KLUKWAN | 331 |
| XLI. | THE ROBBERS AT LAST | 339 |
| XLII. | PYRAMID, SKAGWAY, AND DYEA. — CONCLUSION | 348 |

# ILLUSTRATIONS

|  | PAGE |
|---|---|
| SLEDDING UP THE CHILKAT VALLEY | *Frontispiece* |
| PYRAMID HARBOR, PYRAMID MOUNTAIN IN THE DISTANCE | 26 |
| MAP OF THE DALTON TRAIL | 28 |
| A CURIOUS PHENOMENON BESIDE THE TRAIL | 89 |
| THE CAMP OF THE MYSTERIOUS THIRTY-SIX | 93 |
| "PRESENTLY SOME LITTLE YELLOW SPECKS WERE UNCOVERED" | 131 |
| CHILDREN OF THE WILDERNESS | 192 |
| RAFTING DOWN THE NORTH ALSEK | 265 |
| A HERD OF CATTLE. — YUKON DIVIDE IN THE DISTANCE | 267 |
| FORDING THE KLAHEENA | 325 |
| "SALMON BY THE THOUSAND" | 349 |

# GOLD-SEEKING

ON

# THE DALTON TRAIL

---

## CHAPTER I

### A LETTER FROM ALASKA

IN a large, old-fashioned dwelling which overlooked from its hillside perch a beautiful city of Connecticut, the Bradford family was assembled for the evening meal. It was early in February, and the wind, which now and then whirled the snowflakes against the window-panes, made the pretty dining-room seem doubly cozy. But Mrs. Bradford shivered as she poured the tea.

"Just think of poor Will," she said, "away off in that frozen wilderness! Oh, if we could only know that he is safe and well!" and the gentle lady's brown eyes sought her husband's face as if for reassurance.

Mr. Bradford was a tall, strongly built man of forty-five, with light-brown hair and mustache, and features that betrayed much care and responsibility. Upon him as treasurer had fallen a great share of the burden of bringing a large manufacturing establishment through two years of financial depression, and his admirable constitution had weakened under the strain. But now a twinkle came into his gray eyes as he said, "My dear, I hardly think Will is suffering. At least he wasn't a month ago."

"Why, how do you know?" asked Mrs. Bradford. "Has he written at last?"

For answer Mr. Bradford drew from the depths of an inside pocket a number of letters, from which he selected one whose envelope was torn and travel-stained. It bore a Canadian and an American postage stamp, as if the sender had been uncertain in which country it would be mailed, and wished to prepare it against either contingency.

At sight of the foreign stamp Ralph, — or "Roly," as he had been known ever since a certain playmate had called him "Roly-poly" because of his plumpness, — aged fifteen, was awake in an instant. Up to that moment his energies had been entirely absorbed in the laudable business of dulling a very keen appetite, but it quickly became evident that his instincts as a stamp collector were even keener. He had paused in the act of raising a bit of bread to his mouth, and made such a comical figure with his lips expectantly wide apart that his younger sister Helen, a little maid of nine, was betrayed into a sudden and violent fit of laughter, in which, in spite of the superior dignity of eighteen years, their brother David was compelled to join.

"Yes," said Mr. Bradford, "I received a letter from Will this afternoon. Suppose I read it aloud." Absolute quiet being magically restored, he proceeded as follows: —

RAINY HOLLOW, CHILKAT PASS, Jan. 9, 1898.

DEAR BROTHER CHARLES, — I am storm-bound at this place, and waiting for an opportunity to cross the summit, so what better can I do than write the letter so long deferred?

I have been as far west as the Cook Inlet region, and have acquired some good coal properties. While there I heard from excellent authorities that rich gold placers have been discovered on the Dalton trail, which leads from Pyramid Harbor to Dawson City, at a point about two hundred miles inland. I thought it best to investigate the truth of this rumor, and am now on the way to the designated locality, with an Indian guide and dog-team.

Now, as you know, I was able to take claims for you as well as for myself in the Cook Inlet country, by the powers of attorney which you sent me, but in the Canadian territory to which I am going the law does not allow this, and you can only secure a claim by purchase, or by being here in person to take it up.

I don't suppose you are in a position to buy claims; but it struck me, Charles, that it would be a grand good thing if you could leave that work of yours awhile and rough it in these mountains. You looked worn out when I saw you last, and you need a change. This is a rugged country, but a healthful one if a man takes care of himself, and nothing would do you more good than to take my advice and come. Why not bring the boys along? Too much schooling is n't good for growing lads, and they will lose nothing in the long run.

Come prepared to stay six months. I will write our friend Kingsley at Seattle in regard to your outfit, and will send him directions for the journey. Start at once, for I think there'll be a rush in this direction very soon.

You'll be surprised to find how comfortable you can be in your tent on the snow, even with the mercury below zero. Trust the directions I shall send to Kingsley, and I'll guarantee you against the suffering you read of, most of which is the result of ignorance and carelessness.

I send this letter out by an Indian who leaves here to-morrow.

With love to you all, I am,
Your brother,
WILLIAM C. BRADFORD.

"Uncle Will's a brick!" exclaimed Roly, promptly. "Of course we shall go." Whereupon Helen burst into tears because she was not a boy. David managed to preserve outward calmness, but his eyes sparkled as he thought of the wonders he might soon see. As for Mrs. Bradford, she scarcely knew whether to be sad or glad. She was willing to believe her enthusiastic brother-in-law would not urge his own relatives to face unreasonable dangers. But to think of being separated from them half a year! After all, she could do no better than leave the matter to her husband.

"Well, Charles," she said quite calmly, "what do you propose to do?"

David and Roly trembled in their seats, while Mr. Bradford regarded them thoughtfully.

"I am inclined," he said at last, "to think favorably of Will's proposal, so far as it concerns myself."

At the word "favorably" both boys jumped, but when they heard the last of the sentence they looked very wretched and crestfallen. They did not understand the whole of Uncle Will's letter, but there was absolutely no doubt that he had suggested their coming. David ventured to remind his father that they were both a year in advance of most boys of their age in their school-work.

This argument appeared to have weight with Mr. Bradford. He reflected, too, on the many youthful adventures of his own in the Adirondack woods, which he had often narrated in their hearing. It was but natural that they should wish to go. He was bound to admit that they had studied carefully and well, and had fairly earned an outing. David, dark-haired and brown-eyed like his mother, had reached the age of rapid growth. He was shooting up like a weed, and his face was paler than it should be. Roly was of light complexion, and round and ruddy. Nothing more could be desired of him in the matter of health, yet his father knew how keenly he would feel the disappointment if his brother were permitted to go and he were left behind.

Mr. Bradford looked inquiringly at his wife. "Can you spare them?" he asked.

It was a hard question. Mrs. Bradford would have preferred to keep the boys at home, but she had travelled extensively before her marriage, and knew the value of travel. She was ambitious for her sons and wished them to have every advantage. But it was not without a flood of affectionate tears that she consented at last to let them go.

The matter being thus decided, at a sitting, as it were, the evening was spent in a study of maps and guide-books; and long after they went to bed the boys lay awake and talked over their good fortune.

## CHAPTER II

### BUYING AN OUTFIT

IN spite of his brother's injunction to hurry, Mr. Bradford was unable to complete his arrangements until the first of March.

Mrs. Bradford's heart sank as she said "Good-by" to the three, and watched the train roll away in the distance. Helen, too, was quite awed by the solemnity of the occasion, but was comforted by the thought that her Aunt Charlotte was coming in the absence of the rest of the family.

As for the boys, their spirits rose quickly after the sad moments of parting, it being the pleasant privilege of youth to see only bright skies ahead, and to leave responsibility to wiser brains. Neither David nor Roly had been beyond New York, and the next few days were filled with novel sights and experiences.

How strange it seemed to sit down to one of the little tables in the dining-car, with its white spread and dainty dishes, and calmly make a meal while being whirled through the country at sixty miles an hour!

But that was nothing to the sensation of lying in bed in a long, dimly lighted sleeping-car which seemed to be flying through space. What a delicious sense of motion! What power and speed the swaying on the curves betrayed! Now they hear the hollow roar of a bridge, then presently the deadened sound of the firm ground again; and they know they are passing through a village when they recognize the clattering echoes from freight-cars on a siding. And now the electric lights of a large town gleam through the windows, and the train slows down and stops. There is a babel of voices, the rumble of a truck along the platform, the clink of a hammer against the car-wheels, and at last the distant "All aboard!" and they are off again.

It was a long, long journey, and the boys realized as never before the length and resources of their country. They crossed the snowy prairies of Ohio, Indiana, and Illinois, made a flying change of cars at Chicago, passed through Wisconsin in a night, and found themselves at St. Paul on the Mississippi, where, in the course of their rambles about the city, David petitioned for a camera, — a petition which Mr. Bradford willingly granted.

They crossed Minnesota that night, and North Dakota with its prairies and Bad Lands the next day.

At Mandan the boys discovered near the station a taxidermist's shop in which were finely mounted heads of moose, antelope, and buffalo, — the latter worth two hundred dollars apiece. Stuffed but very lifelike foxes looked craftily out from every corner, and gorgeous birds of various species were perched all about. There were wonderful Indian relics, too, — bows and arrows, head-dresses of feathers, brightly beaded moccasins, and great clubs of stone with wooden handles.

Through Montana and Idaho the surface of the country was diversified by the spurs and peaks of the Rocky Mountains, while in Washington they passed alternately through fertile tracts dotted with ranches, and barren, sandy plains where only the gray sage-bushes thrived.

As in the Rockies, two engines were required to draw the heavy train up the slopes of the Cascade Range. Through a whole afternoon the scenery was of the most beautiful description. They wound about the forest-covered heights, now through a dark tunnel or a snow-shed, now along the edge of a precipice from which they could see the winding valley far below and the snow-crowned peaks beyond. The change from the sandy barrens to the deep snows and rich forests of the mountains was as refreshing as it was sudden. Darkness was falling over the landscape when the highest point of the pass was gained. The laborious puffing and panting of the engines ceased, and the train ran swiftly down the grades by the simple force of gravitation. Late that evening, after a brief stop at Tacoma, they rumbled into Seattle, — six days from New York.

Mr. Kingsley, who had been notified by telegraph of the time of arrival, awaited the Bradfords on the platform.

He shook Mr. Bradford's hand warmly. They had been chums in their boyhood days, and many years had passed since they had seen each other. The boys were then introduced, and he greeted them cordially. He insisted that they should stay at his home while they were in the city, and led the way to a carriage, first cautioning Mr. Bradford against pickpockets, of whom there were many in town at that time.

They were driven rapidly through lighted business streets, then up several steep hills, and presently the carriage stopped before a pleasant house, surrounded by a wide lawn with shrubs and shade trees, some of which were putting forth green buds. Here Mrs. Kingsley and her daughter Flora, aged fifteen, received the travellers.

David was awakened from a most refreshing slumber next morning by the songs of birds outside his window. He roused Roly, and together they jumped up and looked out. Below them to the west lay the city, and beyond it sparkled the waters of Puget Sound. Beyond the Sound towered a range of majestic snowy peaks which, they afterward learned, were the Olympic Mountains. Turning to the south window, they saw in the southeast the graceful form of Mount Rainier looming over fourteen thousand feet into the clouds. It was a glorious morning, bright and balmy.

At the breakfast table Mr. Kingsley said he had received full directions regarding their needs on the trail, together with a rough map of the country through which they were to travel. He was a jolly, red-faced man, and the boys were sorry he was not going to accompany them. He declared, however, when Mr. Bradford suggested it, that he was too stout to walk so far, and would n't be hired to go until he could ride in a railroad-car.

The entire day was devoted to the purchase of the outfit. As soon as breakfast was over, Mr. Bradford and the boys, in company with Mr. Kingsley, boarded a cable-car, which soon carried them down a hill so steep that it was only with great difficulty that the passengers, especially those unaccustomed to the performance, kept themselves from sliding in a heap to the front of the car. Roly thought the sensation a good deal like tobogganing, except that they did not go so fast.

There was a liveliness and stir in the crowds which thronged the business streets, betokening the excitement due to the recent gold discoveries. Hundreds of roughly dressed men crowded into the outfitting establishments. Many of them were picturesque in yellow Mackinaw coats, broad-brimmed felt hats, and knee boots. They came from every State in the Union, but all had a common purpose, and seemed for the most part strong, brave, good-tempered fellows, ready to laugh at hardships and able to overcome all sorts of difficulties.

Entering one of the large stores recommended by

Mr. Kingsley, Mr. Bradford opened negotiations for the necessary clothing, aided by the list which his brother had prepared. Suits of heavy black Mackinaw were selected, and as time was precious and fit not important, Mr. Bradford and David were provided for from the ready-made stock. Roly was just too small for the smallest suit in the store, but the proprietor promised to make him a suit of the right material and have it ready in two days. Stout canvas coats and blue overalls were then selected, and underwear both heavy and light. Blue flannel shirts, rubber gloves for the work of panning, heavy woollen caps, stockings and mittens, stout shoes, and broad-brimmed felt hats were added. Then came rubber boots reaching to the hips, and rubber "packs" for use with the snow-shoes. Creepers, consisting of leather soles studded with sharp spikes, for travel over ice, completed the list of footwear.

Owing to the lateness of the season, it was considered best to take no furs, and very thick blankets and down quilts were substituted for sleeping-bags. Two small mosquito-proof tents and one larger tent were next secured.

The morning's work was completed by the selection of various small articles such as towels, handkerchiefs, mosquito netting to fit over their hats, toilet articles, a sewing kit, and dark glasses to protect the eyes from the glare of the snow. They had brought a partial supply of these things from home, owing to the forethought of good Mrs. Bradford.

That afternoon the boys were given their freedom, as they could be of no assistance to their father in the purchase of the hardware. At Mrs. Kingsley's suggestion, with Flora for a guide, they took a cable-car to Lake Washington, east of the city, where a great land-slide had wrecked many houses.

When they returned it was nearly supper-time. Mr. Bradford had completed his purchases, and the goods had been delivered at the house.

The boys could hardly wait for supper to be over, so eager were they to rush out into the storeroom and inspect the new supplies, but at last they were free to go. There stood three pairs of fine snow-shoes made in Michigan. Mr. Kingsley slyly remarked that he would like to be present when they first tried to use them, but when Mr. Bradford observed that he had already been invited, the jolly gentleman laughed and said he supposed, if he accepted, he would have to be a participator in the gymnastics instead of a spectator, which might interfere with his enjoyment of the occasion.

Mr. Bradford now took from its canvas case a double-barrelled shot-gun of excellent workmanship and very light weight, which he handed to David. The latter thought at once of the bear-skin which he had already resolved to bring back to Flora, to whom he had taken a great fancy. What a delight it would be to own the beautiful weapon now in his hands! He had no idea that his father was about to test his sense of fairness.

"I intend," said Mr. Bradford, "to give this gun to one of you boys. Now, Dave, which do you think ought to have it?"

David found his desire and his generosity at once engaged in a struggle. He had asked for a camera and received it. Ought he to have all the good things? Thanks to his affection for Roly and his strong sense of right, the struggle was brief.

"I think, sir," he replied after a moment, "that if you believe Roly is old enough and careful enough, he ought to have it," and to prove his sincerity he immediately turned the gun over to that delighted youth, who was no less pleased than Mr. Bradford at this outcome. The latter stepped to the corner of the room and presently returned, holding something behind his back.

"Since you have made the right decision," said he, smiling, "I'm very glad to give you this," and he handed to David a fine rifle.

David could hardly realize his good fortune, but he thanked his father again and again and expressed his pleasure as well as he was able.

Mrs. Kingsley asked Mr. Bradford if he did not fear they would shoot themselves or somebody else, to which that gentleman replied that he should personally instruct them in the use of the weapons, and take care that they were competent and careful before he allowed them to hunt by themselves. As for himself, he expected to carry only a revolver.

Outside the door stood three strong sleds, one about six feet long and the others two feet shorter, which were to carry their supplies. Then there were bread-tins, a frying-pan, and aluminum kettles and cups, very light in weight, and made to nest one within another, thus taking up the smallest possible space. The plates, forks, and spoons were also of aluminum; but the knives, which required greater strength and a keen edge, were of steel. There were three handsome hunting-knives and belts.

As his brother had a portable sheet-iron stove, as well as a whip-saw and other tools, Mr. Bradford omitted those articles, but thought it best to provide an axe for himself and hatchets for the boys, some rope, a shovel, a pick, a gold-pan, compasses, fishing-lines and flies, and a supply of medicines.

A rainstorm set in on the following day, but the boys were not to be kept in the house. They visited a shipyard where eighteen light-draught steamers were in process of construction for the Yukon River. Then at Roly's suggestion they went down to the wharves, where countless great sea-gulls flew to and fro, dipping occasionally to pick up stray bits of food. Here they were just in time to witness the arrival of the ocean steamer

"Walla Walla," from San Francisco, with hundreds of Klondikers on board,— a motley collection of rough-looking men, and not a few women. They also saw an antiquated steamer with a very loud bass whistle and a great stern paddle-wheel which churned up the water at a furious rate.

While the boys were thus occupied, Mr. Bradford had been busy with the food supply, and reported at the supper table that he had completed the work, and the provisions had been sent down to the "Farallon,"— the steamer which was to carry the little party northward. Being desired by the boys to make known what sort of fare they might expect on the trail, he read the list of the articles of food, the amount in each case being estimated as sufficient for six months.

Mr. Kingsley asked if it was not the rule of the Canadian mounted police to turn back at the boundary line all persons who did not have a year's supplies, to which Mr. Bradford replied that such was the case on the Chilkoot and White Pass trails from Dyea and Skagway, but he understood that so few miners had yet gone in by the Dalton trail from Pyramid Harbor through the Chilkat River valley that the police had not yet established a post upon that trail.

The provisions upon Mr. Bradford's list included bacon, salt pork, ham, flour, corn meal, rolled oats, beans, rice, crystallized eggs; evaporated fruits such as apples, peaches, apricots, plums, and prunes; evaporated vegetables, including potatoes, onions, cabbages, and soup vegetables; raisins, canned butter, hard-tack, baking powder, sugar, salt, pepper, concentrated vinegar, mustard, tea, coffee, cocoa, condensed milk, and beef tablets.

With such a variety the boys felt sure they could live very comfortably, and were surprised that so many fruits and vegetables, and even butter and eggs, could be had in such convenient forms.

## CHAPTER III

### FROM SEATTLE TO PYRAMID HARBOR

LATE in the afternoon of the following day, the 9th of March, the travellers embarked on the "Farallon," commanded by the genial Captain Roberts. The "Farallon" was not as graceful a vessel as the Eastern steamers to which the boys were accustomed, but she appeared to be stanch and seaworthy, — qualities eminently to be desired in view of the six days' voyage of a thousand miles which lay before her.

Her decks were now thronged with hopeful Klondikers of all ages and descriptions, the majority men, though there were a few brave women who preferred roughing it with their husbands to staying behind in physical comfort, but alone. On the bow temporary stalls had been built for a score of horses intended for use in the coast towns or on the trails.

As the wharf receded David caught a glimpse of a girlish figure and a face framed in wavy light hair, among the crowd. Flora saw him at the same moment and waved her handkerchief. How pretty and winsome she looked! David vowed then and there to bring her that bear-skin at all hazards. At last, when he could see her no longer, he turned toward the stateroom on the upper deck abaft the pilot-house, where his father was stowing away the brown canvas bags which contained their clothing and such small articles as they would need on the trail.

We must pass rapidly over the events of the voyage, filled though it was with experiences quite new to the Bradfords. At Victoria, the pleasant little capital of British Columbia, situated on the southern point of Vancouver Island, where the steamer remained half a day, Mr. Bradford procured two mining licenses which gave himself and David the right to locate claims in Canadian territory, cut timber, and take game and fish. These licenses cost ten dollars apiece, and no claim could be legally staked without one. Poor Roly, not having reached the required age of eighteen, could take neither license nor claim. This business completed, they wandered through the city, David securing a picture of the magnificent Parliament building then just finished.

Two days later, after passing up the sheltered Gulf of Georgia and crossing the broad, blue expanse of Queen Charlotte's Sound, the steamer entered a narrow waterway between islands on the west and the mainland of British Columbia on the east. Here the scenery was of the most bold and rugged description, reminding the travellers of the Hudson where it breaks through the Catskills. On either side rose immense mountain masses, covered below to the water's edge with a virgin forest of spruce, cedar, and hemlock, while from the bleak, treeless summits the snow could sometimes be seen blowing into the air like smoke.

"What a pity," exclaimed Mr. Bradford to David and Roly, as they stood upon the deck gazing about them in admiration, "that the grandeur and beauty of this coast are so little known! We've been travelling for hours through this paradise without seeing a hotel, or a cottage, or even a log-cabin, and yet I believe it will not be long before tourists will throng to this region. Now there," said he, pointing to a level plateau on the top of a forest-covered ridge which rose a hundred feet above the water, — "there is an ideal site for a hotel. It commands a view of the strait both north and south, and of the mountains in every direction. No doubt there is a lake in that hollow beyond it, and the waterfall yonder is its outlet. I should like to spend a summer right here."

That evening they emerged into Dixon's Entrance, where the open Pacific tossed them about for several hours until they came again into the lee of islands. Morning found them at Saxman, a village of the extreme southern end of Alaska, where the "Farallon" stopped to take on a passenger.

At Ketchikan, a few miles beyond, there was a good wharf and a considerable settlement, and here the Bradfords saw for the first time a raven, which the boys mistook for a crow.  Here, too, they first beheld an Indian totem-pole, — a great tree-trunk carved into grotesque shapes of beast and bird, and strange caricatures of the human countenance, all of which doubtless had a significance relating to the tribe, family, and achievements of the deceased chieftain whose memory it perpetuated.

David, with the enthusiasm of an amateur, attempted to photograph this strange column, but as the day was dark and a damp snow was falling, he failed to obtain first-rate results.

At ten in the evening the lights of Wrangel, or Fort Wrangel, as it is often called, being a United States military post, came into view.  Late as it was, the Bradfords decided to go ashore, for this was one of the larger Alaskan towns.  The wharf was unlighted save by the steamer's lamps, but they picked their way without much difficulty.  Most of the townspeople seemed to have retired, and only the saloons and dance halls showed signs of life.  From these places the travellers heard the strains of a fiddle, or the worn, hard voice of some poor girl doomed to sing to a throng of rough men amid the glare of lights and the fumes of beer and bad tobacco.

There were many evidences that the gold excitement had brought a large if transient population to Wrangel.  New frame buildings were in process of erection all along what appeared to be the main street, which was, however, utterly impassable for any kind of wheeled vehicle, being a deep ditch far below the level of the board walk which skirted it. In this hollow what little light there was revealed logs, lumber, boats, and mud, and it was evident that at high tide the water filled it. The buildings were raised on piles to the level of the future highway.

The Bradfords followed the walk with the utmost caution, for some of the boards were missing and others were broken, and in the darkness an ankle might be sprained or a leg fractured by one false step. The boys took turns in going ahead, the leader warning those behind of holes and pitfalls.

After proceeding thus gingerly for nearly half a mile and passing several elaborate totem-poles, they found themselves well out of the business portion of the town and in the midst of a collection of tents interspersed with cheap frame structures. Here and there on tents and houses they could dimly distinguish flaming advertisements of museums and various catch-penny shows, but none of them were open at that hour. The board walk seemed to lead no farther, so the three carefully and slowly retraced their steps to the steamer, where a lively scene presented itself.

Three incandescent lights backed by a powerful reflector had been rigged on board to illumine the forward deck and hold, from which freight was being discharged upon the wharf. Captain Roberts informed them that one hundred tons of freight were to be left at Wrangel, and a number of the horses and dogs.

"Ah!" said Roly, "I'm glad some of the horses are to go ashore here. They haven't had a chance to lie down since we left Seattle."

"No," said David; "and I saw two this morning so tired that they went to sleep standing up. Their eyes were shut, and their heads kept drooping, drooping, and then popping up again like Mr. Dobson's when he goes to sleep in church."

Roly laughed. "I only hope," said he, "the poor brutes will have no worse time on the trail."

Just as dawn was breaking over the town, the "Farallon" took advantage of high tide to pass through Wrangel Narrows,—a tortuous channel between low, wooded shores, where the scenery, though of a subdued character, was exceedingly beautiful. A bark and a barkentine were aground in this dangerous passage, though buoys and lighthouses were plentiful; but the steamer emerged safely in due time into broader waters, and the day passed without special incident until evening, when they had passed the latitude of Sitka, the Alaskan capital, on Baranoff Island to the west.

Not long after supper Mr. Bradford and David were reading in the stateroom and Roly was sitting on the iron grating, through which a pleasant warmth arose from the engine-room, when they all heard a bumping sound and felt the steamer tremble. A second later there came another bump. Instantly bells rang and the engine stopped, while Roly jumped from the grating, and running to the bridge peered forward into the darkness. He could see nothing in that direction, nor could Mr. Bradford and David, who were quickly beside him; but the next moment a huge block of ice and several smaller fragments grazed along the steamer's side, and were dimly illuminated by her lights. Then they understood what had happened.

"She's hit one o' them small icebergs out o' Glacier Bay," they heard a man say on the deck below them. "There's many of 'em hereabouts, I'm told, but they ain't big enough to do damage."

"Not if she hits 'em square," said another voice.

Captain Roberts, however, thought it best to be cautious, especially as he had just broken the bell-wire and could only communicate with the engine-room by speaking-tube. He sent a man to the bow of the vessel to watch for ice, and ordered half-speed ahead.

In a few hours they had reached Juneau. It was so late that the Bradfords did not leave the ship, but they could see by the lights that Juneau was larger than Wrangel, and contained not a few wooden buildings of very respectable size and appearance. It was a mystery how the town could grow any more, however, except straight up in the air like New York, for it was surrounded by water on two sides, and on the others by huge barriers of rock two thousand feet high. Across the strait a few straggling lights disclosed the location of Douglass City and the famous Treadwell gold mines.

The following day was mild, but the scenery became more Arctic. The steamer passed up the long inlet known as the Lynn Canal, on either side of which rose bold peaks crowned with brilliant snow. Glaciers flowed through the valleys between them, — great frozen rivers which no summer sun could melt. Of these, one of the largest and most graceful was the Davidson glacier on the western side of the strait. Ducks were seen here in countless numbers. Porpoises rolled and played about the vessel, and Roly caught sight of a seal which bobbed above the water at intervals.

As they were now nearing the end of the voyage, Mr. Bradford and the boys wrote letters to send back by the purser. Early in the afternoon the course was changed slightly to the west, and the steamer entered Pyramid Harbor, a beautiful circular sheet of water, flanked on the south by high mountains. Near its eastern side rose a pointed mound of pyramidal shape, to which the harbor owed its name.

On the southwest shore, under the shadow of the mountains, lay the little settlement, prominent in which was an extensive salmon cannery. In front of the cannery two wharves projected toward the bay, — one high above the beach, designed for use at high tide; the other a slender affair, longer and lower.

"There must be very high tides here," said Mr. Bradford, observing the wharves.

"Yes," answered a tall, brown-whiskered man who stood near. "Twenty foot, if I ain't mistaken. Reminds me o' the Bay o' Fundy, only there they gen'rally build only one wharf an' give it two stories."

The boys recognized in the speaker the man whom they had heard discoursing of icebergs on the previous evening.

"The cannery does n't seem to be running," observed Mr. Bradford.

"No," replied the other; "I b'lieve they only run it in summer. There ain't no salmon this time o' year."

Mr. Bradford told David to see that everything was ready for landing, and to bring the clothing bags out upon the deck. The steamer had blown her whistle as she entered the harbor, and two men could be seen walking down toward the end of the lower wharf. Mr. Bradford turned his field-glass upon them. Suddenly he uttered an exclamation of surprise and handed the glass to Roly.

"Do you know either of those men?" he asked.

"Why," said Roly, after he had scrutinized them a moment, "the second one looks like — no, it can't be. I

Pyramid Harbor, Pyramid Mountain in the Distance

declare, though, it does look like him! Yes, it *is* Uncle Will! But what a big beard he has!"

David, hearing these exclamations, came running out of the stateroom, and joyfully verified the identification. There could be no doubt that Uncle Will was there, but what had brought him was more than they could conjecture.

## CHAPTER IV

### THE FIRST CAMP

THE "Farallon" was slowly and carefully brought to the end of the lower wharf, though the water was so shallow that her screw stirred up the mud.

Roly and David signalled with their caps and soon attracted Uncle Will's attention, and that gentleman waved his arms delightedly the moment he saw them. Meanwhile the cannery watchman had made fast the steamer's bow and stern lines, the latter to the piling of the higher wharf, and the other to a large rock on the beach. A few minutes later the Bradfords had jumped ashore, and the crew had piled their sleds, provisions, and belongings of all kinds in a promiscuous heap on the wharf. They were the only passengers to disembark there, for the Dalton trail was little used. The "Farallon" presently drew in her lines and backed away with a parting blast of her whistle, to continue her voyage a few miles farther up Lynn Canal to the head of navigation, whither the rest of her passengers were bound, some intending to go to the Klondike by the White Pass trail from Skagway, and others preferring the Chilkoot trail from Dyea.

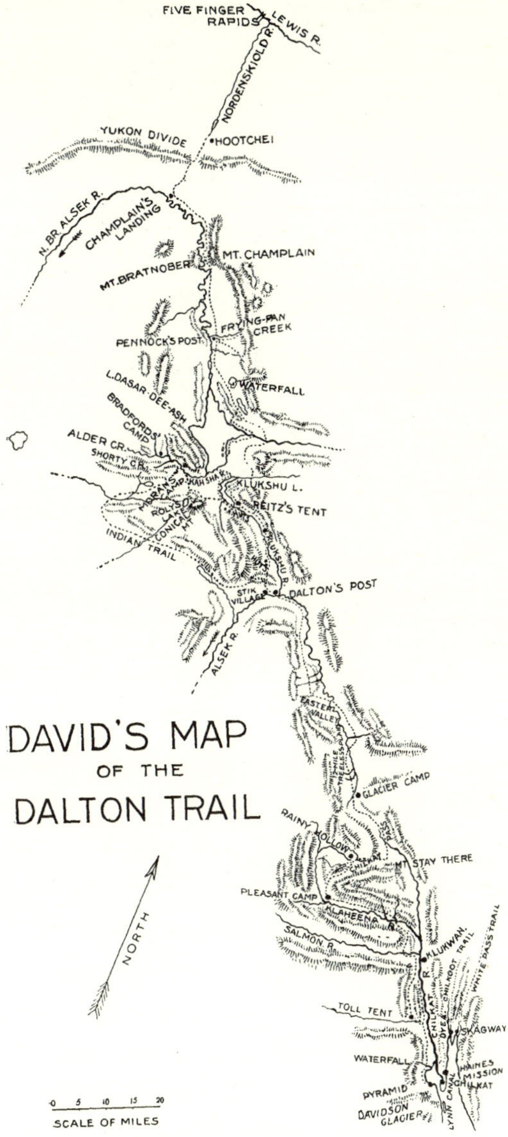


DAVID'S MAP
OF THE
DALTON TRAIL

"I didn't expect to find you here, Will," said Mr. Bradford, as he warmly grasped his brother's hand, "but I'm all the more glad to see you."

"And I'm delighted to be here to welcome you, Charles. I'll tell you how it happened when we have a moment to spare. You've brought the boys, I see. That's right. They'll enjoy the life, and it'll do them good. Why, I hardly knew David here, he's grown so tall! We'll soon have some tan on that pale face of his. As for Roly," and he eyed that healthy specimen of a boy, "about all he seems to need is hard labor and a bread-and-water diet."

Roly laughed, for he saw the twinkle in his uncle's eye, and had no fears that such a course of training would be inflicted, — or at least the bread-and-water part of it.

"Is that good mother of yours well, Roly, and the little girl?" asked Uncle Will.

"Yes," said Roly.

"And how about the 'Maine?'" continued his uncle, turning to Mr. Bradford. "I have just heard that she has been blown up at Havana. Shall we have a war?"

"I hope not," said Mr. Bradford. "It may happen, but such a contest wouldn't last long."

Uncle Will was of the same opinion. "And now," said he, taking command of the little party by the tacit consent of all, since he best knew what was to be done, "let us throw off our coats and carry these goods to a place of safety. The tide has turned and will soon cover the end of this wharf. We must get everything up to the level of the cannery buildings. This is a country of work, — good hard honest labor, of which no man need be ashamed."

So saying, he stripped off his outer coat and, throwing it over a post, picked up a fifty-pound bag of flour and swung it lightly across one shoulder, calling to his brother to place a second bag on the other. Having thus obtained his hundred-pound load, he started up the incline to the cannery. Mr. Bradford now followed him, David swinging up the second bag to his father's shoulder. David took a single bag, finding that he could not manage two, and Roly staggered along with another. On the next trip Mr. Bradford advised Roly to bring a bag of dried apricots, which was lighter, and thus, each carrying what he could, all the supplies were at length stowed safely above high-water mark.

"Next," said Uncle Will, as he resumed his coat and wiped the prespiration from his forehead, "we must have these goods taken over to my camping-place on the west shore of the harbor. Suppose you boys stand guard while your father and I see if we can get a boat. All you'll have to do will be to keep the Indian dogs away from the bacon."

The boys assented to this proposal, and the two men

## THE FIRST CAMP

walked away in the direction of the Indian village, which lay not far from the cannery toward the harbor's mouth, where the watchman said they might find a canoe.

They had been gone but a few minutes when several Indian men and boys approached, dressed in the clothing of civilization, but quite ragged withal, followed by a number of wolfish dogs, which lost no time in running up to the pile of provisions as soon as they scented the meat. David promptly sent a snowball at the largest cur with such good effect that he beat a hasty retreat, while the others, seeing his flight and hearing his howls, for the snowball had struck him in the nose, slunk away and sat down at a respectful distance to await developments.

The Indians now came up and with much curiosity began to inspect the goods. They seemed to take no offence at the treatment of the dogs, much to the relief of the boys, who half expected they would consider it a declaration of hostilities.

"Me Chilkat Indian," said one of the older men, addressing David and pointing to himself.

David nodded to show that he understood.

"Where you go?" asked the Indian.

David did not know that the place to which they were bound had any name, but he remembered how his uncle had dated his letter, so he said, "Rainy Hollow."

"Ugh!" grunted the Indian. "Rainy Hollow there," and he pointed to the north. "You go get gold?"

"Yes," said David.

"Me go too?"

"I don't know," replied David. "Ask my father." He motioned toward a large black two-masted canoe which now made its appearance from the direction of the village. One of the natives and Uncle Will were paddling, while Mr. Bradford was sitting in the stern and steering.

The Indian turned and scrutinized the craft. "Chief's canoe," said he. "Him chief's son."

The canoe, which was quite an elaborate affair, built of wood, with a high projecting prow and stern, was presently brought alongside the wharf, the end of which was already submerged by the rising tide. The occupants jumped out, and the Indian tied the painter to the piling.

"Now, boys," shouted Uncle Will, "off with your coats again, and we'll soon have the goods on board."

They had hardly begun the work when the old Indian approached Uncle Will and renewed his plea, but the white man shook his head and said, "Plenty Indian. Long Peter go." Which lingo the old fellow understood perfectly.

Large as the canoe was, when all the goods were on board, together with the three men and the boys, it was down nearly to the water's edge. There was no wind, however, and the course lay near the shore under the shelter of the mountains.

"There," said Uncle Will, in a tone of relief, as he resumed his paddle, "now we shall be clear of the dogs. They're a great nuisance wherever there's an Indian settlement. I've no doubt they would have kept us awake all night here prowling around the supplies."

"Where are we to camp?" asked David.

"Look along there on the west beach," replied his uncle. "You can see my tent now. It's about half a mile away."

The boys looked with interest at the spot which was to be their first camping-place. Behind the tent was a dark spruce forest which spread back nearly on a level for a short distance, and then mounted the steep, snowy slopes of the mountains. Before long the canoe grated against the small stones near the beach, the Indian jumped out regardless of the water, and carried Uncle Will and then the boys ashore on his back. Uncle Will went at once to his tent, and soon reappeared wearing long rubber boots. Mr. Bradford passed the goods out from the canoe, Uncle Will and the Indian carried them ashore, and there David and Roly received them and took them up the beach above the high-tide mark of driftwood and seaweed. When this work had been accomplished, the Indian was paid and dismissed and was soon paddling back to the settlement.

"Now, boys," said Mr. Bradford, "do you know how to pitch your tent?"

"No," said David, "but we'd like to try it. I guess we can manage it after a few trials. Our tent is like Uncle Will's, isn't it?"

"Yes," replied Mr. Bradford. "You can study on that awhile, or watch me pitch mine."

"There's no need of getting yours out at all, Charles, unless you want to," put in his brother. "My Indian has his own tent back there in the woods, and you can bunk with me."

So it was decided that only the boys' tent should be raised, and they set about it at once, while their father cut some dry spruce boughs on which to pile the supplies.

On examining their uncle's tent they found that it consisted of two parts, — the main tent, really a complete tent in itself and rendered mosquito-proof by having a floor of canvas continuous with the walls, and an entrance which could be tightly closed by a puckering string; and, secondly, the fly or extra roof above the tent proper. Ventilation was obtained by openings covered with mosquito netting at the peak in front and rear.

The tent stood on the beach between the line of snow and the high-tide mark. Underneath it, on the stones, was a thick layer of small spruce boughs. There was no possibility of driving stakes into the stony ground, and the guy-ropes were tied around a prostrate tree-trunk on each side, these side logs being about five inches in diameter and fifteen feet long. There was a straight and

## THE FIRST CAMP

slender ridgepole, to which the roof-ropes were attached, and this ridgepole rested upon two crotched poles at each end of the tent, set wide apart with the crotched ends uppermost and interlocked.

After noting all these things, the boys sought out their tent from the pile of goods and unrolled it to get some idea of its size. They found that it was much smaller than their uncle's tent and had no walls, the roof part sloping to the ground and connecting directly with the floor.

"We won't need such long poles as Uncle's tent has," said David, "nor such heavy side logs either. Suppose you cut a lot of spruce boughs to put underneath, and I'll cut the poles and logs."

Roly assented at once, and the two set off for the woods with their hatchets. There was abundance of spruce, but David had considerable difficulty in finding saplings or bushes which would afford crotched poles of the proper size. He found it a slow and laborious task, too, when he attempted to cut down two larger trees for the side or anchor poles, and was finally obliged to return to the camp for an axe, — a tool which Mr. Bradford let him have with some misgivings and many words of caution. Having succeeded in cutting the poles and spruce boughs, they were obliged to make several trips back and forth before all the material was brought to the beach, the deep snow greatly impeding their progress.

As they were starting out for the last time, a tall young Indian, with cheeks more plump than an Indian's usually are, shuffled along toward them on snow-shoes, drawing a long sled loaded with wood. He smiled good-naturedly when he saw them.

"Me Long Peter," said he, — "Chilkat Injun. Go with Mr. B'adford. You go with Mr. B'adford?"

"Yes," replied David, who concluded that this was the Indian his uncle had mentioned. So the three returned to camp together.

Savory odors were now wafted about from the camp-fire where Uncle Will was getting supper, and the boys hastened their work in order to be ready when he called. They succeeded in untangling the tent-ropes, and after a few mistakes and frequent examinations of the larger tent, their own little dwelling was set up near the other, on a soft bed of fragrant spruce. Then with a piece of soap and a towel from one of the clothing bags they went down to the water's edge to wash.

Presently Uncle Will shouted, "Muck-muck!" and the boys looked around inquiringly to see what he meant. "Supper-r!" he called in the same cheery tone. There was no mistaking the meaning of *that*, and the little party speedily gathered around the fire, where Uncle Will informed them that "Muck-muck" was the Indian term for "Something to eat," and was generally adopted on the trail as a call to meals.

The aluminum plates and cups were handed around, and Uncle Will distributed crisp bacon and potato and rice, while Mr. Bradford opened a box of hard-tack. David meanwhile made himself useful by filling the cups with coffee, and passing the sugar and condensed milk. As for Long Peter and Roly, finding nothing better to do, they attacked the viands at once with appetites sharpened by labor.

"I declare!" exclaimed Mr. Bradford, as soon as he too was ready, "I haven't been so hungry since I was a boy in the Adirondacks. What memories the smell of that bacon calls up!"

He took a seat on a log which Roly had drawn up before the fire, and presently called for a second helping.

"That's right, Charles," said his brother. "It does me good to see you eat like that. Well, well! the boys are ready for more, too. I see I shall have to fry another mess of bacon. Never mind, though! That means just so much less to carry on the trail." And their good-natured cook forthwith cut off half a dozen generous slices with his hunting knife and soon served them crisp and hot.

When the meal was finished, the dishes washed by Long Peter, and fresh wood piled on the fire, Uncle Will deftly lighted his pipe with a glowing ember, then turned to the others, who had comfortably seated themselves around the crackling logs, and declared his readiness to explain his presence at Pyramid Harbor.

## CHAPTER V

### THE GREAT NUGGET, AND HOW UNCLE WILL HEARD OF IT

"LET me see, Charles," he began; "I was at Rainy Hollow when I wrote to you, was n't I?"

"Yes," replied Mr. Bradford.

"And I told you of the rumors of rich strikes about two hundred miles in on this trail?"

"Yes."

"Well, my intention was to go straight to that spot with all possible speed; but as Robbie Burns puts it,

> 'The best-laid schemes o' mice an' men
> Gang aft a-gley.'

I met with an accident, and it's fortunate that I did, for when I reached this place yesterday I found that the stories of gold had leaked out, and already a well equipped party of more than thirty men had just landed here. To be exact, there are thirty-six of them; and owing to the absolute secrecy which they maintain regarding their destination, they are already known as the Mysterious Thirty-six. I have tried to induce two or three of them to talk, but they declared they knew no more about their plans than I did. Only their leader knows where they are going, and what they are to do. Now, I am perfectly convinced that these men are bound for the very spot I wrote you about, and we must get ahead of them, if we are to have the pick of the claims. They are camped now about three miles up the valley, waiting for a party of Indians who are to help them with their sleds.

"It's fortunate I had to return to the coast, for you might not have realized the necessity of outstripping them. Besides that, I have cached most of my goods a hundred and forty miles up the trail, and come back empty-handed, so for that distance Long Peter and I can help you with your outfit, and we can give them a good race."

"Won't that be fun?" cried Roly, excitedly. "I should just like to give them the slip!"

David had a better idea of what it meant. "You won't feel so much like racing, I guess," said he, "after a few miles of it. But, Uncle," he added, "did you say you had cashed your goods? You haven't sold out, have you?"

"Oh, no!" answered Uncle Will. "The word I used was 'cached,' which, in the language of the trail, signifies that I left my goods temporarily beside the way. A 'cache,' if we consider the French word 'cacher,' would mean goods concealed or covered up; but the idea of concealment is not prominent in the miner's use of the term, and in fact there is generally no attempt at concealment. It would be death in this country to be convicted of stealing such supplies, and few Indians or whites would venture to disturb them."

"I understand now," said David, "and beg pardon for interrupting. And now what was the accident you mentioned?"

Uncle Will took a few strong puffs on his pipe, and blew the smoke away in rings meditatively. Presently he proceeded.

"I won't stop to tell you much about my journey, for you will soon pass over the same ground. Rainy Hollow, where I wrote the letter, is about sixty miles from here, near the summit of Chilkat Pass. I pushed on from that point through a grand mountainous country. Day after day I trudged through snowy valleys and over frozen rivers until I reached Dalton's trading-post, the location of which, about a hundred and twenty miles from the coast, you have doubtless noticed on the maps.

"There I rested a day, and fell into conversation with a young German, Al King by name, who told me he had spent all of last summer in prospecting on the coast, and had recently explored the region around Dalton's. He had taken a claim on a stream called Shorty Creek, about thirty miles away and somewhat to the west of the main trail, and thought a man could make about ten dollars a day there, working alone; but I have no doubt,

## THE GREAT NUGGET

from what he told me of the character of the gulch, that operations on a larger scale would pay extremely well, and I resolved to turn aside for a look at the place on my way north. I convinced myself that he had heard nothing of the rumors which had brought me into the region, and had not visited the spot to which I was going, and I thought it best to tell him nothing then, though I hope, if all goes well, to do him a good turn later.

",After leaving Dalton's Post, we — that is, Long Peter and I — continued as far as Klukshu Lake, the point at which we were to turn from the main trail and make a flying trip over to Shorty Creek, which was about fifteen miles distant by the winter route, I should judge.

"We were cooking our supper among the willows near the foot of the lake when we heard the sound of a gun toward the north, followed by a cry. We both jumped up and ran to the shore, in order to get a clear view up the lake. Half a mile away near the east bank we could see what was apparently a man lying on the ice, with a smaller person bending over him, while a dog was running and barking around the two.

"On reaching the place, we found that the prostrate man was a young Indian of the Stik tribe, whose village lies near Dalton's Post. His younger brother, a lad of about fourteen, was with him. Long Peter recognized them both.

"We saw at once that Lucky, the older one, had been shot. As we afterward learned, he had left his shotgun standing against a log on the shore while he went out on the ice to fish. While he was cutting a hole, the dog upset the gun and discharged it, and poor unlucky Lucky had received most of the shot below the left knee.

"His small brother, who was called Coffee Jack, was trying to stanch the flow of blood when we came up, and Lucky was quite coolly giving directions. I bound a handkerchief tightly about the wound, and we helped the unfortunate fellow to our camp, where we made him as comfortable as possible. On the following day, I succeeded in picking most of the shot out of his leg,— an operation which he bore with true Indian fortitude. Then came the question of what to do with him.

"Long Peter was for leaving him right there in care of Coffee Jack. You see, there's not much love lost between the Chilkats and the Stiks. The two tribes used to be continually at war, for the Chilkats wouldn't let the Stiks come out to the coast without a fight. And though the presence of the whites prevents actual war at present, the members of the rival tribes have very little to say to each other, remembering the old feud.

"I was quite unwilling, however, to leave Lucky until I had assured myself that his wound was healing properly, so we remained there with him a week. At the end of that time, as all went well, I made preparations to continue on the journey, intending to leave provisions enough to last the two brothers until they could return to their village, for they had with them, at the time of the accident, a very small supply of dried salmon, and that was already consumed.

"There are two log shanties near the foot of Klukshu Lake. One was in good repair, and the door was fastened with a padlock. I suppose some white man — Dalton, perhaps — keeps supplies there. The other was open to any one who cared to enter, and though the roof was gone, the hut afforded fairly good shelter. Into this hut we carried Lucky, after repairing the roof as well as we could, and cutting some firewood, for it was intensely cold. With a good fire blazing in the centre of the room and Coffee Jack at hand, there was no fear that Lucky would suffer with cold, even though the mercury froze in the tube, as in fact it did a little later in my pocket thermometer when I hung it on my tent-pole one night.

"When all was ready, and Long Peter and I had packed our goods on our sleds, I went into the hut to say good-by to the brothers. Lucky beckoned me to come closer. When I had done so, Coffee Jack shut the door behind me. I thought from their actions that they had something to say, and did n't wish Long Peter to hear it, which proved to be the case.

"Having made sure that Peter was at a distance, Lucky

said in a low tone, ' You good man. You help me. You give me muck-muck. Now me help you. Me find big nug — what you call 'em — nuggit — Kah Sha River — big as my head — four moons. Me show you when snow go away — no find him now.' "

Here Roly interrupted to ask if Lucky's head was as big as four moons.

"Oh, no!" replied Uncle Will, smiling. "He meant that it was four months ago when he found the big nugget. The only month the Indians know is the period between one full moon and another, which is about thirty days.

"After some further conversation with Lucky," continued Uncle Will, "I made out that he had discovered, not a loose nugget, but what I judge is a remarkable outcropping of gold ore in the solid rock. He had no means of breaking out any of the rock, and so had nothing by which to prove his statements, but I have every reason to believe him. Now the Kah Sha River is the stream into which Shorty Creek flows, so the discovery must be in the neighborhood of King's claim. Lucky said that the snow was very deep in the gorge where the nugget is, and it would be hidden for two moons. He promised to meet me at the proper season, and go with me to the spot.

"Long Peter and I then started on our journey; but we had gone only a short distance toward the lake when, in descending a steep bank, all the upright supports on one side of my sled gave way, some of them being split beyond repair, and the iron braces broken. The uprights on the other side were badly wrenched and weakened at the same time, and further progress that day was out of the question. We therefore took everything back to the hut, and cached the goods there. I found it impossible to repair the sled. It was an old one which I never ought to have bought, but I was in a hurry when I started into the country, and took the first one I saw.

"There was nothing to do but return for a strong sled. I could get none at the trading-post, and so came all the way back, and the more readily, because I knew it was time you reached here if you were coming. Long Peter's sled we brought with us, and now I must go over to Dyea or Skagway and get one for myself. Then we shall be in first-rate trim."

"Well, boys," said Mr. Bradford, as Uncle Will finished, "it looks as if we had work ahead, and plenty of it. Better turn in now and get all the sleep you can."

The boys accordingly rose and departed toward their tent. David crawled into that small dwelling first, and Roly handed him a rubber blanket, which he doubled and laid on the canvas floor. Then a down quilt was similarly folded and placed upon the rubber blanket.

The heavy woolen blankets followed, and finally the other quilt. Into this warm nest the boys crept, after removing their shoes and coats and rolling the latter into the form of a pillow. Two minutes later they were sound asleep.

## CHAPTER VI

### ROLY IS HURT

THE camp was early astir. Mr. Bradford examined the thermometer which he had left outside the tent, and found that it registered twenty-seven degrees above zero.

"I expected much colder weather here," he remarked, as they were eating their breakfast of oatmeal, ham, biscuits, and coffee. "We must hurry, or the snow will melt under our sleds."

"Oh, there's no fear of that yet," said Uncle Will, reassuringly. "You see, we still get the influence of the Japanese current of the Pacific, which warms this whole coast. We shall find it colder in the interior. At the same time, we have a long distance to go, and the warm weather will be upon us all too soon. Let me see, this is the sixteenth of March. To-day I must take a sail-boat, and go over to Skagway for a sled. It's hardly possible that I can return until late to-morrow, with the best of luck."

"Can we do anything to hasten matters in the mean time?" asked Mr. Bradford.

"Yes," replied his brother. "To-day you and the boys might take the axes and hatchets to the cannery and have them ground. It's a great saving of time and labor to have the edged tools sharp. Long Peter will look after the camp while you are gone. And to-morrow I advise you to hire that Indian's canoe again, and take everything but the tents to the cave about three miles above here. Peter knows where it is. If the Mysterious Thirty-six are camped there, you can leave the goods a little this side and cover them with oiled canvas."

Immediately after breakfast, in pursuance of these plans, the whole party except the Indian, made their way along the beach to the cannery, where Uncle Will was fortunate enough to secure the services of a boatman just arrived in his sloop from Chilkat across the harbor. The breeze was favorable, and the little vessel was presently speeding along the south shore, soon passing out of sight around the point.

The grinding of the axes occupied an hour or more, after which the three walked over to the Indian village, where they were given a noisy welcome by a score of dogs. The houses were rude affairs, built of hewn boards and logs, but affording much better shelter than the wigwams which the boys had always associated with Indian life. They had seen a few wigwams near the railroad in the State of Washington, but here there were none. In attire, too, these Indians seemed to have copied the white people. Two or three women who were cooking fish outside of one of the larger houses, wore neat hoods, dresses and shoes, but others had greasy red handkerchiefs tied over their heads, and wore torn moccasins and dilapidated skirts.

"I wonder," said David, "if it is true that the Indian women do all the work. I have heard so."

"No," answered Mr. Bradford, "the men hunt and fish, and work for the whites on the trails, but the women do all the domestic drudgery, even to the cutting of the firewood. The men have rather the best of it, for they enjoy a variety and are idle about half the time, while the work of the women never ceases. It's a good deal the same, however, the world over. I have been in parts of Europe where the wives worked in the fields, and even dug cellars for new buildings, while their husbands, I presume, were engaged in the sterner but less wearing duties of army life. Here comes a poor old drudge now."

The boys looked in the direction indicated, and saw an old squaw staggering along toward the village, with a heavy spruce log on her shoulder. She had brought it a quarter of a mile from the hillside back of the cannery. While they watched her, they saw her slip on a bit of icy ground and fall, the log fortunately rolling to one side. With one quick impulse David and Roly ran to help her.

She had risen to her feet as they approached, and was making ineffectual efforts to raise the log. The boys picked it up in a twinkling, — it was not much of a load for them, — and having settled it firmly on their shoulders, they looked inquiringly at the woman, who appeared much surprised at their action, and indeed seemed to fear that they were going to make off with their prize. David, however, motioned to her to go ahead, and gave her to understand that they would follow. In this manner they reached a small cabin a few rods distant, where the log was dropped on a pile of chips near the door.

An old Indian sat on a stump beside the house, smoking his pipe complacently. He had witnessed the whole proceeding, but had not offered to lift a finger to help his poor old wife, much to the indignation of the brothers.

Mr. Bradford warmly commended his sons when they returned, adding, "I'm glad to see you differed from the old native yonder, who was ashamed to do a woman's work."

"We didn't stop to think much about it," said Roly, "but I guess we should have helped her just the same if we had."

They returned to camp about noon, and Mr. Bradford prepared the dinner, as Long Peter was not a competent cook. In the preparation of fish and game the Chilkat was an expert, but such dainties as hot biscuits, baked in Uncle Will's Yukon stove, were beyond his powers, and an omelet of crystallized eggs caused him to open his mouth, not only in expectation, but in astonishment.

After dinner David and Roly were intending to visit the railroad excavation, a quarter of a mile beyond the camp, on the northwest shore of the harbor. A dozen men were cutting through a strip of high land which crossed the line of the proposed road. The work had been going on but a few days, during which the trees had been cleared away, and the snow and earth removed from the underlying rock. It was the intention of the capitalists, so the cannery watchman had informed the boys, to extend the railroad clear to Dawson along the line of the Dalton trail, but he doubted if they would ever complete it, for a rival road was being constructed from Skagway. The excavation was plainly visible from the Bradfords' camp.

"Hurry up, Roly," shouted David, who was eager to start. "The workmen are all in a bunch up there in the hole."

Roly hastily swallowed the remnants of a biscuit, and finished a cup of tea which he had set in a snow-bank to cool. Then he ran down to the beach where David stood. The workmen were now seen to leave the spot where they had been collected. They walked rapidly to their shanty, which stood not far from the hole, and one man who had not started with the others came running after them.

"I believe they are going to fire a blast," said David, and called his father and Long Peter to come and see the explosion.

All the workmen had now taken shelter behind their shanty, and they were none too soon. A great cloud of earth and smoke, mingled with fragments of rock and timbers, puffed suddenly out from the bank, followed by a mighty detonation that echoed from peak to peak of the neighboring mountains. A moment later the Bradfords heard two or three stones strike around them.

Mr. Bradford instantly realized that, great as the distance was, they were not out of danger. As he turned to warn the boys, there was a thud and a cry, and Roly sank to the beach, pressing his hand to his chest.

In a twinkling his father and David were at his side. The poor boy could not speak, but moaned faintly once or twice. His face was white, and he hardly seemed to breathe, but retained his consciousness. They lifted him tenderly and laid him in the large tent, where Mr. Bradford gave him brandy, felt his pulse, and then unbuttoned the heavy Mackinaw overcoat, the inner coat, and the underclothing. As he bared the boy's breast, he could not restrain an exclamation of surprise and pity. Through all that thick clothing the stone had left its mark, — a great red bruise on the fair skin, and so great was the swelling that he feared a rib had been broken. Such happily was not the case, and Mr. Bradford heaved a sigh of relief as soon as he had satisfied himself on that point.

"It — it knocked the wind out of me," said Roly, faintly, when at last he could speak.

"I should think it would have," said Mr. Bradford, with emphasis. "It would have killed you if it had struck you on the other side or in the head. Thank God it was no worse!"

Long Peter, who had been poking around on the beach where Roly had stood, came up to the tent with a fragment of rock, which he handed to Mr. Bradford. It was the mischief-maker without a doubt. One side was smoothly rounded, but the other was rough and jagged, showing that it had been violently broken from the parent rock. It was but half as large as a man's fist, and Roly found great difficulty in believing that so small a stone could have dealt such a blow.

## CHAPTER VII

### CAMP AT THE CAVE

UNCLE WILL did not return on the following afternoon or evening, and the watchers attributed his tardiness to contrary winds. All the second day as well they looked for him in vain. Nor could the little party at Pyramid Harbor accomplish the work they had planned. Roly was in good trim again, excepting a very sore chest, but the Indian canoe which had transported their goods was now on the far side of the harbor, and no other was to be had. Furthermore, the trail followed the beach, which was free from snow, and unfit for sledding. There was nothing to do but wait for Uncle Will and the boat he had hired. In the mean time, letters were written in the hope of an opportunity of mailing them.

Early on the third morning, they saw the little white sail enter the harbor's mouth. Breakfast was hurriedly finished, and by the time the boat's keel grated on the stones the tents were down, dishes packed, and everything ready for embarkation.

The sloop had a capacious cabin, which took up so much of the available space that it was found impossible to put more than one sled on board. She could carry the other supplies, however, and one passenger in addition to the boatman. Uncle Will invited his brother to be the passenger, saying that for himself he would be glad of a chance to stretch his legs on shore.

Mr. Bradford therefore climbed into the boat and seated himself on a sack of rice, while the others waded into the water in their high rubber boots, and pushed the heavily laden vessel away from the beach. Then they took up their march along the water's edge, dragging their empty sleds after them.

In some places it was possible to take advantage of the snow where the ground above the beach was level and clear of trees, but for the most part it was hard travelling, the sleds apparently weighing more and more as they proceeded. Roly found himself looking around more than once, under the impression that some one for a joke had added a rock to his load, but he was always mistaken.

"Whew!" he gasped, as he stopped to wipe the perspiration from his face. "If an empty sled is so hard to pull over these stones, I don't see how we are ever going to draw a loaded one."

"It's a good deal easier to draw a loaded sled on the snow-crust," said Uncle Will, encouragingly, "than it is to overcome the friction of a light weight here. Tomorrow we shall be on the ice, which is even better than the crust."

"How far are we going to-day?" asked David.

"About three miles. We shall not try to go beyond the cave."

The attention of the boys was attracted by the noise of a waterfall which they could see imperfectly through the trees. The water dashed over a perpendicular cliff about one hundred feet high, and was almost enclosed by a sparkling structure of ice.

All this while the boat was in plain view, sailing on a course parallel to theirs, at a distance of half a mile. It had now outstripped them, and Uncle Will said it ought to turn in soon toward the shore. It became evident before long, however, that the craft was in trouble. She was well out from the land, but seemed to be stationary. The shore party, slowly as they moved, now steadily gained on her, and at length they could see the two occupants standing on the bow and thrusting oars or poles into the water in different places.

"She's aground!" exclaimed Uncle Will, after a moment's observation; "and the tide's going out. This is a pretty fix!"

"Can we do anything?" asked David, eager to go to the rescue.

"Oh! we might as well go on to the cave. It's not far now. We'll leave the sleds there, and then see what can be done. I don't think we can wade out to the boat yet, for there are two or three channels this side of her." So on they plodded once more.

The cave was a great hole in the base of a cliff, and would comfortably contain a score of men, being ten feet high, fifteen feet deep, and eight feet wide. The boys wondered if it had ever been the haunt of robbers or pirates, — a fancy which the still smouldering embers of a camp-fire left by the Mysterious Thirty-six seemed to bear out. Indeed, Roly examined the interior carefully, half expecting to see the glimmer of gold coins in the darker crevices, but he found only a piece of canvas which might have been part of a money-bag. A closer examination showed that it was plentifully sprinkled with flour, and probably had never been used for anything more romantic. In all directions the snow had been trampled hard, and numerous bits of rope, and a tin can or two which no keen-eyed Indian had yet appropriated, showed how recently the place had been deserted.

Along the beach was a row of crotched poles, most of them still upright, where the numerous tents had stood. David pointed these out to Roly delightedly, observing that poles and spruce boughs in abundance were ready cut for them.

The receding tide had now uncovered miles of mud flats, and Uncle Will declared himself ready to try to reach the boat. Long Peter was left at the cave to cut firewood, but the boys preferred to accompany their uncle, and started off in high spirits. They advanced with some difficulty, for the mud was often adhesive, clogging their boots at every step until they came to sandier stretches. At all the channels, most of which were easily crossed, although the water was running swiftly seaward, Uncle Will took the lead, prodding the ground carefully with a pole as he walked, to guard against quicksands. In this manner they reached a deep channel a few rods from the stranded sloop.

Mr. Bradford and the boatman had been watching their progress from the other side of this channel, to which point they had brought bacon, hard-tack, and some cooking utensils, in order that dinner might be prepared as soon as they could cross. This being at last accomplished, the supplies were distributed among the whole party, and they made their way to camp.

It was late in the evening when the goods were all snugly stowed in the cave, the boat having been brought up at high tide. The boatman sailed away before the water receded, carrying with him a package of letters which he promised to mail at Chilkat post-office. Hardly had he gone when a damp snow began to fall, with promise of a disagreeable night.

Roly thought it would be fun to sleep under the rocky roof of the cavern; but the smoke from the camp-fire persistently filled the place, and he was obliged to give up the idea. How strange it seemed to the boys to lie there so comfortably under the blankets in the tent and hear the snowflakes tap upon the canvas! The fitful gusts that swept past their frail dwelling threatened to overthrow it, but the anchor logs were heavy and the tent was strong, and it offered so perfect a shelter that, had the occupants not heard the wind, they would not have known it was blowing. They were too wearied with the day's work to lie long awake, even amid novel surroundings, and soon their regular breathing gave evidence of the deep, refreshing sleep which follows out-of-door labor.

## CHAPTER VIII

### SLEDDING

THE following day was Sunday, and they rested in camp.

Saturday night's storm had ceased before daybreak, and fortunately but an inch of snow had fallen, — not enough to interfere with their progress. The tents were brushed clean of the feathery flakes early on Monday morning, before being taken down and folded for the journey.

Breakfast over, Uncle Will declared that no time must be lost in loading up the sleds. It had been decided that for the first day David should draw a load of one hundred and seventy-five pounds, and Roly one hundred and fifty. The remainder was to be evenly distributed between the three long sleds drawn by Mr. Bradford, Uncle Will, and Long Peter, each of whom would have about four hundred and fifty pounds. Such a load could only be drawn where the trail followed ice or level snow-crust. In soft snow or on hills, Uncle Will said they would have to take half a load forward and then return for the rest. The boys were sure they could haul heavier loads than those assigned to them; but their elders pre-

## SLEDDING

ferred not to overtax their strength, feeling that growing lads ought not to go to the extreme of exhaustion.

David selected for his load his clothing bag, which weighed fifty ·pounds, two fifty-pound sacks of flour, a wide flat box of spices, and his rifle and snow-shoes. While his uncle showed him how to distribute the articles to the best advantage, and bind them securely with a lashing-rope passed through the side loops of the sled and over and around the load in various directions, Roly proceeded, with the assurance of youth, to load his sled unaided. He first put on two twenty-five pound boxes of hard-tack, then his clothing bag and a sack of flour, followed by his shot-gun and snow-shoes, and tied them all on as securely as he could. When his uncle had finished his instructions to David, he was surprised to find Roly's sled already loaded and lashed.

"There, Uncle Will," said Roly, proudly, as that gentleman approached, "I've done it alone. You won't have to waste any time on me."

"Ah!" said Uncle Will, "so I see." But Roly did not notice the amusement in his eyes as he surveyed the work.

"Now, boys," he continued, after a moment, "there's one thing more, and you can be doing it while the rest of us are lashing our loads. Do you see those two iron rings just above the forward end of the sled-runner on the right side?"

"Yes," answered David and Roly.

"Well, they are intended to hold the 'gee-pole' in place. Do you know what a gee-pole is?"

The boys had never heard of the contrivance in question.

"It is a pole," explained their uncle, "about seven feet long, which extends forward from the right side of the sled, and serves as an aid in guiding. If you should try to guide your sled with the drag-rope alone, you would find that it would swerve on every uneven spot, and slip sideways on a slope, and dig its nose into the sides of the trail where the snow is soft; but with your right hand on a firm-set gee-pole, you will be able to steady your sled and guide it accurately where the trail is rough or rutty. The sled will answer to the lightest touch on the gee-pole. You can cut four of the poles in that thicket on the hillside yonder, and fit them into the rings. I believe Long Peter has already supplied himself with one."

Roly and David, after several minutes' search, found four straight saplings of the required length and thickness, and cut them down with their hatchets. The large ends they trimmed to the right size, and inserted them through the rings of the sleds, making them firm by driving chips wedgewise between the iron and the wood.

At eight o'clock all was ready, and the procession started with Long Peter in the lead. Behind them lay the mud flats, with the shining water in the distance.

Before them to the northward stretched a broad and level expanse of snow, with here and there a patch of ice swept clean by the wind. The snow was almost as hard as the ice, and afforded a good running surface for the sleds. On either side of this broad valley of the Chilkat rose high, wooded hills, and behind them glittering peaks from which the snow would not entirely disappear even in midsummer, so Long Peter informed them.

For this kind of travelling the spiked "creepers" were a necessity, enabling the feet to obtain a firm hold on the alternate lanes of ice and icy snow. They were worn beneath the rubber shoe-packs, and fastened to the feet by leathern thongs.

They had not proceeded far, when they came to a low ridge or bank, so steep that Uncle Will was obliged to go to the assistance of the Indian. When the first load had been forced up the incline, the Indian returned with Uncle Will, and the two pushed up the second sled. Mr. Bradford and David followed with the third, the former pulling on the drag-rope, and his son pushing on the rear of the load. David was able to draw his own light load up the slope without assistance, and Roly came close behind him.

Unfortunately for Roly, he did not attack the ridge directly but diagonally, which brought one sled-runner higher than the other. In an instant over went the sled upon its side.

"What's the matter, Roly?" shouted Uncle Will, who had been watching from the other side of the bank.

"My sled's upset," answered Roly, ruefully, "and the load is all loose."

"And why should your sled have upset when none of the others did?"

"I suppose it was because I didn't go up the hill straight."

"That's only a part of the reason," said Uncle Will, good-naturedly, as he came up and scanned the pile. "I expected this very thing. Don't you see why? You put the cracker boxes, the lightest part of your load, underneath, and the heavy flour sack and clothing bag above. The whole affair is top-heavy. And everything is loosened by the fall, because you did not cinch your lashing-rope. Now let us load up properly. First put the two bags on the sled, then the boxes on top of them — so. Now the load doesn't *look* as well as it did before, nor seem quite so capable of maintaining its balance, but you will find that, as a matter of fact, it will ride much better.

"Pass the lashing-rope over or around each article separately, and then back and forth over the whole load, cinching it at each side loop as you pass it through. Now, should your final knot loosen, it will not affect the whole load, but the boxes on top, and the trouble can be remedied instantly, the cinches holding the rest of the load firm all the while. It is not always a waste of time, my lad, to take instructions when they are first offered, but I wanted you to have a practical demonstration of the results of poor loading. Now we shall get along famously."

At noon, when they halted for a luncheon of cold salt pork previously cooked, hard-tack, and cold, clear water from a spring on the eastern hill under which they were resting, Uncle Will estimated that they had covered nine miles, — an excellent morning's work. They had crossed the Chilkat River once at least, and possibly several times, but as river and gravel flat were here alike covered with ice and snow, they were unable to distinguish the one from the other.

"I could n't eat such a piece of fat pork at home to save my life!" declared Roly, as he took a huge bite from a generous slice. "It would make me sick."

"I rather think it would," said David; "but here nothing seems to hurt us. How good and sweet it tastes! My! but I 'm hungry."

"And I too," said Mr. Bradford. "I can feel my old-time strength coming back with every breath of this air. In a week or two, Will, I shall be as rugged as you are."

"I 've no doubt of it," said his brother; "and your beard is getting a beautiful start, too. The boys won't be able to tell us apart after a little."

"Never fear, Uncle," laughed David. "Unless you

give up smoking, or Father begins it, we shall have no difficulty. You and your pipe are inseparable."

"True enough," said Uncle Will. "My pipe is home and wife and children to me." He lighted a match, and was soon puffing away with great satisfaction.

"How far are we to go this afternoon?" inquired Roly, abruptly.

"Are you tired?" asked his uncle, before he answered.

"No," said Roly, stoutly. "I could keep on all day, if the country is as level as this."

"Well, then," said his uncle, "we'll try to make nine miles more. But if you get very tired, don't hesitate to say so."

After an hour's rest they proceeded, halting at intervals, as they had done during the morning. While travelling they were too warm to wear the Mackinaw coats, and these were thrown across the loads, but at every halt they were resumed to prevent too rapid cooling. At times they saw the "creeper" marks of the Mysterious Thirty-six, and Uncle Will said he felt sure that the large party left the cave on the very morning of the day they — the Bradfords — had reached it. If that were the case, he thought they could be overtaken soon, for, as a rule, a small party could move more rapidly than a large one.

Late in the afternoon, the treeless expanse of the river-bottom became narrowed by broken ground covered with a forest which encroached from the west. The trail followed by the Indian led them into the midst of this forest, taking the course of a small stream which wound through it. In places, no ice had formed along the bank, and the bottom of the brook could be seen to consist of a rusty red mud. Long Peter drank very sparingly of this water, and cautioned the others, saying several times, "No good, no good."

"Why isn't it good?" asked Roly, to whom the water looked clear enough.

"It may be swamp water," answered his uncle, "or it may be heavily charged with minerals. Perhaps it would not hurt you, but it is always best to follow the advice of the natives in such matters. They are careful to choose only pure streams or springs for drinking purposes, and this brook appears to be impregnated with bog iron, so probably the water comes from some stagnant pond."

Soon after five o'clock, when Mr. Bradford and the boys were growing very weary, and even Uncle Will, who was accustomed to the work, had admitted that the march was a long one, Long Peter gave a satisfied grunt and pointed forward. The others looked, and saw a row of tent-poles on a low bluff. They had reached the spot where the Thirty-six had spent the previous night.

"Good!" exclaimed Uncle Will. "We've made as long a march as they did, sure enough, though we have n't come more than seven miles this afternoon. We will camp right here, and thank the mysterious gentlemen for the use of their poles and boughs."

On the succeeding day, there was a well-defined trail, much cut up by the heavy sleds of the party ahead, for the snow was now deep and rather soft. In spite of the excellent manner in which the three long sleds were loaded, and the care with which they were drawn, upsets occurred quite frequently, and even the light loads of Roly and David sometimes overturned in the deeper ruts. Re-lashing was seldom necessary, however, thanks to the instructions of Uncle Will.

As the sun mounted higher, the snow became softer, and progress increasingly difficult. To deviate from the beaten path was to sink hopelessly, while to remain in it was to encounter hollows and ruts, from which two men could hardly extricate a single sled. They were constantly obliged to help each other, and at last Uncle Will gave orders to wait until the snow hardened again in the afternoon. By nightfall, they had covered about nine miles, reaching a point opposite the Indian village of Klukwan, which lay on the eastern bank of the river. Here again they found a deserted camp.

## CHAPTER IX

### KLUKWAN AND THE FORDS

THE boys had been too thoroughly fatigued to closely observe the settlement of Klukwan by the waning light of the afternoon, but in the morning they gazed with interest at the village across the Chilkat. The shore was lined with canoes of various sorts and sizes, and the river at this point was free from ice. They could hear the barking of dogs, and see men, women, and children moving about among the houses, which extended along the shore in a nearly straight line for a quarter of a mile. There were, perhaps, a score of buildings in all, most of them not unlike two-story New England farmhouses, neatly painted and well preserved.

"You would hardly believe that such a village contains no white inhabitants, would you?" said Uncle Will, who, with Mr. Bradford, now joined the boys on the river-bank.

"No," replied David. "How does it happen that the Indians own such good houses?"

"I'm told," said Uncle Will, "that this was a Russian post before the United States bought Alaska in 1867. The Russian traders built the houses; and when the territory was sold, they moved out and the Chilkats moved in. And not only are the Indians well housed, but, through the influence of the traders and missionaries, they have adopted the dress and, to a large extent, the manners of civilization. One of them even owns a horse and cart, which he drives across the flats, carrying on a kind of express business between Old Village — which is the meaning of the Indian word 'Klukwan' — and Pyramid Harbor."

Roly had been staring at a curious figure directly opposite. It appeared to represent the head and fore-legs of a frog, surrounded by a circle of black paint, the whole being portrayed upon several upright boards which stood side by side.

"What in the world is that thing?" he asked, when his uncle had finished. "It reminds me of the African dodger at the circus last summer. A colored man put his head through a hole in a sheet, and if you hit him you got a cigar, — and I did hit him, but the proprietor said I was too small to smoke, so he gave me a stick of candy."

The others laughed, and David proposed that Roly should throw a snowball at the frog, and see what he would get.

"That would hardly do," said Uncle Will, "even if he could throw so far, for this is no African dodger, but a totem-figure, similar to those on the totem-poles.

The ashes of some Indian of the family which has the frog as its symbol are entombed in a little house behind those boards, and Roly would be more likely to get a bullet than a stick of candy if he injured that image."

On turning back from the river-bank, they found Long Peter looking intently at a group of people a short distance to the north.

"White people — two men — two women!" he exclaimed, as they approached.

"Women?" repeated Mr. Bradford, incredulously; "this is a queer place for white women."

"So it is," said Uncle Will. "They must have come from that disabled steamer, bound for Copper River, which landed her passengers at Pyramid Harbor a fortnight ago. I met a few of her people on this trail when I came out to the coast, but didn't see this party. They must have camped off the regular trail, and have evidently travelled very slowly. I think they are on this side of the Salmon River, which empties into the Chilkat opposite the north end of the village."

Uncle Will's theory proved the true one. The Bradfords, having made everything ready for the day's march, soon covered the short distance which separated them from the party ahead, which consisted of two young men, a tall and rather slender young woman, and a matronly person whom they at first supposed to be the mother of the others. After pleasantly greeting the new-comers, however, and noting their expression of surprise and interest, the elder woman took it upon herself to offer an explanation.

"I don't wonder, gentlemen," said she, "that you are surprised to see ladies in such a place as this, though I do not doubt there are many on the more frequented trails. We were bound for Copper River; but our steamer proved unseaworthy, and was obliged to land her passengers at Pyramid Harbor. There were rumors of gold on this trail, so we determined to reach the spot if possible."

"I admire your pluck, madam," said Uncle Will, gallantly.

"But wasn't it a rather rash undertaking?" suggested Mr. Bradford.

"Yes, I admit it was. In fact, we didn't let our friends and neighbors back in Ohio know what we intended; because if we had, and then failed, we should be the laughing-stock of our town. All our friends thought we were making a pleasure trip to the Pacific coast."

"Well, well!" exclaimed Mr. Bradford. "And this is a family party, then?" and he wondered what his wife would think of making such a trip.

"Yes, practically so. I am Mrs. Shirley. These are my nephews and my niece."

"And we are all Bradfords, except the Indian," said Mr. Bradford, in return for this information.

## KLUKWAN AND THE FORDS

"But how in the world do you manage to move your supplies with only two men and no Indians or dogs?" asked Uncle Will.

"Oh, my niece and I help with the sleds. We have to make a good many trips, though, over the same ground, for we have a year's provisions with us. It is very slow work, especially since one of the boys is quite disabled. He cut his foot badly with an axe a few days ago."

Uncle Will looked at the bandaged foot, and asked if it had been properly cared for.

"Yes," replied the young man, "thanks to my aunt."

"Very fortunately," said that lady, "I am a physician, and so was able to dress the wound. There was a medical man with a large party which recently passed, who offered his services, but they were not needed."

"And how do you expect to cross this wide river?" asked Mr. Bradford.

"Oh, my uninjured nephew has been carrying the goods over piece-meal. It is simply a matter of time and perseverance. Three days ago, we had stopped at the first of those shallow streams which you must have passed yesterday, when we were overtaken by that numerous company of white men and Indians. They made light work of the fording, carrying their sleds over bodily, loads and all, as many men taking hold as could find room; and when their own loads were across, they generously came back for ours. Finally a big, strong man whom they called Paul, took my niece, my injured nephew, and myself over on his back, one after another, — and they did the same thing for us at the other streams that day; but before we reached this river they were out of sight."

"Well," said Uncle Will, "we mustn't let them outdo us. It's surely our turn now, and we shall be very glad to help you, madam."

"Thank you," replied Mrs. Shirley, gratefully. "I am very unwilling to cause you extra labor and delay, but in our present unfortunate situation I can not refuse assistance."

Preparations were at once begun for crossing Salmon River. The Bradfords took from each of their long sleds half its load. Then Long Peter, facing forward, firmly grasped the front of his sled, while Mr. Bradford and Uncle Will, one on each side, held to the ends of a shovel thrust under the forward part above the runners. David and Roly took the ends of another shovel similarly placed under the rear end, and the only able-bodied man of the other party, who insisted on doing his share, grasped the sled from behind. In this manner they lifted their load, and started down the snowy bank into the water, which was shallow at first, but grew deeper as they neared the opposite shore. It was quite necessary that all should keep step, but as they entered the deeper water David and Roly found it difficult to do this, for the current was very strong, and almost forced their feet from beneath them. The icy water surged and bubbled higher and higher against their rubber boots, — a fact which the boys noticed with some dismay. At length they entered the lowest part of the channel, where the depth of the stream was about two feet and a half.

"There!" exclaimed Roly, ruefully, as he took a step forward and braced himself as well as he could against the current, "the water came into my boots that time. There it goes again. O-o-h! but it's cold."

"Are n't you glad you came?" said David, provokingly.

"Y-yes," stoutly stammered Roly, who saw that his brother was also wet, and resolved that he, too, would make light of the wetting. "But I did n't expect ice-water bathing."

A moment more and they were out of the river and up on the further bank, where they set down the sled and paused to recover their breath. The men, being taller and wearing higher boots, had escaped dry-shod, but the boys felt anything but comfortable.

"Never mind the water, boys," said Uncle Will, cheerfully. "It won't hurt you to get wet in this country. Pour the water out of your boots, if there's much in them, for you need n't go back again. Just stay right here and load up the sleds as fast as we bring them over."

The men swished back through the water, carrying the

empty sled for the other half of its load. In half an hour all the supplies of both parties had been brought across.

"Now, Mrs. Shirley," said Uncle Will, with a smile, "have you any preference as to the manner of transportation? I trust I'm as strong as the kind-hearted Paul."

"I've no doubt of that," replied Mrs. Shirley, with a slight trace of embarrassment. "But really, if another way could be found, I should prefer it. You have an unloaded sled on the other side, — could you not take us over on that?"

"Yes," said Uncle Will, "we can."

The sled was promptly sent for, and upon its arrival Mrs. Shirley requested her niece to go first. The young woman accordingly seated herself upon it, grasped the sides firmly, and was borne lightly over the river by the four men. Her brother went next, and finally her aunt.

The two parties remained together all that day, as there were other channels to be crossed, and a few miles farther a second great river, the Klaheena, also flowing into the Chilkat from the west. It was nightfall before the fording was completed and the way lay clear before them.

## CHAPTER X

### A PORCUPINE-HUNT AT PLEASANT CAMP

AS the Bradfords were able to travel more rapidly than Mrs. Shirley and her companions, the two parties separated on the following day. The trail turned to the west, ascending the gradual incline of the Klaheena River valley — a valley similar in character to that of the Chilkat — to a point called Pleasant Camp.

Although the distance from Klukwan to Pleasant Camp was about the same as that from Pyramid Harbor to Klukwan, they were five days in covering it, since for much of the way the snow was soft, and progress correspondingly difficult. There was no more ice to travel upon, and the snow-crust would not bear them during the warmer part of the day. In fact, they could seldom walk upon it at all without their snow-shoes, the use of which the boys learned after a few hours' practice, — not, however, without some of those gymnastic performances predicted by the genial Mr. Kingsley.

They crossed one wide but shallow stream by throwing brush into the water, which raised the sleds enough to keep the loads dry. At another point a considerable delay was caused by a steep hill which the trail mounted at one side of the valley in order to avoid a difficult ford. Uncle Will pointed out a tree at the top of this hill, the bark of which was worn off in a circle a few feet above the ground, remarking that the Mysterious Thirty-six had evidently rigged a block and tackle there, and drawn up their sleds by a long rope. After following a rough, wooded ridge for perhaps a quarter of a mile, the trail led down again to the river flats.

Each day brought them nearer the great range of snowy mountains, at the foot of which lay Pleasant Camp. There they would turn to the right and cross the mountains, which were in British territory, by the Chilkat Pass. The boys thought they had never seen a more beautiful valley than that of the Klaheena. In every direction were glistening peaks, their bases clothed with green spruce forests, which here and there spread out over the levels near the river, where they showed a sprinkling of bare-boughed poplars, willows, and alders.

At one of their camps, where a small stream known as Boulder Creek flowed into the Klaheena from the north, the weather turned suddenly cold, with a bitter wind which the huge camp-fire hardly tempered. It was so cold in the tent that the boys slept in their Mackinaw coats, which usually they removed and rolled up for pillows. Nestling deep down into the blankets, they were warm enough, except when one or the other turned

## A PORCUPINE-HUNT AT PLEASANT CAMP 79

over, disturbing the coverlets, and drawing a blast of cold air over their necks and shoulders. They did not take the precaution to pull their caps over their ears, relying on the protection of the blankets, but unfortunately, while they slept, their heads became entirely uncovered. Both boys found their ears slightly frost-bitten and very painful in the morning.

When they attempted to draw on their shoe-packs, which had been left outside the tent, the leather tops and lacings were frozen so stiffly that it was necessary to thaw them out before a fire. Mr. Bradford's pocket thermometer registered three degrees below zero when they crept out into the crisp morning air and with numb fingers took down the tents and made ready the sleds.

"This is about as chilly as we shall have it," said Uncle Will, as he deftly turned the bacon in the frying-pan; "and it's nothing to what I had on my first trip in. Fifty below is a nice bit colder than three. It's too late in the season for any more of that, and I'm not sorry. We shall be unlucky though, if we don't reach the Alsek River before the ice breaks up, for cross-country travelling in that region is a hard proposition."

"How far away is the Alsek?" asked David.

"About thirty miles on the other side of the Pass."

"And where do you suppose the mysterious gentlemen are now?"

"Oh, they are doubtless working up toward the summit. If they cross first, we can hardly hope to catch them, for I have no doubt the Alsek ice is firm yet, and on that they can move as fast as we can."

"Why is it we have n't overtaken them?" inquired Roly.

"I suspect they don't stop on Sundays as we have."

"Then it's not a fair race," said Roly. "They have an advantage over us."

"Only an apparent one," observed Mr. Bradford. "They are likely to wear themselves out with such unremitting labor. We shall see."

Two days later Pleasant Camp was reached, and the sleds were drawn up from the river flats to the top of a low plateau covered with a fine forest, mostly of spruce. To the west and north rose the massive white summits of the Coast Range, like giants guarding the gateways to the interior.

A small party of Indians who had camped there were about to leave when the Bradfords arrived. Their household goods, consisting of blankets, kettles, pans, dried salmon, and a gun or two, were packed upon sleds, several of which were drawn by small, weak-looking dogs. There was one very old Indian who drew a light load upon a sled, while his wife, who was younger and stronger, bore a considerable burden upon her back. Her face was blackened to protect the skin from the blistering glare of sun and snow. The only other woman in the party carried on her back a baby warmly rolled in a blanket. She wore a sort of hood, a skirt which reached to the knees, and deer-skin leggings and moccasins, and travelled easily over the drifts on light, narrow snow-shoes of native manufacture.

When these Indians had disappeared up the mountain trail, Long Peter, who had cast admiring glances at David's rifle and Roly's shot-gun whenever the boys had removed them from their cases, came forward with a tempting proposal.

"You come with me," said he to the boys. "Plenty porc'pine here. Take guns and snow-shoes. Porc'pine much good."

The boys were on their feet in an instant at the prospect of a porcupine-hunt. At last they were to have an opportunity to test their new weapons. But first they must obtain permission to go.

"Are n't you too tired?" asked Mr. Bradford, when they bore down upon that gentleman.

"Oh, no!" shouted both together.

"Well then, you may go; but I think I 'll go with you. I 've no doubt you 've listened very carefully to all my instructions, but you 'll be pretty sure to be absent-minded in the excitement of the hunt. Do you remember the first rule, David?"

"Yes," said David. "Never point a gun, loaded or unloaded, at yourself or any one else."

"Correct," said Mr. Bradford. "What was the second rule, Roly?"

"Never leave a loaded gun where it can fall down, or be thrown down, or disturbed in any way."

"Right again. It was a violation of that rule which caused Lucky to be shot at Klukshu Lake, as your uncle told us. Now, David, the third rule."

"Unload the gun before climbing over fences, walls, and fallen trees, or entering thickets, or rough or slippery ground."

"Good," said Mr. Bradford. "That is a rule which is often disregarded, and neglect of it has caused many accidents. You won't find any fences here, but there will be plenty of rough ground and fallen timber. The fourth rule, Roly."

"Let me see," said Roly, biting his lip with vexation as he tried in vain to recall it. "Oh, yes! I remember it now. Wherever possible, keep the hammers at half-cock."

"Now," said Mr. Bradford, "if you will bear those few rules in mind, you need not trouble yourselves about any others at present. Get your snow-shoes and guns and a few cartridges, and I'll be ready when you are."

The boys started off with high anticipations a few minutes later, led by the Indian, and followed by their father. They all wore snow-shoes, for in the forest back of the camp, where the snow had not alternately frozen

## A PORCUPINE-HUNT AT PLEASANT CAMP

and thawed as it had in the open valley, there was very little crust over the deep drifts. They wound in and out among the spruces, the Indian carefully examining the snow for tracks as he shuffled lightly along at a pace which the others could keep only with the greatest exertion, for their snow-shoes were heavier and wider than his, and they were not yet skilled. They had not gone a quarter of a mile when Long Peter paused at a fresh track which crossed their course at right angles, and led toward a little gully where there were several young spruce-trees with thick branches.

"Good," said he, and immediately started on the animal's trail.

Roly became excited at once, and in swerving to the left to follow the Indian, he forgot to manage his snow-shoes with the care that is necessary, stepping upon his left snow-shoe with the right one, so that he could not raise the left foot for the next step. In an instant, carried forward by his own momentum, he plunged head-first into the soft, white, yielding drift, which closed over his head and shoulders.

David, who was close behind, struggled in vain to choke a peal of laughter, and was thankful that Roly was not likely to hear it with his head in the snow. Long Peter, who had no scruples, laughed long after Roly had emerged. They all rushed to aid the struggling youngster, who was so hampered by the big shoes that there seemed no possibility of his regaining his feet until they were disencumbered. David, after warning his brother not to kick, quickly loosened the moose-hide thongs and removed the snow-shoes, which done, the fallen youth picked himself up, and brushed the snow out of his eyes, mouth, and neck.

"Whew!" he sputtered; "how did I happen to do that?"

"You turned the corner with the wrong foot," said his father. "Where's your gun?"

The gun was nowhere to be seen until Long Peter fished it up out of the snow, where it had fallen underneath its owner.

"Is it loaded?" asked Mr. Bradford.

Roly thanked his stars that he could answer "No," and added, "I took this to be rough ground."

"You were right, Roly," said his father, much pleased. "There was no need to carry a loaded gun here, for you always have plenty of time in shooting at this kind of game. You can readily see what kind of an accident might have happened. Now wipe off the gun as well as you can, and let's see where this track leads."

They passed down into the gully, where many of the trees had been stripped of their bark and killed by the little animals. After following it a few rods, they turned up the farther bank, where the Indian paused at the foot of a dense spruce. All about the base of the tree were the porcupine tracks, but they did not appear beyond.

"Porc'pine here," said the red man, circling around the tree and gazing intently into its bushy top. A moment later he exclaimed, "I see him! You, Dave, bring rifle here."

David slipped a cartridge into his gun, and looked where the Indian pointed. He could see a dark body close to the tree-trunk among the upper branches. As he raised his rifle to his shoulder, he was surprised to find himself trembling violently.

"Well, well, Dave!" exclaimed his father, noticing his nervousness, "you've got the buck fever over a porcupine, sure enough. Hadn't you better let me shoot him?"

"Oh, no! I'm all right," said David, bracing up mentally if not physically, and pulling the trigger.

A few spruce needles and twigs rattled down as the shot rang out, but the porcupine was apparently unscathed.

"No good," said Long Peter. "You no hit him."

"You fired too high," observed Mr. Bradford, "and you shut your eyes. Keep at least one eye open, and be sure it's the one you sight with. Aim low and don't jerk."

Roly petitioned to be allowed the second shot; but his father, seeing that David was much chagrined, ruled that he should have another chance. Carefully observing directions, David fared better at the second trial. Through the smoke as he fired, he saw the porcupine come tumbling heavily down from branch to branch till it dropped into the snow and lay there motionless. It was quite dead, and Long Peter, with a grunt of satisfaction, took it up gingerly by the feet, taking care not to be pricked by the sharp quills which bristled all over the animal's back.

"Hurrah!" cried Roly, "now we shall have fresh meat."

"Yes," said Mr. Bradford, "a porcupine stew will be a welcome change from bacon, — but we ought to get one more at least. Long Peter here could eat the whole of this at one sitting without any trouble at all, eh, Peter?"

The Indian smacked his lips, and his eyes glistened, for the prickly little animals are considered such a delicacy by the natives, that they will gorge themselves even to sickness when they have the opportunity.

A second porcupine was treed not far from the first. Roly brought it down at the first shot, — a feat which would certainly have puffed him with pride, had he not retained a vivid remembrance of his late inglorious downfall.

They returned to camp in triumph, and found supper waiting. The porcupines were thrown into the fire, that the quills might burn away, Uncle Will remarking that such chickens needed a great deal of singeing. Long Peter prepared them for the stew, and they were served up in fine style on the following morning, with rice and soup vegetables. The meat had a distinct flavor of spruce bark, the food of the animal; but it was not at all disagreeable, and the stew was voted an unqualified success.

## CHAPTER XI

### THE MYSTERIOUS THIRTY-SIX

FOR nearly a week, the little party struggled with the most difficult portion of the trail. At Pleasant Camp they had reached an elevation of about five hundred feet above the sea, but the rise had been so gradual through the forty-five miles of river valleys that it had hardly been noticed. From that point, however, it was all mountain work, and they had to ascend three thousand feet more in about fifteen miles, to gain the summit of the Chilkat Pass and the high interior plateau. The trail often led uphill only to lead provokingly down again on the other side, so that the gain was thrown away, and had to be earned all over again. Then, too, the snowdrifts increased the roughness of the path. It was out of the question to move full loads under such conditions, and half-loads were taken forward a few miles and cached one day, and the remainder brought up the next. Some of the slopes were so steep that even the ice-creepers barely gave the sled-pullers a foothold, and often the sheer weight of the loads dragged them back again and again.

A Curious Phenomenon beside the Trail

Under this terrible strain their feet grew sore, and the frequent dipping of the gee-poles, as the sleds dove into the hollows, gave them cruelly lame backs. To make matters worse, the tugging on the ropes, coupled with the usual dampness of their mittens, caused the skin of their fingers to crack deeply and painfully at the joints. Many times the sleds overturned, or jammed against stumps and roots. Altogether it was a severe and thorough training for the boys in patience, endurance, and perseverance.

"What will become of Mrs. Shirley's party here, I wonder," said Roly, after a hard day's work.

"If they are wise," replied Uncle Will, "they'll stop at Pleasant Camp. The two young men can make a dash in for claims when the lame one has recovered, but those ladies can never stand this kind of work."

David declared that never before had he appreciated the picture in his room at home, of Napoleon's soldiers dragging cannon over the Alps. He was quite sure he would groan with genuine sympathy when he saw it again. In the mean time, in spite of all discomforts, he was daily securing beautiful and interesting views of mountains and valleys, of camps and the sledding, and of all the unique phases of his outdoor life.

At one point, he photographed a curious phenomenon beside the trail. The stump of a tree bore upon its top a great skull-shaped mass of snow, while underneath on every side the flakes had been packed against the bark by the wind, the whole forming a colossal figure of a human head and neck, which appeared as if carved in purest marble.

Now and then they observed traces of the company ahead. Sometimes it was a broken gee-pole, again a deserted camping-ground or fireplace, and frequently bits of rope, empty cracker boxes and tins, or a freshly "blazed" or notched tree to indicate the trail. But the Thirty-six themselves were as elusive as if they all wore seven-league boots, and the Bradfords never caught sight of them during these days, no matter how hard they worked.

In the forest through which they were travelling, spruce gum of fine quality could be picked from many of the trees, and the boys found it useful as a preventive of thirst in a country where open springs were far between. Often, too, they carried beef tablets in their pockets, and these served to alleviate hunger as well as thirst, — for so severe was the work, and so stimulating to the appetite the mountain air, that they were fairly faint between meals.

Once, while on the march, they were startled by a deep rumbling, which seemed to come from the bowels of the earth. Uncle Will said that this was the sound of an avalanche on the high mountains across the Kla-heena valley.

Porcupines were so numerous as to be obtainable as often as needed, but Roly one day discovered a new kind of game. He espied a large dark bird sitting on a low branch of a spruce near the trail, and called Uncle Will's attention to it.

"Ah!" exclaimed the latter, "that's a spruce partridge, and very good eating. Is your revolver loaded, Charles?"

The guns were packed in their cases on the sleds, but Mr. Bradford's revolver was loaded and ready. He took careful aim at the partridge and fired. The bird, not thirty feet away, merely cocked its head to one side, and calmly eyed the discomfited marksman.

"Missed," said Mr. Bradford. "Suppose you try a shot, Roly. I've been out of practice too long."

"Yes," said Roly, "let me try. But why didn't the partridge fly away? They're awfully 'scary' at home."

"This is not the ruffed grouse, or partridge, of New England," explained his father, "but a different species. It is often called the 'fool hen,' because it is so stupid. You might fire a dozen times without inducing it to fly, and you can go up quite close to it if you wish. It's more sportsmanlike, though, to give the bird a chance."

Roly accordingly stood where he was, fired, and missed. Uncle Will then brought down the bird with his revolver, and later, David and Roly plucked and dressed it, with some assistance from Long Peter, and cooked it for their supper.

David awoke, one morning, to find his younger brother observing him with a curious expression in his eyes, the cause of which he was at a loss to discover.

"What in the world is the matter with your face, Dave?" said Roly, as soon as he saw that his tent-mate was awake.

"Matter with my face?" repeated David, sleepily. "Why, nothing. What makes you think so?"

"You don't look a bit natural," said Roly.

"Oh, come!" muttered David. "What are you talking about? I'm all right, I tell you;" and he gazed drowsily up at the canvas above him, through which the morning light filtered.

"Oh! you are, are you?" said Roly. "Well, I advise you to look in a mirror before you go outside, that's all."

But David neglected the warning. His appearance, when he crawled forth from the tent, was the signal for a loud burst of laughter from Long Peter, who was making the fire, and this, more than anything else, convinced the boy that something was really wrong. He retreated into the tent and consulted a small pocket looking-glass, whereby he discovered that his countenance was as black as the ace of spades.

"April Fool!" shouted the irrepressible Roly, with great glee, and dived head-first out of the tent to escape

THE CAMP OF THE MYSTERIOUS THIRTY-SIX

a flying shoe. "My dear brother, permit me to inform you that this is the First of April." This last explanatory speech was delivered with telling effect from a safe distance.

David was at first much vexed, but having washed his face, he joined at last in the laugh against himself.

Taking the idea from the blackened faces of the Indian women, Roly had carefully gone over his sleeping brother's face with soot from the bottom of a kettle. The youngster confessed, however, that, owing to anxiety lest David should awaken first, his fun had cost him half his night's sleep. It brought upon him, too, some words of counsel from his father, who reminded him that practical joking often provoked serious ill-feeling, and it was only owing to David's good sense that it had not done so in the present instance.

That day's march was a short one. Early in the afternoon they saw a thin blue column of smoke rising through the trees ahead, and a few minutes later, to their unbounded delight, they entered the camp of the Mysterious Thirty-six, whose tents were scattered through the grove wherever the snow was level, or a tree or bank afforded shelter. Such members of the company as they saw greeted them pleasantly, and congratulated Uncle Will on making so rapid a journey. They could far better afford to be distanced by the small Bradford party than the Bradfords by them, and showed no trace of ill-humor.

Uncle Will declared, however, as the Bradfords were pitching their camp in the edge of the timber, that it was too early to crow yet.

"What place is this?" asked Roly, as he fetched a kettleful of water from the one open spot in a brook everywhere else buried deep under the snow.

Uncle Will hung the kettle over the fire and answered, "Rainy Hollow."

"Ah!" exclaimed the boy, with sudden recollection, "this is where you wrote your letter."

"Yes," said his uncle, "and the place was well named. It storms here most of the time, consequently the crossing of the summit is usually difficult and often quite dangerous. We are close to the summit now, and this is the last of the timber."

"And how far is it across the summit?"

"About twenty miles to the timber on the other side."

After supper the boys paid a visit to the large camp, having a desire to see how the Mysterious Thirty-six looked and lived. As they entered the camp the familiar "Muck-muck" was shouted from the entrance of a large cooking-tent by a jolly, red-faced man, whose general appearance, together with a big spoon which he waved dramatically above a kettle of beans, indicated that he was the cook. The call was taken up in various directions, and repeated to the farthest tents, and presently white men and Indians appeared from every side and

## THE MYSTERIOUS THIRTY-SIX 95

took their places indiscriminately in a line before the tent. Each carried an aluminum plate and cup, with knife, fork, and spoon. As fast as they were served, the men either seated themselves on logs and boxes, or stood in groups, eating their beans, bacon, and biscuits, and drinking their hot tea with great relish. The boys saw several sly young Indians finish their rations almost at a gulp, lick their plates clean, and immediately re-enter the line, by which trick they received a double portion, the cook being evidently unable to distinguish them from new-comers.

When all had been served, a white man approached the tent and asked, "Do we get a second helping to-night, Jack? I'm as hungry as I was before. Appetite's just getting whetted."

"No, Si, my boy, there's nothing left. Only one round, — that's the orders to-night."

"H-m," said Si. "I'll bet those Indians did n't go hungry, though. I saw one of 'em go back into the line."

"Well," said the cook, "the Cap'n will have to see to it, then. I can't watch 'em all."

"I suppose not," said Si. "It's a shame, though." He looked around to satisfy himself that the leader was not within hearing. "I'd have pitched that Indian into a snowbank if it was n't directly against orders. The Cap'n says we're to have no rows with the redskins, or they'll leave us, so we've got to be sweet an' nice to the rascals. By the way, Jack, has anybody spoken for that kettle?"

"You're first on that," replied the cook, handing out one of the bean kettles, in the bottom of which clung some half-burned scrapings. "Get all the satisfaction you can out of it, old man."

"Trust me for that," said Si, calling to a friend to come and share his prize.

Several others came up to ask for a second helping, but they were disappointed, — all except the one who followed Si. He received the other bean kettle.

"I'm glad we don't have to figure so closely," said David. "It must be pretty tough to go to bed hungry after a hard day's work."

"That's what it is!" exclaimed a young man who stood near, and overheard David's remark. "If they doubled our present rations it wouldn't be too much, considering the work we have to do in these mountains. I've had only two really satisfying meals since we left Pyramid Harbor, and those consisted of porcupine stew."

"Why don't they give you more, then?" asked Roly.

"Oh! I suppose it's because we can't carry much food on these sleds, and what we have must last until June, when pack trains of horses can bring us more. Would you boys like to look around the camp?"

"Yes, indeed," answered David.

"Well," said their guide, who, as they learned, came from their own State, "let's have a look at the fireplace."

This was near the cook-tent, and consisted of a circular hollow at the foot of a tall spruce. At the bottom of the cavity a bright fire blazed, and several kettles were hung over it by forked sticks suspended from a horizontal pole, which was supported at each end at the proper height by a crotched stake.

"There was quite a hole here when we came," said the young man, "and we enlarged it with our shovels, and deepened it until we reached the ground. The heat of the fire has made it still larger. You can get a good idea of the depth of the snow from this hole, for, as you see, the head of the man who stands in there by the fire does n't reach within a foot of the surface. There's about twice as much snow here as there was in the valley."

They next visited the dwelling tents, which were exactly like the diminutive tent of David and Roly, each barely accommodating two men; but here in some cases four men had joined, and by spreading their two tents and the two flies over a framework of poles, they secured a sort of canvas hut which was quite roomy, and sheltered the occupants from the wind on three sides, while a fire of logs before the open fourth side made the improvised dwelling comfortable and cheerful, and served also to dry the moccasins, coats, and blankets which had become damp on the march.

In the distance they now heard some one calling off a list of names. Their friend listened intently.

"There," said he, with a woful face, "I'm wanted. I suppose it's my turn on guard to-night."

"Do you have to stand guard?" asked David, with some surprise. "We never do. What is there to guard against?"

"I don't know, I'm sure," said the young man, replying to the latter question. "Perhaps our Indians would meddle with the supplies, or it may be the rule was made in the interest of the cooks, for the last guard calls them up in the morning. Then, besides, there are generally beans to be boiled at night, and the guards do that, and, of course," he added with a grimace and a smack of the lips, "we have to sample those beans to know when they are done. That's the one redeeming feature of guard duty."

The boys laughed, and declared the guards were not to be blamed under the circumstances.

"How long is your watch?" asked Roly.

"Two hours. We draw lots for choice of watches. There are so many of us that the turn doesn't come round to the same man oftener than once a week, but it is pretty hard then to be pulled out of the blankets in the middle of the night after a long day's labor.

Well, I must leave you. Good-bye!" and he was off to see about the guard duty.

The boys returned to their camp, passing on the way the large tent of the Indians, who were singing a weird, monotonous native chant, varied by the occasional insertion of religious hymns which they had picked up at Haines' Mission. Uncle Will was telling his brother the information he had gathered in the neighboring camp.

"They arrived here yesterday," he was saying, "so their leader told me, and to-day they carried part of their goods forward five miles, where they cached them. The men returned from that trip just before we came. To-morrow they plan to take another and longer journey, moving their remaining supplies ten miles and then returning here. That will be a good twenty-mile march, and it will use them up so that I think they'll have to rest one day at least. Their leader, who was willing enough to talk about his present plans, said that as soon as possible after they had made the second cache, they would take an early start from here, and try to reach the timber on the other side the same day. You see they'll have virtually nothing to carry except tents and blankets until they reach their first cache, which they will pick up, leaving the second untouched. In other words, they will travel five miles with very light loads, and then fifteen with half-loads, — twenty miles in all. They will return from that advanced camp the next day to their second cache and take that forward."

"I suppose," said Mr. Bradford, "we shall have to employ the same tactics to some extent. We can't carry forward our whole outfit in one march."

"That's true," answered his brother. "I think it would be wise to first carry half-loads ten miles. If the boys give out before we get back, we'll draw them. I'm convinced that if we're to beat the big party, we must do it here, and work as we never worked before. One thing I'm thankful for, — our loads are lighter than theirs, for you see we've already taken provisions for myself and Long Peter as far as Klukshu Lake, and we two are now moving a share of yours. Besides, these fellows have an unusual amount of clothing and other truck in their clothing bags, and a great deal of heavy hardware. What did you learn from their Indians, Peter?"

Long Peter smiled and looked wise. "Injuns say they no go to-morrow. Big snow come. White men no keep together; some get lost. No wood for fire. But *we* go if no wind. Me know t'ail [trail]."

This was a long speech for Long Peter, and it meant much. The morrow would decide the race.

## CHAPTER XII

### THE SUMMIT OF CHILKAT PASS

THE prediction of snow was fulfilled to the letter. When the Bradfords awoke, they found the air thick with feathery flakes, which came gently and noiselessly down on tent and tree and drift. Already the green boughs of the spruces were heavily laden. In Mr. Bradford's thermometer the mercury stood at twenty-five degrees above zero.

Long Peter noted the direction of the wind, which was so light as hardly to be perceptible. Then he examined the snowflakes, which were damp and large, indicating that the cloud currents of the air were not intensely cold.

"We can go," said he to Uncle Will.

Breakfast hurriedly disposed of, the sleds were loaded with half the supplies, oiled canvas being bound over the goods to keep them dry. Uncle Will knew that Long Peter was one of the most experienced path-finders in his tribe, and would not undertake the march if he were not well able to bring them through in safety. By seven o'clock they were on their way, the Indian leading and treading a path with his narrow, turned-up snow-shoes. The others followed easily in his track, all wearing snow-shoes, for otherwise they would have broken through the thin crust of the old snow, and the sleds would frequently have been stalled.

As they had camped in the edge of the woods, they were quickly out of sight of the trees, and traversing a barren, snowy waste which presented a gentle upward incline. The falling snow cut off the distant prospect, and in the absence of all landmarks the Indian was guided solely by the slope of the ground and the direction of the wind. Uncle Will, however, verified his course from time to time by a small compass.

After travelling thus about a mile, they arrived at the edge of a bank or bluff, which sloped steeply down to a level space fifty feet below.

"Devil's Slide," said the Indian to Uncle Will, in a tone of satisfaction.

"Yes," replied the latter. "I remember this place and its curious name very well."

"I don't see how we are going to get these loads down," said Roly. "It's awfully steep."

Long Peter, so far as his own sled was concerned, quickly solved that problem. He drew his load to the edge of the bluff, and then, with apparent recklessness, threw himself upon it just as it toppled over the brink. The others held their breath while man and sled went down, as Roly said afterward, "like greased lightning;" but the runners cut through the snow at the bottom of the hill, and the outfit brought up safely.

Mr. Bradford declared that might do for Long Peter, but *he* didn't care to risk it. He accordingly let his sled go alone, which it did gracefully enough until halfway down, when it swerved, upset, and rolled over and over, the gee-pole finally sticking in the snow and ending its wild career. It was necessary to repack the whole load.

Uncle Will's sled fared better. As for the boys, they ventured to coast down as Long Peter had done, and reached the bottom in a whirl of snow without any mishap.

Near the foot of the slide they entered a narrow ravine, — the bed of a mountain brook now buried deep under the drifts, — and followed it up for a mile or two, emerging at length upon an almost level expanse, which Uncle Will said was one of the highest places on the pass.

"Indeed," said he, "we may as well call this the summit, although for many miles we shall continue at about this height. There is a shallow lake in the little hollow ahead, Long Peter tells me, but you wouldn't guess it to look at this unbroken snow-field."

On their right they could now dimly see, through the falling flakes, an abrupt mountain peak, whose lower slopes they were already skirting. Its top was cut into several sharp points like saw-teeth. Uncle Will informed his friends that it was one of the best landmarks on the pass, being visible in fair weather for miles in either direction, — in fact, it was such a steadfast, reliable peak that it had earned the name, "Mount Stay-there." To the left was a low ridge of rounded hills, beyond which nothing could be seen in the thick air. It was here that the Bradfords discovered the first, or five-mile cache of the Mysterious Thirty-six, — a huge pile of boxes and sacks protected from the weather by oiled canvas.

Drawing their sleds into the lee of the goods, they seated themselves for a brief and much needed rest, for both of the boys were complaining of their backs, and Mr. Bradford suffered considerably in the same way. Their feet, too, protested with almost equal insistence against the present journey, coming as it did hard upon the excessive strain of the preceding week. No one thought of calling himself disabled, however, and the pain was borne patiently, and for the most part silently. The soreness in their faces and fingers continued too, but that was a minor evil.

Roly presently turned his head and listened intently. "What is that noise?" he asked, — "that clucking which sounds so near? I can't see anything, though I 've heard it several times."

"You'll have to look sharp to see those visitors,"

answered Uncle Will. "What you hear is the call of the ptarmigan, a bird which in summer is brown, but in winter is white as the snow."

"So we're in a ptarmigan country, are we?" said Mr. Bradford. " I believe that bird is considered quite a delicacy."

"There's nothing finer," said his brother. "We shall have plenty of ptarmigan from now on."

"What do the birds live on?" asked David. "I don't see anything but snow here."

His uncle replied that there were places where the wind kept the ground bare, allowing the birds to pick seeds from the grasses, and buds from the willows.

"There!" exclaimed Roly, who had been gazing steadily into the storm, "I see two of them on the little knoll yonder. They're not quite as big as the spruce partridge."

The boys wished to add them to the larder, but as revolvers were the only available weapons, and it would not do to stray away from the party, Mr. Bradford vetoed the proposition, saying that they would undoubtedly have better opportunities.

"What a funny note they have!" said Roly. "I do believe they are calling Long Peter. Listen, now. 'Peter, Peter, Peter; come over, come over.'"

The others agreed that this was a very fair interpretation, and the Indian exclaimed, "Me come over bime-by; make ptarmigan sick," — whereat they were all amused, and for the moment forgot their pain and discomfort.

It would not do, however, to rest too long, for they were becoming chilled, and stiff in every joint. With much limping until renewed exercise had limbered their sore muscles, the little band resumed the march, making brief halts when their breath gave out on the hills, but gaining ground the rest of the time slowly but steadily. Long Peter turned to the left from the base of Mount Stay-there, and for several miles followed the northeastern slope of a range of low, rounded hills, descending gradually until he reached the valley of a brook which Uncle Will said must be one of the sources of the Chilkat, since it flowed to the south. The brook was buried under the snow for the most part, but near noon an open place was discovered, to which, with mouths parched from toil, they all rushed, for there had been no water to drink since leaving the brook at Rainy Hollow, and eating snow was prohibited, owing to repeated warnings from the Indian that it would "make sick." Had it not been for the beef tablets, they would have suffered more than they did.

Here they ate a cold repast of salt pork and hard-tack, and never did food taste better than those thick slices of fat meat. The dry, tough crackers, too, now that there was water in plenty, seemed sweeter than the sweetest morsel at home. Thus do hunger and hard work transform the rudest fare.

After the meal, and a half-hour's rest, the snow became increasingly sticky, clogging beneath their snow-shoes in hard, icy masses, and making those articles extremely heavy, so that it was necessary to halt often and rap off the frozen particles. The boys were getting very tired, and in spite of their light loads were fain, time and again, to pause for breath and a rest. Hour after hour hardly a word was spoken, no one having any surplus energy to expend in that way. David was really more exhausted than Roly, for though the older, he was the weaker, owing to his rapid growth; but, with an elder brother's pride, he would have dropped rather than complain first. So for the greater part of the afternoon he struggled on in silence, scarcely able to drag one foot after the other, but pluckily dogging his father's sled, though at last his head swam so that he fairly wavered as he walked. Poor fellow! he realized, as never before, how light in reality were the tasks of home and school, which had seemed so often distasteful and hard. He thought of his mother and Helen by the comfortable fireside, and then of a bright-haired girl waving her handkerchief to him from the wharf, — and then he knew no more.

It was a cry from Roly which gave the others the first intimation of David's collapse. Roly had been close behind him, bringing up the rear of the procession, and had seen his brother pitch forward like a log into the snow and lie there motionless. Mr. Bradford and Uncle Will ran back in alarm, and while the former placed a coat under David's head and rubbed his forehead with snow, the other, after feeling his pulse, drew forth a flask of brandy, which he carried for such emergencies, and poured a little between the boy's lips. It was several minutes before he opened his eyes and asked where he was, and what was the matter.

Seeing that he was reviving, the others held a hurried consultation. It was now about four o'clock. Uncle Will and Long Peter, both of whom were well fitted to judge, were of the opinion that in spite of many rests and a snail-like progress, they had fully covered ten miles, as they had planned to do. The return journey with empty sleds was still before them, and must be accomplished before nightfall. Long Peter moreover looked skyward, and shook his head ominously.

"Wind come bime-by," said he. "We stop here — make cache — go back quick. Too much wind no good!"

"That's just what we've got to do," said Uncle Will, observing the signs of the storm's increase. "Off with the goods, and don't lose a minute!"

Boxes and bags were hurriedly loosed from the lashings, and piled in a high heap, so that the topmost ones would remain visible above the deepest snow-fall. The

## THE SUMMIT OF CHILKAT PASS

cache was then covered with oiled canvas held in place by boxes, loose ropes were gathered up and fastened upon the sleds, and all was ready.

Now came the question of what to do with David, who was sitting up, faint and dazed, but undaunted. He insisted that he could walk in a few moments, but the others would not hear of it, for no sooner did he try to rise than he fell back again weak and dizzy. It was decided that he should lie upon a long sled and be drawn by the three men in turn, at least for an hour or two, until he recovered more fully.

In this manner, therefore, they started at once to retrace their steps, Mr. Bradford taking the first turn at drawing his disabled son. The snowflakes were whirling and driving now before the rising gusts, and the air felt colder. David was accordingly wrapped in the heavy coats of the others, he being the only one who could not keep warm by exercise.

The rest and the ride refreshed him greatly, so that at the open brook where they had lunched, he declared, after a drink of cold water, that he would not be drawn any farther. He threw off the coats impatiently, not forgetting, however, to thank his faithful friends, and standing up, found himself strong enough to walk. Uncle Will now insisted that Roly should ride for a while, though that youth, tired as he was, did not think it necessary, and only yielded with reluctance. So wearied was he, however, that no sooner had he stretched himself on the sled than he fell fast asleep, and rode in that manner much farther than he had intended, the others having no heart to wake him.

The valleys and slopes were comparatively easy to identify and follow with the aid of Uncle Will's compass, until Mount Stay-there was reached, but by that time it was between six and seven o'clock, and darkness was settling down. Meanwhile, the wind had increased, and the snow was drifting. It was very evident now why the Indians dreaded a storm on the summit. Terrible indeed would it be, to become confused in such a place! Here was no hospice of St. Bernard, sending out its men and dogs to the rescue, but only a howling, uninhabited, frozen waste for miles.

For a little while yet, the Bradfords were in no danger of losing their way. It was not difficult to find the head of the ravine which they had ascended that morning, and it led them straight to the Devil's Slide. But the last mile from there to camp lay across the bleak, windswept upland. They were never in more need of the compass than now, but, alas! they could no longer see it.

With great difficulty matches were lighted at intervals, and though these were invariably blown out directly, they enabled the party to determine their course. Side by side and close together they walked, in order that no one might lag behind or be lost in the blinding storm.

It was a wild experience, and one which the boys will never forget, nor their elders either, for that matter.

Suddenly they heard the Indian exclaim, "Trees!"

They had struck the timber line at last, some distance from their camp, but presently, having ascertained their whereabouts, they covered the remaining interval, and with glad hearts flung themselves into the tents.

## CHAPTER XIII

### DALTON'S POST

THE storm continued all the next day, which was Sunday, and both parties remained in camp, the Bradfords according to their custom, and the others because of the weather.

"We stole a good march on them yesterday," said Uncle Will at breakfast, "and I believe we shall come out ahead. While they are making their ten-mile cache and returning here, we can make a straight march and camp on the other side. We shall be just one day ahead of them then, and I think we can hold that lead. At the same time, we must not overtax the boys. I would rather lose all the gold in the universe than injure their health."

The plan suggested by Uncle Will was carried out, and camp was pitched in due time among the straggling spruces beyond the pass. Nothing worth mention occurred on that march, save the discovery of a sulphur spring at a place called Mosquito Flats, and the shooting of several ptarmigan, from which was concocted a delicious stew with real dumplings and gravy.

Being far too tired after their long tramp to search for tent-poles and soft boughs in such an unpromising place, the boys decided not to raise their tent. Instead they laid it flat upon the snow, spread the blankets and down quilts upon it, and covered the whole with the rubber blanket. They turned in soon after supper, curling far under the coverlets, in which they arranged a small opening for breathing purposes, and slept warmly and well. What was their surprise, when they awoke, to find that snow had fallen during the night and covered them, so that the ptarmigan, seeing only a white mound, were clucking and calling almost within arm's reach. So tame were these birds that even when the boys jumped up and shook the snow from their bed, they only flew to a distance of twenty or thirty feet, where they paused to eye the strangers curiously.

The Bradfords brought in their cache that day, in spite of violent snow-squalls which evidently prevented the Thirty-six from making their final dash across the summit. Thus they gained another day in the race.

They were now at a place called Glacier Camp, near the headwaters of the Alsek River, which flows first to the north for fifty miles, then makes a great sweep to the west past Dalton's trading-post and the village of the Stiks, and finally, turning to the south, cuts the massive St. Elias Range, and enters the Pacific at Dry Bay. They were glad to take advantage of the smooth and level surface of this river, with its alternate patches of ice and firm snow, but there were considerable stretches where, to avoid the windings of the stream, the trail took the shortest course through the woods, in spite of soft snow and the many irregularities of the ground.

For a week they travelled in this manner through the varied scenery of the Alsek valley, now traversing wide plains, now passing sublime mountains and frowning cliffs, and meeting with sundry new experiences. On one occasion they enjoyed the novel sensation of feeling their high-piled sleds blown merrily over glare ice by a strong south wind. When this impetuous ally took hold, Roly longed for a pair of skates, that he might glide easily in front of his sled. As it was, his spiked ice-creepers dug in at every step, the sled was continually on his heels, and all the gliding he could do was in his imagination.

David had imprudently neglected to wear his dark snow-glasses, and the sun being now high and the snow dazzling, he was attacked with snow-blindness,—a malady no doubt aggravated by the pungent smoke of the camp-fires. When he sat down to supper one evening, he found it difficult to keep his eyes open. Prickly pains darted through the eyeballs, and the vision was seriously impaired. On the following day he could hardly see to walk, in spite of the glasses which now — too late — he wore. Fortunately Mr. Bradford had included in the medical stores an eye-wash for this painful affection, and after two or three days' treatment the inflammation subsided, and normal vision returned.

Hardly a day passed in which the travellers succeeded in keeping entirely dry. To go to sleep in wet stockings was the customary thing; they were sure to dry during the night from the bodily warmth, and no one thought of taking cold. On one memorable march a damp, clinging snow fell in enormous flakes, which melted upon their coats, soaked through, and finally ran down into their shoes, and it required a roaring fire that night to restore the little company to a fair degree of comfort.

None too soon they arrived at Dalton's Post, one hundred and twenty miles from the coast, for signs had not been wanting that the ice was about to go out of the streams.

How novel it seemed to stand under a roof once more! How delightful to sit down in a chair beside a roaring stove and bid defiance to the elements! This little settlement, so far from anywhere in particular, was a very oasis of civilization.

The storekeeper, Mr. Martin, usually called "Ike," was a small, wiry man, whose black hair was sprinkled with gray. He was very glad to see the new-comers, and welcomed them hospitably, inquiring whence they came and what was the news in the outside world. For months he had been the only white man at the trading-post, Jack Dalton, the owner, being absent on a journey to the coast. The advent of prospectors now and then was the only break in his monotonous existence.

On entering the substantial log store, the boys surveyed the interior with interest. It was not unlike that of a country store at home, the shelves being piled high with calicoes and ginghams, shoes, hats, tin pans, plates, and cups, while from the roof-beams depended kettles, pails, steel traps, guns, and snow-shoes. Ike informed them that he kept a small stock of flour, bacon, rice, sugar, and other provisions, in a storehouse near at hand, and that the establishment traded principally with the Stik Indians, whose village lay nearly a mile down-stream to the west. The natives paid for the goods, either with money earned by packing on the trail, or with the skins of bears, foxes, and other fur-bearing animals.

"What do you charge for your goods?" asked David, after his father and uncle had departed to select a camping-place. He had heard of the exorbitant prices of the Klondike.

"It depends a good deal on supply an' demand, same as anywhere else," answered Ike. "But we commonly give the Indians a lower rate than white men. You see, the Indians are our regular customers, an' it's for our int'rest to give them the preference. They have to depend on us entirely for many of the necessaries of life, while white men should not come in here without bringing what they need. Just now we're running short o' flour, — wouldn't sell a fifty-pound sack to a white man for less than twenty-five dollars. There hain't been trade enough with whites up to this year to make it worth while to carry a big stock, for, as you probably know by this time, it's a hard job to get supplies over the summit."

"Have you heard about the big party behind us?" asked Roly.

"Yes, Al King told me about them the other day, when he passed here."

"Will you sell provisions to them?" asked David.

"They've been on short rations right along."

"Not in large amounts. They must look out for themselves. If they should want a few sweets to munch on, we might let them have raisins at fifty cents a pound, or candy at one dollar."

"Candy?" repeated Roly, eagerly. "Just let me see some if you please, Mr. Martin."

The storekeeper laughed, and produced a cheap, mixed grade,— the best he had, of which luxury the boys bought quite a quantity.

While Roly was describing how the Thirty-six had been distanced on the summit, two Indian women entered and addressed the storekeeper in the native language, with which he seemed perfectly familiar. He rose, and going behind the counter, weighed out some salt, answering meantime a number of questions which seemed to have reference to the boys, at whom the women glanced occasionally.

"They wanted to know all about you," said Ike, when his customers had gone. "They belong to Lucky's family. Your uncle knows Lucky, don't he?"

"Yes," said David. "Uncle Will took care of him when he was shot. Is he well again?"

"Oh, yes! Off trapping now somewhere in the woods. He's a shrewd one, that Lucky. Brings in more furs than any other man in the tribe. He's a tall, wiry chap, with big cheek-bones an' little foxy eyes, an' the reg'lar Indian virtues an' vices. He's brave, an' he's enduring, an' a splendid hunter, but he's sly an' lazy. Little Coffee Jack, his brother, is going to be just like him."

"There's Father calling us," said David, presently. "They probably want water. Where do you get it, Mr. Martin?"

"You'll find a hole cut in the river ice," answered the storekeeper, "if you follow the path straight out from the door. You can't miss it. You want to be careful, though."

Having procured kettles at the camp, the boys easily found the path, and the hole to which it led. So great was the combined thickness of snow and ice that the opening was about five feet deep, wide at the top, but narrowing toward the bottom. A sort of shelf or ledge had been hacked out about halfway down, upon which the person drawing the water could stand, and as an additional safeguard a pole had been set horizontally across the hole. So rapid was the current that the water did not rise in the hole, but fairly flew beneath it.

"I don't wonder Mr. Martin told us to be careful," said David, with a shudder. "One slip on that icy ledge, and down you'd go into the dark water and under the ice in a jiffy."

"Just think," observed Roly, "if Mr. Martin had ever fallen like that when he was here alone, no one would ever know what had become of him. The hole would soon get filled up, and his disappearance would be the kind of a mystery you read about. Probably the Indians would be suspected."

"Yes," said David, "I've no doubt of it. But now let's get the water. You stand up here, and I'll do the dipping. You see," he added, concealing with an air of mock pride the real responsibility he felt, "superior age makes it my duty to take the post of danger," — with which heroic burst he scrambled quickly but carefully down and filled the kettles without accident, though they were nearly jerked from his hands by the force of the current. It is safe to say, however, that had Uncle Will known the dangerous character of the water-hole, which only Long Peter had visited on his earlier trip, he would have fetched the water himself.

## CHAPTER XIV

#### FROM THE STIK VILLAGE TO LAKE DASAR-DEE-ASH

THE Bradfords passed through the Stik village early the next day, after leaving letters with the storekeeper to be sent back when opportunity offered. This Indian settlement consisted of about a dozen houses, some built of rough logs, others of hewn boards. A few possessed the luxury of glass windows. Over the door of one of the more pretentious was nailed a board on which was painted the name of the chief, John Kah Sha. The Indians, many of whom appeared abjectly dirty and ignorant, gazed stolidly for the most part at the travellers, but a few nodded and smiled as they passed, and called away the swarm of curs which yelped or fawned at their heels.

Beyond the village the trail turned north and left the river valley, ascending eight hundred feet by a sharp ridge to the top of a great table-land. The snow had melted from the ridge, and it was necessary to unpack the sleds and carry up the goods piecemeal, — an operation which required many trips and the severest labor, and occupied the entire day.

## STIK VILLAGE TO LAKE DASAR-DEE-ASH

In the nick of time Lucky appeared with his younger brother, and having begged to be allowed to accompany the party, — a request which Uncle Will granted at once, — he fell to work with such energy and good-will that the boys were inclined to think the storekeeper had erred in calling him lazy. Coffee Jack, too, struggled with flour sacks nearly as heavy as himself, and won golden opinions from everybody. The truth is, an Indian is every whit as ready as a white man to show gratitude for kindness.

Reaching the brow of the hill breathless and warm after the first ascent, the Bradfords threw their loads upon the ground and paused to rest and look back. A wonderful panorama was outspread before them. Green spruce forests were sprinkled over the snowy surface of the Alsek valley and its bordering plateaus. Below them lay the Indian village, while to the east in a clearing rose a column of blue smoke from the chimney of the trading-post. They could trace the river for many miles in its great curve to the south, where on the far horizon glittered the mighty summits of the St. Elias Range. To the southeast, perhaps ten miles away, loomed a grand cluster of unnamed mountains, and another to the southwest, while, to perfectly balance the picture, similar isolated mountain groups appeared over the tree-tops in the northeast and northwest.

It was here that a trim, long-tailed bird was first observed, whose plumage was mostly black, and whose note was loud rather than musical. Uncle Will said it was a magpie, a bird which, in captivity, can be taught like the parrot to imitate the human voice. Another bird, of a gray color, made its appearance at dinner-time, and showed a great fondness for bacon rinds, coming close up to the party to snatch the coveted morsels. This was the butcher-bird or shrike, very common in all the northwestern country, and an arrant thief when there is meat in sight.

Sledding was resumed next morning. The enlistment of Lucky and Coffee Jack had swelled their number to seven, and without increasing the loads to be carried added to the working force, so that in spite of the softness of the snow good progress was made. Lucky had brought an old sled, cast aside by some prospector; but as it was too weak to carry a full load, Uncle Will relegated it to Coffee Jack with one hundred pounds, while Lucky drew the sleds of the others by turns.

The boys soon had occasion to observe the shrewdness of their young Indian friend. The gee-pole of Coffee Jack's sled broke on a steep down-grade, and he was obliged to halt for repairs. The Indians invariably take much pride in their powers as swift, strong packers and sledders, especially when in the company of white men, and Coffee Jack was now at his wits' end to maintain his position and keep the young pale-faces behind him. He rose to the emergency, however.

"You got hatchet?" he asked innocently, as David approached. "Sled broke."

"Yes," said David, handing over that article and sitting down good-naturedly on his sled while the Indian boy went to cut a new pole. He supposed that as soon as Coffee Jack had secured the pole and driven it into place, he would return the hatchet, without waiting to re-fasten the drag-rope and lashings, which it had been necessary to loosen.

This, however, was just what Coffee Jack did not propose to do. Seeing, as he had hoped would be the case, that David had stopped to wait for the hatchet, and Roly had stopped rather than make so long a détour out of the trail through the deep snow, he pretended to need the hatchet after the pole was in place, giving a rap here and a tap there, and all the while adroitly fastening the ropes in place again.

But Yankees have a reputation for shrewdness as well as Indians, and David and Roly were quick to perceive Coffee Jack's trick. While the Indian boy's back was turned, the two exchanged signals; then David quietly turned out of the trail, passed Coffee Jack's sled, though only with considerable difficulty, and came into the trail again, closely followed by Roly.

Perceiving that his plans were discovered and frustrated, and realizing that he had met his match, Coffee Jack laughed and surrendered the hatchet.

During the next few days, while they were ascending the comparatively narrow valley of Klukshu River, a small stream emptying into the Alsek above Dalton's Post, winter made his last dying effort. It was now the middle of April, and the sun was so high that the snow softened greatly at midday. It had become impossible to make satisfactory progress except by rising at two o'clock in the morning and starting as soon as there was light. For three successive nights the mercury sank to zero, and the air was so keen and frosty that their fingers were nearly frozen when, in the early dawn-light, they removed their mittens to loosen the knots of the tent-ropes; yet by noon it was invariably so warm that the snow was melting and the sleds stuck fast.

The Klukshu River was not so thoroughly ice-bound as the Alsek, and, already swollen with the melting snows, it had broken its fetters in many places, so that it was impossible to follow the stream itself. Twice, however, the trail crossed it, — first from west to east by a jam of tree-trunks and debris, and then back again by a narrow span of ice which cracked ominously and threatened to go down-stream, even as they passed over it.

Here they met Grant Baldwin, Al King's partner, — a young man not much older than David, who was travelling alone to the coast with a sled drawn by two dogs.

At length, after many a tussle with hills and willow thickets and stumps and roots and ruts, all of which seemed in league to oppose them, the Bradfords reached the lower end of Klukshu Lake, a long but narrow body of water at the eastern side of a broad valley. Except a small spot near the outlet, it was covered with ice and snow. Four miles to the west among others rose a peak so perfectly conical as to serve for an excellent landmark, while to the northwest and ten miles away they could see the extensive mountain system in which lay Al King's claim.

Uncle Will at once examined the cache which he had left in the deserted Indian shack. Finding it intact and in good condition, he determined to keep it there for the present, and the whole party pushed on up the lake, which proved to be about four miles long, curving to the east at its upper end. Here a long hill was surmounted in the same manner as at the Stik village, after which a trail through the woods brought them over a divide to a larger lake called Dasar-dee-ash, whose outlet, in contrast to that of Klukshu, flowed from the northern end. This lake was solidly frozen as far as the eye could see, its surface being a succession of snowy windrows separated by streaks of ice. The grand mountain chain which they had seen in the distance rose from its western edge, while the opposite shore sloped gently back in wooded hills. Mr. Bradford estimated that the lake was fifteen miles long, and about twelve broad at its widest part.

That evening the Bradfords in council decided that the three Indians should bring up Uncle Will's cache on the morrow, they, in the mean time, making a flying visit to Shorty Creek for the purpose of staking claims. To be sure, the Kah Sha River and all its tributary creeks, Shorty included, would be buried deep under snow and ice, and claims would have to be chosen at random, but even this was better than ignoring a district where gold was known to be. Later, when they had visited their principal goal, some thirty miles distant, they could return, hunt for Lucky's big nugget, and see what kind of claims they had drawn from the Shorty Creek grab-bag.

## CHAPTER XV

### STAKING CLAIMS

A DAY'S delay was occasioned by a snow-storm, but the second morning opened bright, and the Indians early departed on their errand. The Bradfords started soon afterward, crossing a bay of the lake and making for the western shore at a point near the southern base of the mountains. A valley, mostly wooded and several miles in width, extended straight back in that direction; and after following it about six miles, Uncle Will, who had previously questioned Lucky as to the route, turned to the right toward a deep gap which now came into view. This was the gorge of the Kah Sha River, — a stream named after the old chief of the Stiks.

They had made fairly rapid progress, having brought but one sled with food for two days, tents, blankets, cooking outfit, two axes, and a gold-pan. It was necessary, however, to wear snow-shoes the entire distance. This in itself was fatiguing, and rests were frequent.

Near the mouth of the gorge they came out of the woods into a wide, clear space, which, later in the season, when the snow was gone, they found to be due to an immense deposit of stones and gravel thrown out by the stream through many generations. This open tract led them directly to the gorge, and presently they passed in between high bluffs of sand and gravel, which soon gave way in places to abrupt cliffs of dark, slaty rock several hundred feet in height. The river could be heard dashing impatiently over its stony bed under huge banks of snow, which had drifted in upon it to so great a depth that the water could seldom be seen. It was a wild and wonderful canyon such as the boys had never dreamed of, and they felt the spirit of adventure rise within them as they realized that this was a land of gold. Who could tell what treasures lay at last beneath their feet? They could hardly refrain from scrutinizing every rock for the gleam of yellow metal. They gazed long and earnestly at the bare patches of sand on the slopes, till at length they were obliged to confess that it looked quite like the barren sand of New England.

Their elders only smiled on perceiving their enthusiasm, warning them, however, not to go close to the cliffs; and hardly had the word been spoken when, as if to emphasize the warning, a mass of crumbling rock fell with a roar just behind them.

Two or three miles of this kind of travelling brought them to Al King's tent, which stood to the left of the stream on a small level plot. On the opposite side a rocky wall rose straight from the water's edge a hundred feet and cut off all view, so that it seemed to the boys a rather dreary spot. Yet here, as they presently learned, one lone man had passed the entire winter, with no better shelter than a tent.

This man was the recorder of the district, Tom Moore by name, a grizzled veteran of many a hard campaign of mining and prospecting. His tent was near that of Al King. On a tree before it had been nailed a slab from a box, bearing the inscription, "Recorder, Last Chance Mining District, T. Moore."

The Bradfords received a hearty welcome from Al King and the recorder, the latter, by reason of his long exile, taking especial delight in the sight of new faces. King's fine dog "Bess" was even more demonstrative in her welcome than the two men, and bounded from one to another of the little group, licking their hands and receiving their caresses.

In company with Moore and King, who volunteered to guide them, they passed the mouth of Shorty Creek, — so named from the Indian who discovered gold there, — a small brook flowing in from the left. Neither of the guides thought it worth while to stop there, for the best claims were already taken. They believed that Alder Creek, a larger tributary above on the same side, now offered the better chance, and the Bradfords were quite willing to take their advice, since there appeared no motive for deception. Up Alder Creek they accordingly went, through a valley wider and less rugged than the Kah Sha gorge and leading toward a shapely mountain about two miles away, where the valley divided, that to the right being known as Union Gulch.

Here they found a discovery claim, located the previous year by the miner who first found gold on that creek. By right of discovery he had claimed five hundred feet of the valley, or twice the length of an ordinary claim, and naturally he had chosen what he believed to be the most promising spot. The stake which marked the upper end of his claim was the stump of a poplar tree which had been cut off about five feet from the ground. It stood on the bank of Alder Creek just above its junction with Union Gulch. For a foot below the top it had been squared with an axe, and on the smooth white wood was written in pencil, "Discovery Claim, five hundred feet, down stream. J. Barry, September 4, 1897." There was also a stake which marked the lower end of the claim.

Uncle Will looked the ground over carefully. Below Union Gulch was a level expanse of gravel ten feet higher than the stream and covered with snow except along the edge of the bank. This gravel rested upon solid rock at about the level of the water. He took the gold-pan and set out, with Mr. Bradford, the recorder, and King, on a tour of investigation, bidding the boys cut stakes similar to those on the discovery

"Presently some little yellow specks were uncovered"

claim. David and Roly would have preferred to go with their elders, but being accustomed to obey orders without question they set off at once on the less romantic quest for straight young poplars. Occasionally, however, they paused to watch the gold-seekers down the valley.

The stakes having been cut and trimmed, the boys brought them all down to the discovery claim. They were four in number, sufficient for three adjoining claims.

"What luck, Uncle Will?" shouted Roly, as they ran to join the others.

"Plenty of colors," answered that gentleman, smiling. "I've no doubt I could get more if I had brought a shovel. The gravel is frozen so hard that I can't scrape much together."

"What are colors?" asked David.

"Colors," explained his uncle, "are little thin flakes of gold, as distinguished from heavier pieces called grains or nuggets. Look in the pan here, and you'll see what colors are."

In the bottom of the pan lay a small quantity of dark sand, which Uncle Will told them was called "black sand" and consisted mainly of iron. Dipping up a little water, he allowed it to wash back and forth over the black sand, and presently some little yellow specks were uncovered. These were the colors of gold, which, being relatively heavier than even the iron, had sifted down to the very bottom.

"Hurrah!" cried Roly, joyfully, as he caught sight of them, adding with more force than elegance, "that's the stuff!"

David, maturer and less boisterous, was not a whit less pleased. He expressed a desire to see how the panning was done.

Uncle Will accordingly drew on his rubber gloves to protect his hands from the icy water, rinsed out the pan, and with some difficulty scraped together with the head of an axe a panful of dirt and gravel from the bank as near bed-rock as possible, explaining that the most gold was found as a rule at the lowest possible point. He carried the gravel to the edge of the stream, where he allowed the water to flow in, not too swiftly, upon it. He now rinsed off and threw out the larger stones, after which he took the pan in both hands and shook it vigorously for a few seconds with a circular motion, finally letting the water flow rapidly out, carrying with it some lighter portions of earth and gravel. Then with his hands he pushed out of the pan the upper part of its contents to the depth of about half an inch.

Roly was alarmed at once. "Look out, Uncle," said he. "You'll lose some of the gold, won't you?"

"Not a bit," said Uncle Will, complacently. "When I shook the pan the gold went down, aided by the water. There isn't a single color in the top of this gravel now."

So saying, he shook the pan again as before, and pushed off a little more of the contents, and sometimes he allowed the water to flow in and out several times, carrying with it on each occasion the lighter particles. In this way the amount of gravel was gradually reduced, and in less than ten minutes there remained apparently only a quantity of black sand and a few pebbles. The latter, Uncle Will deftly removed with his thumb. Then he proceeded to reduce the amount of black sand, using greater caution than before, and letting the water flow very gently in and out.

Presently a yellow speck was uncovered, then another and another, to the great delight of the boys; and, best of all, a little nugget of the size of buckshot made its appearance, which Uncle Will said might be worth fifteen cents.

All this was highly encouraging, for the Bradfords had not counted on a gold district here when the expedition was planned. It only remained to set up the stakes and write the names and dates thereon. As the discovery claim included only the upper end of the bank where the nugget was found, Uncle Will took two hundred and fifty feet next below, followed by Mr. Bradford and David in turn. Roly, as we have said, was under eighteen, and had no license.

"There," said Uncle Will, when all was finished and the stakes firmly braced with stones, "I believe we've taken the cream of the creek. The Thirty-six will probably stake the six claims next below, then they will have to leave the next ten for the Canadian Government and begin again below that, and so on. There's no telling what would have been left for us if we had n't come first."

"That's so," said Tom Moore, with a grin. "I guess ye'd 'a' ben up on the glacier or down in Dasar-dee-ash Lake."

The party camped that night near the tents of King and the recorder, the latter entering the claims in due form and collecting ten dollars per claim, according to law.

## CHAPTER XVI

### A CONFLAGRATION

WHEN the Bradfords returned to Lake Dasar-dee-ash, they found Lucky, Long Peter, and Coffee Jack awaiting them with all the supplies. The course lay across the lake to its outlet, a stream bearing the Indian name of "Kaska Wulsh," but generally known as the north branch of the Alsek, since, after flowing north for fifty miles, it turned to the west and south like the other branch, which it joined many miles below Dalton's Post.

After a consultation it was decided to cache a part of Mr. Bradford's supplies, and all of Uncle Will's except certain tools, on the western shore, within six miles of Kah Sha gorge, for they would eventually return to look after the Alder Creek claims, and it was, besides, advisable to lighten the loads and hasten forward before the snow and ice were gone. Uncle Will accordingly took Lucky and Long Peter and set out across the bay of the lake with three sled-loads, leaving his brother and the boys to rest after their labors. Late in the evening he returned and reported that he had built a strong platform of saplings high up between three trees and enclosed on all sides. There he had left the goods covered with oiled canvas, and felt confident that they would be safe alike from dogs, wild beasts, and stormy weather.

It was now thought best to dismiss Long Peter, since the remaining thirty-five miles consisted of level lake and river, and furthermore it was necessary to husband the provisions. The Indian seemed sorry to part with his white friends, but took the matter good-naturedly, the more so, perhaps, since he was confident of finding employment with the Mysterious Thirty-six, who could not be far behind. He left on the following morning, happy with a present of a fine hunting-knife in addition to his wages. Uncle Will wished to buy his sled, in order that Lucky might use it, but Long Peter was unwilling to part with it, and Lucky was obliged as before to take turns with the sleds of the others and act as general assistant.

The surface of the lake proved more unfavorable for sledding than was anticipated. Exposed as they were to the uninterrupted glare of the sun, the snowy ridges were soft and slushy except at night. To make matters worse, a north wind blew strongly in their faces. Toward noon they descried several black specks on the ice to the rearward, which gained steadily upon them, and were at length seen to be three men, a sled, and a team of dogs. The men proved to be the leader of the Thirty-six, a miner named Cannon, and a very tall native known as Indian Jack, the owner and driver of the dogs.

The "Cap'n," as the leader was called, gave no hint as to his destination, but Uncle Will surmised that he was going forward to look over the ground upon which he proposed to locate his men. He was willing to say, however, that the rest of his party would turn aside to Kah Sha River, as the Bradfords had done, and that they ought to reach there in about three days. Several of his men were sick or exhausted, one was suffering from a sprained ankle, two were snow-blind, another had been cut with an axe, and still another had blood-poisoning in a finger. He thought they might lose a day or two from these causes. Without waiting to talk further, he gave the word to the Indian, who in turn cried out "Chuck!" to the dogs, and away they went as fast as they could walk, much faster indeed than the Bradfords could follow. The Indian guided the sled by the gee-pole, but the dogs did all the pulling, and tugged vigorously as if they quite enjoyed it, — David meantime catching a picture of the whole outfit as it went by, with the Dasar-dee-ash Mountains for a background.

Not more than four miles had been covered when camp was pitched on the eastern shore that afternoon. As the night promised to be comparatively warm and fine, Roly proposed to his father that they should make a big canvas hut with two tents as some of the Thirty-six had done at Rainy Hollow. Neither Mr. Bradford nor Uncle Will objected to humoring the boy, and the hut was set up forthwith on a framework of poles, with the open end to the south away from the wind. The blanket beds of the four occupants were then laid in place side by side upon spruce boughs strewn on the snow.

When supper had been disposed of, a roaring fire was built before the open side of the hut, filling the place with a cheerful warmth and glow, and the four reclined comfortably on the blankets, telling stories and watching the curling smoke and crackling flames, until Mr. Bradford declared that if they did not turn in, they would surely sleep overtime in the morning, for there was neither cock nor clock to arouse them here. Something else there was, however, which proved quite as effectual, and roused them long before daybreak.

Roly was dreaming that he was at home and sitting by the kitchen stove. Suddenly, he thought, the lids flew off, and the flames rose in a bright column to the ceiling, while sparks fell all over him and about the room. He tried to rise and alarm the household, but some strange power held him fast, and he could neither stir nor cry out. The next instant he felt a thump in the ribs and awoke with a sense of choking, to hear his uncle exclaiming excitedly, "Wake up! wake up! everybody! We're all afire here! Quick, quick, Charley! Take your hat or coat or anything, and beat down the flames. David, Roly, get out of this in a hurry!"

The boys grasped the situation in an instant. The wind had turned to the south while they slept, and a flying spark had set fire to the canvas over their heads. The dry cloth was now flaming up brightly, while burning pieces were falling on the blankets. They jumped up, seized their caps, and fell to work with a will to help their father and uncle, who were beating away desperately at the blazing side and roof.

It was quick, breathless work. Not only must they prevent the spread of the flames overhead, but they must also take care of the bedding and whatever clothing was in the hut. David, after extinguishing the fire immediately around him, dropped his cap and pulled both blankets and clothing in a heap out into the snow, where he spread them all out, carefully quenched the sparks, and then ran back to the hut, where the flames were presently brought under control. This was not accomplished, however, until nearly half the roof and all of one side were gone.

The fire-fighters, panting and exhausted, gazed ruefully at the ruins. It was too dark now to ascertain the exact amount of the damage, but there could be no doubt it was very serious. No one, however, was disposed to cry over spilled milk; and Uncle Will, who had known many disasters of various sorts in the course of his rough experience, even laughed grimly and declared that what he regretted most was the singeing of his beard, of which he had lost fully two inches. Both men complimented the boys on their efficient work, which contributed to a large degree toward the saving of the contents of the hut, as well as that part of the hut itself which remained.

"I believe Lucky and Coffee Jack slept through it all," said Mr. Bradford, peering through the darkness toward the beach, where the Indians had pitched their rude tent.

As he spoke, there was a crackling and a flash of light behind the hut.

Not three feet from the rear of the structure rose a tall dead spruce. Fire from the burning canvas had been communicated to a dry vine leading into a network of small branches at the foot of this tree, and a tiny flame, silent and unseen, had been stealthily creeping toward this mass of tinder.

"Down with the hut, boys!" cried Uncle Will, instantly realizing the new danger. "Quick, before it gets too hot! Never mind the tree,—you can't put *that* fire out!"

This last was addressed to Roly, who had promptly

## A CONFLAGRATION 141

attacked the burning branches with his cap, but only succeeded in tearing that article on the twigs without much effect on the flames.

Knots were untied with nervous haste, and where they proved refractory they were cut. That part of the canvas nearest the tree was first folded over out of harm's way, and soon the whole was loosened and dragged to a distance, and none too soon. The fire ran up the dry twigs with startling rapidity and a roar that presently aroused those sound sleepers, Lucky and Coffee Jack, who came running up in surprise.

The tree quickly became a gigantic torch which lighted up the country for miles, and sent a dense column of white smoke rolling skyward. By good luck there were no other trees close enough to be in danger, and the whole party withdrew to a comfortable distance, as soon as the hut was safe, to watch the brilliant spectacle. The best part of it was soon over, for the branches were presently burned away, but portions of the trunk flamed and smoked for hours. Nobody but the Indians thought of sleeping any more that night. The boys curled up in their blankets where they could watch the tree; while Mr. Bradford and Uncle Will, wrapped in their heavy coats, sat on a log near by, — the former telling stories of Adirondack fires, the latter, who never seemed to have smoke enough, puffing away at his pipe.

## CHAPTER XVII

### THROUGH THE ICE

WITH daylight it was seen that the tent of David and Roly, which had formed the western end of the hut, was almost wholly destroyed; but with the exception of several holes in a corner of the fly, the large tent had escaped injury. This outcome was fortunate, for an extra small tent had been provided. As for the bedding, the fine gray blankets were not harmed in the least, but the down quilts, which had been spread over them, suffered numerous punctures from the falling sparks, so that the feathers flew in clouds whenever the quilts were moved, and it was necessary to sew up the holes before setting out on the day's march.

The outlet of the lake, which they reached at noon, was a stream fifty feet in width, and passed at first through a swampy region. Here, in the tall dry marsh-grass, there were pools of open water. Camp was made on a bluff, — the first high land beyond the swamp. A warm south breeze blew steadily, and Uncle Will said it was doubtless the wind known in the Pacific States as the "chinook." It might be expected to continue without intermission for two or three weeks, and would make a quick end of the sledding. Already the southern slopes of the hills were bare, and many of them were green with killikinick, a low plant with red berries and small evergreen leaves, not unlike those of garden box.

"I'm sorry for our mysterious friends," said Mr. Bradford, as he finished pitching the large tent. "They'll be stranded on bare ground pretty soon."

"That's so," said Uncle Will. "They'll cross the lake all right, but I think the ice will go out of this river in two or three days. We're none too soon ourselves. Hello! the wild geese have come." He pointed to a dozen great gray birds, flying in a wedge-shaped flock, and crying, "Honk! honk!"

"They're coming down," exclaimed Roly, excitedly. "Mayn't I go over there, Father? I'm sure I could shoot some of them."

"Yes," replied Mr. Bradford; "but I'll go with you, because the ice is treacherous in the swamp, and, besides, you are not quite expert yet in the use of the gun."

"Bring us the fattest bird in the flock," shouted Uncle Will, as they departed; "and we'll have a royal supper." So saying, he fell to mending the gee-pole of his sled. With David's assistance, the pole was soon as good as new.

"Now," said Uncle Will, "where's your rifle, Dave?"

"Packed on my sled."

"Go and get it. I saw some ducks in a stretch of open water back here, and maybe we can do a little hunting on our own account."

This proposal tickled David immensely. He brought the rifle and a handful of cartridges, and the two set off in a direction not quite parallel to that taken by Mr. Bradford and Roly. A half-mile walk brought them in sight of the ducks, five of them, near the icy edge of a small opening; and by lying flat on the ice, they were able to creep and slide toward them under cover of a clump of tall reeds. At length Uncle Will whispered to David to take careful aim at one of them and fire.

David was already sighting along the gun-barrel — his finger on the trigger — when the report of Roly's shotgun rang out behind a small thicket of willows. The ducks at once took flight, to David's great disappointment, but at the same moment the geese appeared, flying in a confused manner directly toward their ambush.

"Quick, Dave, give me the gun," cried Uncle Will.

David instantly passed it over, and wonderingly watched his uncle as he tossed it up to his shoulder.

"Bang!" went the rifle, and down tumbled a big bird from the centre of the flock, — as fine a fat goose as ever graced a table. David fairly danced with delight.

"There!" said Uncle Will, with a merry twinkle in his eye; "I'll wager that this was the very goose Roly meant to kill."

"Don't you think he shot any, then?" asked David.

"I fancy the chances are he didn't."

And so it proved, when the four hunters reunited and compared notes. David described his uncle's marksmanship with great enthusiasm, and Mr. Bradford and Roly were quite ready to admit the brilliance of the feat.

In two places, next morning, the stream, on whose frozen surface they travelled, broadened into lakelets, where progress over the smooth ice was rapid and easy, but as soon as these were passed and the stream narrowed again, difficulties appeared. Water was beginning to flow over the ice through numerous cracks, and as the day advanced, many openings had to be avoided. Often the centre of the river was wholly free from ice, only a narrow strip remaining along each bank. In such cases, they proceeded with great caution. The banks themselves were usually impassable, by reason of thickets and trees, and the ice-strips offered the only highway, but they were tilted at such an angle that the sleds were constantly slipping sideways toward the water. At the worst spots the united efforts of the party were required to move each load safely past.

At length a point was reached, where they seemed absolutely blocked. The firm ice on one side abruptly ended on a curve of the stream, and it was necessary to cross to the other side. There was ice in the centre at this point, but evidently too weak to bear a man's weight.

The boys could see no solution of the problem, except that of retracing their steps. But the ice in the centre had been weak for a long distance, and nobody wished to go back over such a weary course on the slim chance of finding a crossing. It was Mr. Bradford who overcame this emergency.

"Let us build a brush bridge," suggested he. "I believe it would distribute our weight, and make the passage safe."

"The very thing," said Uncle Will, approvingly. "Strange I didn't think of so simple a scheme."

All hands fell to work at once, chopping down willows and alders. Two strong poplar saplings were laid across the weak ice three feet apart, and the brush was thrown thickly over them. The Indians tested this rude bridge, and the others followed, all passing over in safety.

But they were not destined to unbroken good fortune. It was soon necessary to cross to the east bank again. This time, although there were three inches of water on the ice in mid-stream, the ice itself appeared to be reinforced by a second layer which had been thrust beneath it. Coffee Jack and Lucky examined the situation with care, then crossed with two sleds. Roly, David, and Mr. Bradford followed without mishap. Then Uncle Will, the heaviest of the party, attempted to do likewise; but in the very centre of the river the rotten ice gave way without a moment's warning, and down went man and sled into the cold, muddy water. It was deep, too, — so deep that Uncle Will did not touch the bottom, — and as for the sled, only the tip of the gee-pole remained above the surface. Fortunately, the current here was not swift.

"Stand back, boys!" commanded Mr. Bradford, who saw in an instant the thing to be done. Rushing to the shore, he cut a long willow with one sweep of his knife, then, running to the edge of the hole, where his brother had managed to support himself by treading water and grasping the broken ice-cakes, he held out the end of the branch. Uncle Will caught this, and was pulled to the edge of the strong shore-ice, where he was seized by willing hands and drawn forth, his teeth chattering, but his usual undaunted smile still in evidence as he remarked, "They s-say it's a good th-thing to keep c-c-cool in case of accident. N-nobody can say I'm not c-cool!"

This unexpected sally drew a burst of merriment from the boys, who, now that the danger was over, were quite ready to appreciate the humorous side of the incident. They admired their uncle more than ever for his happy way of making light of discomforts.

But the sled and its precious provisions were still in the water, and no time must be lost in rescuing them. How to do it, was the question. The gee-pole was too far from the strong ice to be reached. If the thin ice, against which it rested, were broken, it would probably sink out of sight altogether.

Lucky finally fished up the drag-rope by means of a long pole, and thus the sled was drawn toward the shore ice. All now took hold, and their combined strength sufficed to haul it out of the water. Its load was quickly unpacked, the sacks of flour were set on end in the sun to drain and dry, as the dampness had not penetrated more than half an inch through the canvas, and the contents of the clothing bag were spread upon a log. A bag of sugar was the only total loss. Meantime, a huge fire was built on the bank, in the warmth of which Uncle Will changed his clothing.

Further progress that day was unadvisable, and indeed, Uncle Will declared that if they had covered seven miles, as he believed was the case, they were practically at their journey's end.

## CHAPTER XVIII

### BUILDING THE CABIN

A TOUR of investigation convinced Mr. Bradford that Frying-Pan Creek, the stream for which they were searching, flowed into the river from the right, not a quarter of a mile distant. Lucky was familiar with all the streams of the region, but he was often unable to identify them by English names, and, in this instance, the white men were obliged to base their conclusions on a description of the district previously given to Uncle Will.

The goods were moved forward overland to a low hill which sloped gradually to the creek on one side, and fronted the river in a fifty-foot bluff on the other. Here there was abundance of spruce timber, much of which, though still standing, had been killed by a forest fire, and was perfectly seasoned.

Nearly a mile to the west, across the river, was a long granite cliff, a thousand feet or more in height, which limited the view in that direction. To the north, as they looked down the valley, they beheld two mountains fifteen miles away, between which the river flowed. The western one rose sharply three thousand feet, the other, much greater in bulk, four thousand. The Indians called these elevations Father and Son, but the western had come to be known among white men as Mount Bratnober, while the other was soon to be named Mount Champlain, after a member of the Thirty-six who climbed it. From Mount Champlain on the north, a range of lesser peaks extended clear around to the southeast, bounding the valley on that side, and it was among these mountains that Frying-Pan Creek had its source, five miles distant. With so many landmarks, they felt no doubt about their position.

Uncle Will declared that at the earliest moment they must set off to the headwaters of the creek on a prospecting trip, but to go while ice and snow remained would hardly be advisable, so long as the Thirty-six were not in sight. It was therefore decided to begin a log cabin. The boys, who had always cherished a longing to live in the woods in a house of their own building, hailed this project with enthusiasm, while Mr. Bradford observed that they would now appreciate the situation and circumstances of their ancestors in the wilderness of New England.

First a site must be chosen, dry, level, and sheltered from strong winds. Several places were examined, but only one of these satisfied every requirement. It was a small plot of level ground, free from trees, near the top of the hill where it sloped to the creek. To the south and west, the hill-top sheltered it, while to the northwest and north stood tall, dense spruce-trees. Eastward the country was more open, and creek, valley, and mountains were in plain view. The cabin was to face in this direction. Its dimensions on the ground were to be eighteen by twenty feet.

So large a structure would hardly have been planned, had it not been for the wealth of light, dry timber around them. The weight of green logs of the required size would have taxed their strength most sorely.

Lucky and Coffee Jack were set at work clearing the ground of snow, of which but little remained; while Mr. Bradford and his brother took their axes, and began to fell the straightest of the dead spruces. The boys trimmed off such branches and stubs as survived. Whenever a trunk was nearly cut through on one side, the choppers would give the warning, and, when the way was clear, a few strokes on the other side brought down the forest giant with a crash.

To drag the logs to the chosen spot was harder and took more time than the felling. Then the ends had to be notched, so that they would join perfectly at the corners of the cabin, each log having two feet of extra length to allow room for the notching.

It was thought the Thirty-six would not arrive before the fourth day, and the elder Bradfords agreed that it would be wise to drop work on the cabin on that day, and stake claims along the headwaters of the creek. But alas for human calculations! About noon of the third day, voices were heard in the direction of the river, and presently six of the mysterious party put in an appearance. They were surprised at finding the Bradfords, who, they supposed, had continued northward.

"Hello!" exclaimed a thick-set man with a reddish beard sprinkled with gray, — "how are you, gentlemen? We heard your axes, and thought we should find strangers. You're doing the very thing we've got to do."

"Yes," said Uncle Will, "but how in the world did you get here so soon, Pennock?"

"Oh! we've been working like slaves to get as far as we could before the ice went out. It would freeze a little every night, and we would make a few miles, but in the middle of the day we had to build bridges every few rods. Half a dozen of our men have broken through first and last, — sleds too. We left Patterson, Lewis, Colburn, and Whitney, on the Kah Sha claims, and now we six are ordered to stop here and do some prospecting. The rest will try to go on."

"Ah!" said Uncle Will, much relieved by this last information; "so the rest are going on? Well, I'm sorry for them. The ice won't last two days."

"That's true as you live," replied Pennock. "Well, we must get back. We're camped temporarily just below here. Maybe I'll see you again this evening."

"All right," answered Uncle Will. "Come up any time."

"I believe," said Mr. Bradford, as soon as the visitors were gone, "he wants to join forces, at least, in the building of the house."

"I think so too," said Uncle Will. "It wouldn't be a bad idea either. The cabin is easily big enough for all twelve of us. With their help, we can finish it in no time. I even think it would be well to work with them in prospecting, if they are agreeable. Let's see — there are only nine claims to be taken between us. We ought all to be able to get good ones, if there are any."

It was accordingly determined that evening, by conference with Pennock's party, to combine for the present. To prevent disagreements, the details of the arrangement were drawn up in writing, Pennock readily engaging to give the Bradfords first choice of claims, for two reasons, — first, because they were first to arrive, and, second, in consideration of the work they had already done on the cabin.

Next morning, the Bradfords went to the top of the bluff overlooking the river, and saw the main body of the Thirty-six, now reduced to about twenty-five white men, and half a dozen Indians — including Long Peter — resuming their march. After skirting the shore on a fringe of ice for some distance, they made a short cut across a narrow tongue of land, where the snow was entirely gone and the sleds could only be moved with the severest toil.

"Flesh and blood can't stand that a great while," said Uncle Will; "especially on short rations. They'll have to abandon their sleds soon, and carry what they can on their backs. I wish I knew how far those poor fellows are going."

"They're making a desperate dash for somewhere," said Mr. Bradford, "and their pluck is certainly admirable. I wish them success with all my heart."

"And I too," added Uncle Will, emphatically.

Work on the cabin was resumed as soon as possible, and the walls rose like magic with the increased force of builders. In a few days these were completed. An opening was sawn in the front for a door, and smaller ones in each side for windows, the sawn ends of the logs being held in place by the door-frame and window-frames, which consisted of small hewn strips of spruce wood nailed in place. The roof was now constructed of poles laid side by side from the ridge-logs to the upper logs of the front and rear walls. David and Roly gathered great quantities of green spruce boughs, which were laid on the top of the roof-poles. This proved to be a mistake, but in the hurry of building, nobody thought of it. Later, as soon as these boughs dried, the needles came rattling down through the cracks upon the slightest provocation, and were a great nuisance when cooking was in progress. A layer of damp moss should first have been spread upon the poles, then the spruce, and finally a thick layer of moss over all. This upper layer was duly applied, and being soft and spongy, contributed in no small degree to the waterproof quality of the roof, which was rather more flat than such a roof should be. As an additional protection against rain, several tents were spread above the moss, and now the cabin was complete, except for the "chinking," and interior furnishings.

"Chinking" is the filling of the cracks between the logs. The boys soon became skilled in this work, and most of it was left for them to do, while the men were engaged in heavier labors. Small dead spruces, slender and straight as bean-poles, were first cut down in large numbers. These were trimmed as nearly as possible to the size and shape of the cracks, and driven firmly into place with the blows of a hatchet. Such crevices as still remained were stuffed with moss and clay.

The door consisted of a light framework of poles, covered with cheese-cloth, of which Pennock had a supply; and the windows were of the same material. Though not transparent, it admitted a goodly amount of light, and promised to keep out insects and the wind.

Within the house, a sheet-iron stove was set up in the opening left for a fire place, which was then enclosed above and on the sides and rear, with poles set close together and chinked, an aperture being left for the stovepipe. Sleds were so arranged as to form a dining-table and seats.

The boys had set their hearts on building bunks to sleep in. This was approved of by their father and uncle, since it was undoubtedly healthier to be off the ground, and they suggested that two double bunks be built in the southwest corner, large enough to accommodate the four. The boys were left to exercise their own ingenuity in this work, and they succeeded in turning out two very good berths, constructed wholly of spruce poles, and arranged like those of a steamer's stateroom. Soft boughs were spread upon the berths, and then the blankets, in which rude quarters they slept as comfortably as they ever had at home. The upper berth, too, served David as a shelf, upon which to develop his photographs.

This nucleus of a city it was voted to call Pennock's Post.

How refreshing it was, as they surveyed the finished product of their labors, to feel that they had reached their destination, that there was no exhausting journey to be resumed on the morrow, and that at all times they could be sure of a warm, dry resting place with a roof over their heads!

## CHAPTER XIX

### THE FIRST PROSPECT-HOLE

IT was now the first week in May. The snow was entirely gone from the lowlands, melted by the breath of the chinook. The creek was swollen to twice its normal size, and had overflowed its banks in many places, bursting its icy bonds and stranding the ice-cakes high among the bushes. As for the river, that, too, had freed itself, and its muddy current was rising inch by inch. On the mountains they could almost see the snow-line creep higher and higher each day, and soon on the lesser heights no snow remained except in the gullies, giving to the mountains a streaked aspect.

Robins and song-sparrows put in an appearance, and ducks were everywhere. On the very first warm day, bees, flies, and a mosquito or two were thawed into life, and hummed and buzzed in the sunshine as if there had never been any winter. In every sandy bluff and bank the ground-squirrels, beautifully mottled little creatures, came out of their holes, and sat up on their haunches as stiff as a ramrod, with their fore-paws demurely folded on their breasts, and sunned themselves and cast curious glances at their new neighbors.

Purple crocuses blossomed in abundance, and everywhere grass was growing green and buds were starting. Spring had come!

"What do you think of a prospecting trip?" asked Uncle Will of Pennock, one morning. "I believe we can sink a shaft now."

"That's a good idea," said Pennock. "The frost ought to be out of the upper soil by this time. If it isn't, we can thaw it with fire."

"The one thing I don't like about this place," continued Uncle Will, "is that the creek seems to be deserted. We heard rumors of extraordinary richness here, and if there's any truth in them, there ought to be some signs of life hereabouts."

"That's so," admitted Pennock. "It was Cannon who advised the Cap'n to leave a few men here. He said he sunk a hole last year and found gold enough to make it worth while to explore more fully. What really brought our party into this country, though, was a report of a rich strike up above. That's where the rest of them have gone; but I don't know just how far it is.'

"Well," said Uncle Will, "the stories I heard may have been misleading. We'll see what there is here anyhow, and take our chances. By the way, there's another creek to the southeast yonder, where you see that gully in the mountain. We might send a party there."

To this proposition Pennock assented. Accordingly Mr. Bradford and Roly, with Large, Nichols, and the two Indians, set off toward the gully, which was about six miles distant, while Uncle Will, David, Pennock, Reitz, Adair, and Johnson started for the headwaters of the creek beside which they had camped, — a journey of four miles. We may as well follow the fortunes of the latter party.

There was no trail worthy of the name, but once or twice hoof-marks were discovered, probably made by Cannon's pack horse the previous season. Sometimes they entered forests of standing spruce and poplar, either growing or fire-killed, and now it was a district of fallen trees, where it was almost impossible to advance, from which they emerged with a sigh of relief into some open grassy meadow near the stream, where walking was pleasant and easy. Presently they ascended a clay bluff a hundred feet high, skirting its edge where it was free from timber. From this vantage ground they could see the snowy peaks of the Dasar-dee-ash Mountains, thirty miles to the south, on the other side of which lay the claims they had taken in April. Uncle Will examined the fine clay of the bluff, and gave it as his opinion that it would make excellent bricks and pottery.

In an hour and a half, they came to the foot-hills, where the stream fell noisily over a bed of boulders in a pretty glen. A sharp lookout was kept, but no signs of Cannon's work were seen. At length it was decided to sink a hole on the south bank where a bed of gravel had been deposited by the water. From the nature of the rocks about them, they concluded that bed-rock was not far below the surface. Picks, shovels, and a gold-pan had been brought, and the men took turns at the digging. It was hard work, for many large stones were encountered frozen into their places, and these could only be pried loose at risk of a bent pick. When a depth of twelve inches was reached, Pennock filled the pan with a sample of the gravel, and took it to the stream, while the others, except Adair, who was swinging the pick, gathered around him, eager to know the result of the test. Not a color was found, but there was black sand and in it two small rubies.

The discovery of the rubies did not seem to offset the disappointment of the men at finding no gold, — a fact at which David wondered, until his uncle informed him that those gems were quite commonly found in the Northwest, and such small ones were of little value. David resolved, however, to look about for himself, and, in a mound of sand thrown up by ants, he found a dozen or more, some of them a little larger than the ones in the pan. These he carefully picked out, and put in his match-box for safe keeping.

Meanwhile, the work in the prospect-hole went steadily on. At a depth of two feet a small color was found, by

## THE FIRST PROSPECT-HOLE

which time it was noon, and work ceased for an hour. By the middle of the afternoon the hole was three feet and a half deep, and solid rock was gained, though toward the last so much water entered that digging was difficult, and bailing had to be resorted to. At the bedrock, where all their hopes rested, were found a few insignificant colors, — nothing more.

Uncle Will, usually so cheerful, was quite downcast at this result. He had heard the rumors of gold from men whom he trusted, and was obliged to conclude that they had themselves been misled. Indeed, it seemed to be one of those instances in which a very small tale, by long travelling and frequent repetition, becomes strangely magnified and distorted. The Thirty-six had detached few men here because the story, as they had heard it, had located the wealth in a different place. Still there might be a good deal of gold on this creek, for a single hole is usually not enough to determine the character of a gulch. At least one more shaft must be sunk where the gravel was deeper, before all hope need be abandoned. Even if worst came to worst, there still remained the Alder Creek claims, and Lucky's nugget.

It turned out that the other party, under Mr. Bradford, had met with even less success. Rubies they had found, but not a single color of gold. However, they had not reached bed-rock at the end of the first day.

Uncle Will and his companions returned to the cabin

a few minutes before the others. Seated on the ground outside the door, they found an Indian family, consisting of an old bent squaw, two young women, and a thin, weak-looking young man. The old squaw, evidently the mother of the others, waved her arms in token of welcome as soon as she saw the white men. Then, touching the young man's breast she exclaimed, "Him sick, you savvy?"

"Sick, is he?" repeated Uncle Will, looking at the pinched features and wasted frame.

"Sick — yis — you savvy [understand]?" said the squaw.

"Consumption," said Uncle Will to David. "It's very prevalent among the Indians, and carries off hundreds." Then turning to the old Indian woman he added, "I savvy, — very bad, very sick. Have some tea?"

"Tea! Yis, yis," answered she, eagerly, for tea is considered a great luxury by the Indians, and this family, dressed in ragged, cast-off clothing, seemed too abjectly poor to buy anything at the trading-post. Indeed, the only food they had was dried salmon, though the man carried an antiquated shot-gun.

Uncle Will made some tea, and the natives drank it delightedly in the cabin, which they entered without invitation as soon as the door was opened.

It must be explained here that the door was fastened

by a sliding pole which ran some distance along the inner side of one of the front logs, and was held in place by wooden pegs. The pole was shoved across the door by means of a knife-blade inserted from the outside between two logs at a crevice left for the purpose five feet from the door. In this manner the door had been locked that morning when the two parties set off. Doubtless the Indians had tried the door; but finding it secure, and seeing no means of opening it, they had not ventured to break in, but waited for the return of the miners.

Both Uncle Will and Pennock realized the desirability of keeping the secret of the lock from the visitors, and this they attempted to do when the door was opened, Uncle Will attracting the attention of the Indians, while Pennock softly stole up to the crevice and pried back the bar.

But though the natives did not see the door opened, they intended none the less to know how it was done, and that was why they so promptly entered the cabin with the others. However, the white men thought it best to say nothing, for it might be that they would drink their tea and go out without noticing the door. Pennock, who was a Colorado man and had no liking for the "redskins," kept an eye on them from the moment of their entrance.

The old squaw, after a quick inventory of the contents of the cabin, glanced furtively toward the door, and at once discovered the long bar, but she did not know exactly how it was managed. So presently she shuffled unconcernedly up to the front of the cabin, and, turning about, faced the centre of the room. To all appearances, she was idly leaning against the logs, but both Pennock and David noticed that her hands behind her back were busily fumbling with the bar, and moving it cautiously back and forth. The "game was up." Knowing the existence of the bar, and its height from the ground, she would easily discover from the outside the crevice through which it was controlled.

"The rascally old witch of an Injun!" muttered Pennock through his teeth; but he knew it was of no use now to make a fuss. He broke out violently, however, when the visitors were gone and it was discovered that a nearly empty butter-can outside the house had disappeared with them.

"They're all sneak-thieves, every one of 'em," he declared angrily; "and the worst of it is that the old squaw learned the secret of our lock. I saw her fumbling round. Now we've got to leave somebody here every time we go away. I'd just like to —!"

This sounded very much like the preface to a dire threat; but Mr. Bradford, who had arrived some minutes previously, interrupted it by observing that the Indians would not be likely to take food or clothing.

"No," said Uncle Will. "They'll make off with

empty cans, or any little thing they think won't be missed, but they would n't take goods of value. That's too dangerous in this country. Besides, we 've treated them well, and they 're pretty low-down creatures if they steal from us now."

"All the same," said Pennock, "there was half an inch of good butter in that can, and I was intending to make a coffee cup of it as soon as it was empty. They 're a shrewd lot, if they are dirty and ignorant. I hope they 've gone for good."

It was a vain hope. A little later, a column of smoke half a mile up the trail northward showed that they had camped.

## CHAPTER XX

### ROLY GOES DUCK-HUNTING

FOR many days, no game of any kind had been secured in abundance, and Uncle Will, who saw the pork and bacon disappearing too rapidly, cast about for some means of eking out the supplies. With this end in view, he prevailed upon his brother to let Roly spend a day in hunting, knowing full well that nothing would please the lad more. Roly had been careful with the shot-gun, and had fairly earned this privilege.

The days in that high latitude were now so long that, even at midnight, there was a twilight glow over the summits of Father and Son in the north. At three in the morning, it was broad daylight, and Roly, as he awoke into delightful anticipations, heard the "quack, quack" of big brown mallards, and the whistling wings of smaller ducks, as they flew to their feeding grounds. He was out of the bunk in an instant, and slipping on his jacket and long rubber boots, which, with his cap, were the only articles needed to complete his attire, he snatched a hasty breakfast, put a piece of corn-bread in his pocket, and then, gun in hand, softly opened the cabin door, and stole out into the fresh morning air. The joy of youth was in his heart, and a sense of freedom and adventure came with the thought of hunting all alone in that great wide valley, and made the blood tingle to his finger-tips.

There were ponds and marshes in every direction, but Roly decided to cross the river and walk southward, for he observed several ducks flying that way. He therefore made his way down the face of the bluff, through the sliding sand to the river-bank, where a raft of three logs had been moored. Loosing this unwieldy craft, he laid the unloaded gun upon it, then seized the long pushpole, and sprang on board. It required considerable effort to free the lower end of the raft from the mud, but finally it swung out into the stream. Roly pushed and paddled lustily for some moments before he succeeded in urging the heavy affair to the farther shore, for the current was strong and carried him down the stream fully two hundred yards. He fastened the raft to a clump of alders, picked up the gun, and set off up the stream to the south, keeping a sharp lookout for any kind of game.

After penetrating a tangled thicket, he saw that he was coming out upon a long, open swamp. There might be ducks here, and he paused to look carefully at two or three pools which gleamed at some distance. Seeing nothing, however, he skirted the edge of the swamp to the higher wooded land beyond, where he was startled by the sudden chattering of a red squirrel in a spruce over his head. He could have shot the squirrel easily, but felt it would be unmanly to kill any creature wantonly. The little animal was too small to have much value as food, and, besides, cartridges were precious. So he passed on, in the hope of seeing larger game.

On every sandy bank the ground-squirrels sat, and while they were larger than the red squirrels, they were very lean after their long winter sleep. They were plentiful near the cabin, and Roly thought he could catch them with traps or snares, as soon as they were in better condition. For the present, therefore, the ground-squirrels were also left in peace.

Everywhere were traces of rabbits, but no rabbits were to be seen. Lucky had explained this one day by saying, "Rabbit come bime-by — plenty rabbit — all gone now," — which Mr. Bradford interpreted to mean that the animals migrated from place to place, and at some seasons would, no doubt, fairly overrun the country, while at other times they would be very scarce.

At length Roly caught a glimpse of a long, swampy pond between the trees ahead, and on its smooth surface, near the centre, he could see three ducks, one small, the others larger and of a dark-brown color, — doubtless mallards. Hardly had he made this discovery, and paused to consider how he should approach, when up flew two little ducks, one variegated, and the other an even brown,

— the male and female, — from a near arm of the pond which had escaped his notice. The boy trembled, lest the other three should also be alarmed; but they went on dipping their bills under the water quite unconcernedly, while the small one occasionally dived.

Near the bank stood a green spruce, the branches of which came thickly down to the ground on the side toward the water, forming a splendid cover. Roly thought that if he could only reach this tree, it would be an easy matter to bag a duck or two, so he started cautiously on tiptoe, keeping the tree between himself and the birds. But there were many dry twigs and little bushes in the space over which he had to pass, and the two mallards — most wary of Alaskan ducks — presently took alarm at the almost imperceptible crackling on the shore. Up they flew, quacking loudly, and making a wide sweep in Roly's direction, so that he felt sure he could have shot one of them on the wing. Indeed, he would have tried it, had not his father given strict orders to the contrary. Cartridges were too precious here to be spent on experiments. Roly had never practised wing-shooting, and his father knew he would waste a great deal of ammunition before acquiring the knack. Where sport was the object, not food, and ammunition was plentiful, Mr. Bradford would have advised his son to shoot only at birds on the wing, that being more sportsmanlike, and giving the birds a chance. But here it was simply a matter of food, and every cartridge must count.

Roly, therefore, after one longing look at the now distant mallards, crept up under the tree, and, kneeling on the moss, took aim through an opening in the branches at the small duck, which seemed much less timid than the others, though it had paddled a short distance toward the farther shore. There was a puff of smoke, and the report rang out sharply on the still morning air. The duck flopped once or twice, then lay motionless on the water, on perceiving which, Roly executed an immediate triumphal war-dance under the tree.

It was now a question whether the pleased youngster could secure his prize. The wind was too light to blow it ashore, and the longest pole he could use would not be long enough. The water looked dark and deep, but at least he would try it; so, pulling up his rubber boots to their full length, he stepped carefully out into the pond. To his surprise, he found that the mud on the bottom was solidly frozen, and the water was nowhere more than two feet deep. The duck was therefore quickly reached and brought back to the tree, where the young hunter ambushed himself again to await developments.

He now bethought him of the empty shell in his gun, and had hardly thrown it out, preparatory to snapping another into place, when two fine mallards appeared from the southward, and plumped heavily down upon the water, not thirty feet from his hiding place. Alas that, of *all* times, the cartridge should stick at *that* golden moment! But stick it did, refusing to go in, or even to come out again. Roly fairly bit his lips with vexation, and tugged with nervous fingers at the mechanism of the breech, keeping an eye on the ducks all the while, and trying to be as quiet as possible. It was all to no purpose. A bit of dirt had found its way in somewhere, and he had to shake the gun violently before the cartridge would move. The mallards could not be expected to turn a deaf ear to this commotion. They raised their heads, and then with one impulse fluttered up and away, and poor Roly nearly cried, as the obstinate cartridge slipped easily in, ere the birds were fairly out of sight.

It was yet early, however, and the lad knew that he had only to wait patiently, to find another chance. He could occasionally hear the whistle of wings as a flock flew past, and sometimes he could see the birds from his covert. He had watched and waited a half hour, when four ducks settled down at the remote end of the pond. They were out of range, but soon began to come closer. Two were like those he had first frightened from the narrow arm of the marsh, small in size, the male brightly plumaged, the female a smooth brown. It was a male of this species which he had shot. The other two seemed much larger, but in other respects almost exactly like their companions. They kept quite near each other, and splashed or dived unconscious of danger.

Roly watched his opportunity, hoping they would bunch together, so that he might kill more than one at a shot. He had not long to wait. As they came in range, the two larger birds and the smaller female were exactly in line, one beyond another. It was the favorable moment. He aimed at the middle one and fired.

The small male duck, which had been out of the line, seemed bewildered rather than frightened by the noise. He dived, came up at a distance, and paddled away without taking flight. The two larger birds were instantly killed, while the small female beyond was crippled, and fluttered around in a circle. Roly felt justified in using another cartridge at once to put her out of suffering. Then he waded out and brought in his prizes, the fourth duck having escaped into the swamp-grass.

He wondered if the others back at the cabin had heard the shots. It was not unlikely, for they would be stirring by this time. Having seated himself again, he fell to thinking over the strange life he had been leading for the past two months, so different from that at home. His reverie was interrupted by the arrival of a fine mallard, which was bagged without delay.

No more ducks visited the pond, though he waited until the middle of the morning, when they ceased flying. He therefore prepared to return. The legs of the birds were tied together, and they were slung over the barrel of the gun, which he then raised to his shoulder, and found he had something of a burden.

But he was destined to carry still more. He had not proceeded far when he heard the clucking of a ptarmigan in the woods to his left, so leaving the ducks where he could easily find them, he stole softly in the direction of the sound. The clucking soon seemed very near, — so near that he did not dare to go a step farther, for fear of frightening the bird, but, look as he would, he could see nothing of it. He scanned the ground for a glimpse of white, forgetting entirely that the ptarmigan becomes brown when the snow disappears, and was just giving up in despair when he sighted the bird perched on the dead branch of a tree across a little glen. And, what was better, there were two in the tree. Roly manœuvred till he had the birds in line, and it was such an easy shot that both fell stone dead at once, amid a shower of feathers.

"Well done, Roly, my boy!" said Mr. Bradford, heartily, when the prospectors returned late that afternoon and found Roly's bunch of birds. "Let's see, here's a mallard, two golden-eyes, two little butter-balls, and two ptarmigan, — seven birds in all. And how many shots did you fire?"

"Five," said Roly, with pardonable pride. "There were no large flocks to fire into, but I meant to make every shot tell."

"Yes," said his father, "and you've done very well, especially for a beginner."

"And how many did you get, Johnson?" asked Uncle Will. Johnson had been on a similar errand for the other party.

"Five ducks and a white rabbit," was the reply. "On the whole, Roly has carried off the honors, for I fired six shots."

So the campers obtained fresh meat, and all were very glad to abstain awhile from bacon. Both Roly and David went duck-hunting often after that, and always with good success throughout the migrating season.

## CHAPTER XXI

### LAST DAYS AT PENNOCK'S POST

THE Indian family hung about the premises more or less, hoping, no doubt, for more tea or another butter-can. They set steel traps in the neighboring sand-banks, and caught many ground-squirrels, some of which they offered to the white men for twenty-five cents a pair; but while ducks, ptarmigan, and occasionally a wild swan or rabbit could be shot, no one was inclined to buy. David and Roly thought, however, that it would do no harm to catch ground-squirrels for themselves, and they set about making snares.

These were simple, and consisted of a strong but slender willow branch, fixed firmly in the bank high above the hole in a nearly horizontal position, a stronger stick similarly set between the other and the hole, and a piece of string with a slip-noose at one end. The other end of the string was tied to the extremity of the upper willow branch, which was then bent down until the noose hung over the hole. A small loop, slipped over the point of the lower stick, held the noose in position.

All being ready, it was expected that Mr. Squirrel, coming out to take an airing, would run his head through the noose, carrying it along with him until the loop slipped from the lower stick, thus releasing the elastic upper stick, which would jerk poor Mr. Squirrel into the air, and hang him for no greater fault than his ignorance. The theory was perfect, but in practice Mr. Squirrel displayed more cleverness than he had been given credit for. Sometimes he pushed the noose aside, and again he would slip through it, and though occasionally a snare was sprung, the denizens of the sand-bank always managed to get away.

The boys therefore decided to try to buy two traps from the Indians; and one day, when the whole family was present, David gave them to understand by signs what was wanted. He shut his hands together with a snap, then held up two fingers. The old squaw quickly nodded her head, and jabbered some unintelligible gutturals, which might have been taken for a fit of choking, but it was evident that she was willing to sell two traps, and on the following day she brought them.

"Probably," said David, as he gave her two fifty-cent pieces, "she is giving me the oldest and rustiest she has."

"Yes," said Pennock, "you can depend upon that. Better see if they'll work, before you buy 'em."

The boys therefore snapped them once or twice, to make sure that they were in order.

"Now," said Roly, "we must get her to show us how to set them in the holes," — whereupon he made a number of signs, which she quickly comprehended. She took the traps to the nearest hole and placed them in the entrance, covering them with dry grass, so that the animals would not hesitate to walk over them. The traps proved so old and worn that very few squirrels were caught at first, but Mr. Bradford doctored them one day with a file, after which they were quite effective.

Not many days later, the old squaw fell ill, and her consumptive son and one of her daughters came down in haste to the cabin, in the hope that the white men would aid them. It chanced that no one was at home but Pennock, he who most of all detested the Indians.

The young woman, by signs and the few English words she knew, made known the state of the case, and urged the white man to come in person, while her brother, with a sweep of the hand toward the east, repeated the word "gold" over and over. He well knew what white men most covet. Pennock, however, did not believe the Indian knew any more about gold than he did. Furthermore, he was not a medical man, and felt that he could do no good by visiting the patient. But he made out that the trouble was a cough, and so without more ado he looked over his slender stock of medicines and picked out a mustard plaster, which he gave to the young woman, showing her by signs to dampen it and lay it on her mother's chest. The two Indians appeared genuinely grateful for the plaster, and offered fifty cents in payment, which of course Pennock refused. So they went off with light hearts, to try the white man's remedy.

"Ah!" exclaimed Uncle Will later, when Pennock related what he had done; "for all your blustering the other day, you've a soft spot under your waistcoat, I see. That's what I call returning good for evil."

"Maybe it was," said Pennock. "I couldn't refuse the poor wretches."

Whether the mustard plaster proved effective or not, the dwellers in the cabin never knew, for a day or two later the Indians disappeared, probably continuing their journey toward Hootchi, a Stik village fifty miles to the north.

For a time nothing was learned of the fortunes of the large party which had toiled down the valley in April, beyond the fact that they had not been able to drag their sleds more than three miles. This news was brought by one of their number, who said that the sleds and most of the goods had been cached, and he had been left in charge. The others had taken from fifty to one hundred and twenty-five pounds, according to their size and strength, and had pushed ahead.

A few small bands of Indians visited the cabin, but as they came from the south they had no news of the gold-seekers. With one of these bands were two dogs of moderate size, staggering under loads of forty and fifty pounds, while their lazy masters carried absolutely nothing but the clothes they wore. Another party brought fresh whitefish, which they bartered for flour and coffee. Four cups of flour and a pound of coffee were accepted in exchange for seven fish, and both parties seemed pleased with the bargain.

This incident prompted the Bradford boys to fish in the creek and river, but they met with no success, and concluded that it was yet too early. Coffee Jack, however, made a most welcome contribution to the larder one day, by coming in with his hat full of duck's eggs, which he had found in a swamp.

At last, on the fifteenth of May, the leader of the Thirty-six returned with five white men and four Indians. Some of them were so worn with hunger and fatigue as to be hardly recognizable, and all were utterly discouraged. Their hopes were dispelled; they had found no gold.

The big party had advanced more than fifty miles with their heavy loads, and had built two cabins to serve as starting-points for further explorations. The men who had remained there would have to draw on the cache near Pennock's Post very soon, and the leader had given them orders to raft these supplies down the river twenty-five miles to the point where the stream turned westward from the trail, and there establish a storehouse. Meanwhile, those with the captain were to go to the Kah Sha River claims and help the four who had been originally left there. The captain himself intended to go to Pyramid Harbor with the Indians, and bring in a fresh supply of provisions on pack horses, as soon as there was grass enough along the trail for the subsistence of the animals.

The men were given a hearty supper at Pennock's, for they sorely needed it. Indeed, they declared it was the first "square meal" they had enjoyed in two weeks. After a good night's rest and breakfast, they resumed their journey in better spirits.

Five days later came a startling piece of information. Mr. Bratnober, a mining man well known on the Dalton trail, with a young man named Onderdonk and two Indian packers, stopped at the cabin on his way north. He said that war had broken out between the United States and Spain in April, and that Admiral Dewey had won a great victory at Manila.

As may be imagined, this news wrought David and Roly up to the highest pitch of excitement.

"Just think," said they, — "war for a month, and we did n't know it!"

For a moment, they almost regretted that they had come to such a far country, and they thought longingly of the stirring times at home. Their father and uncle were also much moved, and their first impulse was to drop everything and hasten back, — the one to protect his family, the other to enter the army or navy. But as they talked the matter over, they saw there was little likelihood that the Spaniards could effect a landing on the American coast; and as to Uncle Will's enlistment, though that would have just suited his roving temperament, he decided, upon his brother's urgent request, to await fuller information. All agreed, however, that it would be wise to return at once to the Kah Sha River, a distance of thirty-five miles.

There were several reasons for this move. The first and most imperative was the fact that their provisions at Pennock's would last but one week more. In the second place, they had demonstrated to their entire satisfaction that there was no gold worth mining in that vicinity, and the Thirty-six had found none farther north. Thirdly, there certainly *was* gold on their Alder Creek claims, and Lucky's nugget was probably now uncovered. Finally, they would be within thirty miles of Dalton's Post, and likely to hear more news from incoming prospectors.

## CHAPTER XXII

### A HARD JOURNEY

PREPARATIONS for departure were begun that evening. The Bradfords overhauled all their belongings, and decided what they would take and what they would have to leave. There was even less food than they supposed, — barely enough for three days, — but tents, blankets, cooking utensils, tools, guns, ammunition, clothing, and various small articles promised to load them heavily, and it was seen that a part of their goods must be abandoned.

The sleds, of course, were no longer of any use. Most of the Mackinaw clothing was now too heavy. The ice-creepers and snow-shoes would not be needed, and the former were thrown out at once, but David and Roly could not part with their snow-shoes, which they desired to take home and hang upon the walls of their room. The rubber shoe-packs were nearly worn out, and were discarded. David regretfully abandoned the two steel traps, which were heavy, and not so necessary as some other things. The down quilts which had served them so well were too bulky to be taken along, though not of much weight. So they went through the whole list, retaining this, rejecting that, until they were ready to make up their packs.

Next morning, Nichols, a Bostonian who usually cooked for Pennock's party, obligingly prepared breakfast for the Bradfords, who were busily completing their packing. Large, a tall, gaunt San Diego man, — whose initials were A. T., so that, as he was fond of pointing out, he was always "At Large," — gave them useful hints about binding the packs. He was a veteran of the Civil War, and remembered his travels with knapsack and blanket. Reitz and Adair, also from San Diego, and Pennock and Johnson, assisted in various ways.

After several failures, the boys acquired the knack of making up and binding a pack. To accomplish this, they first arranged their goods in the least possible space, and rolled them in tent or blankets, — for David had the latter, and Roly the tent, — thus forming a flattened cylindrical bundle. A lash-rope from a sled was wound once lengthwise and twice widthwise around the pack, the latter windings being about ten inches apart. The bundle being set on end, a strong canvas pack-strap two inches wide and three feet long was inserted under the lower winding at its junction with the lengthwise rope, and the ends were made fast to the upper winding about ten inches apart, leaving the two lengths of the strap somewhat loose, so that the packer could thrust his arms through these loops. Thus the straps passed over his shoulders and under his armpits. To prevent them from slipping from the shoulders, they were bound together by a cord passing across the chest. By means of the long, loose end of the pack-rope, brought over either shoulder and grasped by the hands, the load could be shifted a little from time to time if it became painful.

At seven, all was ready, and the Bradfords took leave of their friends and cast a last look at the little cabin.

"I guess you'll see some of us before long," said Pennock, as he bade them good-by. "There's no sort of use in our staying here. Remember us to the boys, and leave us some of the gold."

Uncle Will motioned Lucky and Coffee Jack to lead the way, and off they started through the open timber to the main trail, which passed but a few hundred yards from the cabin. The hoofs of horses and cattle, travelling to Dawson the previous season, had clearly defined it, and one would have thought it a cow-path in a pasture, had it been in New England instead of the Northwest Territory. For two miles it was smooth and hard, and the walking was excellent, except that sometimes a tree had fallen across the path.

Each of the three men carried a load of seventy-five pounds, though Lucky would have thought nothing of one hundred and fifty, being trained to the work from childhood. David had fifty pounds, and Roly and Coffee Jack forty each.

Before they had gone half a mile, the boys realized that the journey they had begun would be a severe test of endurance. The pressure of the straps caused pain in their shoulders, and soon their arms and hands tingled with the prickly sensation which arises when the blood cannot circulate freely. They were obliged to avoid sticks and stones with great care, for a sprain or bruise might easily result from stepping upon them so heavily. Even Uncle Will, who had done a good deal of packing, was quite ready to rest when pain compelled the boys to halt. They secured temporary comfort by seating themselves in front of a fallen tree so that the packs would rest upon it, and the prickly sensation in the arms was relieved by loosening the straps a little. Fortunately all had been well rested and strengthened by their stay at Pennock's Post, and were fortified to endure both pain and fatigue. Mr. Bradford was as strong now as his rugged brother. David had grown muscular, and gained in weight. Roly looked much as usual, but his muscles were certainly harder than they had ever been at home.

Following the east shore of the river, they came to the mouth of the creek whose headwaters Mr. Bradford had explored. It was crossed by a single narrow log twenty feet long, a rude and dangerous bridge for any one who had not a clear head and steady nerves. The water, six or eight feet below, was still and deep and muddy. To fall into it with a heavy pack meant almost certain death, if assistance were not at hand.

Lucky and Coffee Jack, however, crossed unhesitatingly, and Uncle Will performed the feat without betraying dizziness; but when Mr. Bradford's turn came, he looked somewhat doubtful, declaring that he had done no tight-rope walking since his boyhood days, and he feared that if his head swam, the rest of him would soon be swimming too. On the whole, he thought it wise to remove his pack and carry it in such manner that he could drop it if he fell. He then advanced over the log slowly and cautiously, for its upper surface, hewn level and smooth, was but four inches wide. The boys carried their packs across in the same manner, for though they were good at balancing and had no fear of dizziness, yet to transport a top-heavy, swaying load was very different from making the passage unencumbered.

Beyond the creek the land was swampy, and travelling more difficult. They circled one of the small lakes which they had crossed on their northward march, and came at length to a hill two hundred feet high. This was climbed slowly and with several pauses, for they found themselves out of breath the instant they left the level ground, and the perspiration fairly dripped from their faces. At the top, David threw himself down before a log with his pack resting upon it, but Roly thought he could improve on this arrangement by sitting on the trunk itself and letting the pack come against the great upturned roots. Unfortunately, in the act of seating himself, he leaned too far backward, and instantly his load overbalanced him. Over he went on his back on the other side of the tree, pack down and heels up, to the amusement of his friends and his own discomfiture, for, try as he would, he could not move.

"Roly seems to have come to anchor," observed Uncle Will, with a most provoking twinkle in his eye. He and his brother had seated themselves at a little distance.

"Yes," said Mr. Bradford, smiling as he contemplated Roly's fruitless efforts to turn over; "and perhaps it's just as well. We shall know where to find him."

"I should think you would," said poor Roly, laughing in spite of himself. "I can't get up till somebody helps me, and I did want to look at the valley."

"Oh, no!" put in David, with exasperating composure; "the sky is far prettier. Just see those beautiful white summer clouds sailing along."

"Let them sail if they want to," said the prostrate youth, impatiently. "I don't care. Have you all conspired against me? Give me your hand, Dave, you're nearest."

"Oh, I don't know," answered David, without moving. "Do you remember a certain April Fool's trick, young man?"

"Yes," groaned Roly.

"Don't you think you ought to be punished?"

"Not any more than I am. My pack will punish me enough for twenty tricks before the day is over."

"True enough, youngster," said David, with swift repentance, as he thought of his own sore shoulders and the growing pain in his back. "Here's my hand. You had my forgiveness long ago."

"That's right!" said Mr. Bradford, who had been on the point of going to Roly's assistance when this dialogue began. "Don't lay up resentment, my lad."

So Roly came up smiling, and they all took a good look at the valley of Pennock's Post, the whole length and breadth of which lay spread before them. There in the blue distance northward were the Father and Son, with the narrow pass between. Nearer was the granite cliff to the west of the cabin, and even the sandy bluff that fronted the river was distinguishable. But the little house was hidden in the forest.

Soon after the march was resumed, a small and beautiful lake was skirted, lying east of the trail. Beyond it towered a mountain, upon whose green slope gleamed a white waterfall, while near the hither shore emerged an islet crowned with trees. Uncle Will looked particularly at the ice, which had melted away from the margin of this lake, but still appeared firm in the centre.

"There's about an even chance," said he, "that we can cross Dasar-dee-ash, instead of going clear around it. We

# A HARD JOURNEY

must make the short cut if possible, for our food is almost gone. I think the ice will bear us, if we can only get upon it."

With every step, the packs became more painful. Shoulders and hips grew sore, backs ached, and feet grew lame. It was now necessary to rest every quarter of a mile. They passed another lake, along whose shores the trail was rough and swampy. Wooded ridges rose on either side of them. In some places they found small berries of the previous season, which, being pleasant to the taste and harmless, were eagerly eaten.

The Indians at length left the trail and turned through a cleft in the hills in the direction of Lake Dasar-dee-ash, which lay three miles to the west. Only here and there could the white men distinguish faint signs of an old path which Lucky and Coffee Jack followed with wonderful acuteness. On reaching the lake, the Bradfords estimated that they had carried their loads at least fourteen miles, and it was with a great sense of relief that they threw their burdens to the ground and proceeded to pitch the tents with what little energy remained.

At this spot an old Indian and his family were fishing. They were evidently well known to Lucky and his brother, whom they entertained that evening with a supper of salmon and whitefish, — a fortunate circumstance, since the provisions of the Bradfords were running so low that they barely had enough for themselves.

The second day's march was even more severe than the first. It was needful to hasten, for the old Indian could spare no fish when the Bradfords offered to buy, and even Lucky could procure but half a dozen small ones for himself and Coffee Jack on the journey. Rations were therefore reduced, for it was plain that it would be well along in the third day before they could reach Uncle Will's cache, even should it prove possible to cross upon the ice; while if the crossing should seem too dangerous, it would require a fourth day to go around by the rough, wooded south shore.

At the old Indian's camping ground, the outlook was anything but favorable. It was now the twenty-second of May, and so warm that the green buds were swelling in every tree. As far as the eye could see, the ice had retreated from the beach, leaving a strip of open water from fifty to a hundred feet wide. There was nothing to do but follow an old trail along the eastern shore in the hope that somewhere conditions would be more encouraging.

The heavy packs were strapped on once more, and off they tramped across a wide marsh, now jumping as well as they could from hummock to hummock, now wading through water knee-deep. Beyond the marsh they had a bad trail, or no trail at all, for the remainder of the day, sometimes forcing their way through thickets, sometimes clambering through a region of fallen timber, where the great trunks were piled in such intricate confusion that a passage seemed utterly hopeless, and again crossing a newly burned woodland where dry dust and ashes lay several inches deep, and rose from beneath their feet in stifling clouds. A river a hundred feet in width was crossed by a convenient jam of logs and trees. Late in the afternoon they took to the beach, where the rough cobblestones offered the lesser evil, and after a mile of this painful walking came to a little cove where at last was a sight so welcome that the boys gave a glad shout. A narrow spur of ice was seen, bridging the strip of blue water.

## CHAPTER XXIII

### THE LAKE AFFORDS TWO MEALS AND A PERILOUS CROSSING

WHILE the Bradfords were pitching the tents, Lucky set off to try the ice preparatory to the morrow's attempt to cross. Coffee Jack, instead of accompanying his brother, made Roly understand that he wanted a line and a hook.

"Going fishing?" asked Roly, eagerly.

"Yes," said the bright-eyed Indian boy. "Big feesh — yes."

So Roly dove into his pack, which lay unbound on the shore, and presently produced a fish-line wound around a chip. A small hook was already attached. Coffee Jack took the line and examined it doubtfully, as if he feared it might not be strong enough. Young as he was, he had learned many tricks of hunting, fishing, and woodcraft from his brother; and as Roly was glad to acquire such knowledge, he watched the Indian boy carefully.

First about thirty feet of the line were unwound and then doubled, so as to give a length of fifteen feet for the double line.

CHILDREN OF THE WILDERNESS.

## THE LAKE AFFORDS TWO MEALS

"Cut?" asked Coffee Jack, drawing his finger across it, to represent a knife.

"Yes," said Roly; "you can cut it."

So Coffee Jack cut the line and handed back to Roly the part he did not need. He now took one of the small whitefish which he had obtained from the old Indian that morning, and cut off the rear half of its body with the tail attached. This he cut open, and trimmed down with his knife until it resembled a large shiner. The whole hook was then placed inside the body, and the opening sewed up with a needle and thread supplied by his friend.

The Indian boy was now ready to set his double line in place. Accompanied by Roly, who was warned by his father to be extremely careful, he warily crossed the ice-bridge to the firmer ice beyond. In places this ice was a foot thick, but it was so honeycombed by the sun's rays as to be very treacherous. There were numerous openings of various sizes to be avoided, as well as places where the ice had been reduced to an unsafe thinness. Coffee Jack walked out to a point several hundred yards from the beach, having first cut a long pole and a slender stick, the latter about three feet in length. He selected an opening in the ice two feet in diameter, the sides of which were thick and safe to stand upon; and having tied the small stick firmly across the centre of the pole, so that a foot of it was on one side, and two feet on the other, he notched the short end and made the line fast to it.  The pole was then set across the hole, and the bait allowed to sink down through the clear water.  It was evident that if a fish swallowed the bait and attempted to swim away with it, the pole would hold him prisoner, while the short stick would tip up and announce the capture.  Roly had seen the pole and pointer used in New England, but the idea of sewing the hook inside of the bait-fish was a novel one.

"Good!" said Coffee Jack, as he contemplated his contrivance a moment, and then turned back toward the shore.  "Big feesh — to-morrow!"

Roly was inclined to wait for developments, but as the call to "muck-muck" was now heard on the shore, he also withdrew.  It was a very frugal supper which the tired trampers ate, ere they threw themselves into their tents for a long sound sleep.

The morning broke cool and cloudy.  Mists trailed low along the sides of the Dasar-dee-ash Mountains across the lake, and hid their snowy summits from view.  There was a dampness in the air which betokened rain, and that quickly.

Roly gave little thought to the weather, however, when he awoke.  His first glance, as he peered from the tent, was directed toward the little stick away out on the ice, and great was his excitement when he saw that it was pointing straight up.  Without waiting to arouse any one — not even Coffee Jack, who, he rightly reasoned, cared much for the fish, but very little for the sport of catching it — he walked as fast as he dared, out over the surface of the lake. A south wind was rising, and now and then he felt a drop of rain on his cheek.

How his fingers tingled with anticipation when he grasped the taut double line! There was certainly something heavy at the end of it. In another moment the boy could dimly see a great fish coming slowly toward the surface. Presently it took alarm and struggled to swim away in various directions. Fearing that the line would be sawn in two against the icy edges of the hole, Roly hauled in as fast as he could, hand over hand, and now up came the big fish, and out it flopped upon the ice, to be hurriedly dragged to a safe distance. As the bait was in good condition, it was dropped back into the hole.

Roly immediately set out with his prize for the shore, where he raised the camp by a series of whoops which would have done credit to the whole Stik tribe. Nobody knew the name of the fish; but Lucky and Coffee Jack, the moment they caught sight of its long head and body, and mottled brown and yellow skin, looked disappointed and said, "No good."

"That may be," said Uncle Will; "but, good or not, we're going to eat it, for we've precious little else," and he gave it to Coffee Jack to clean.

When it was cut up and sputtering in the frying-pan,

the odor was certainly appetizing, and the Indians made no objection to receiving their share in the distribution which followed. The Bradfords found that the skin was full of a strong — almost rancid — oil, but the flesh, though rather flavorless, was not bad.

"This reminds me of the candle-fish," said Uncle Will, "which runs up Alaskan rivers. It's a small fish, the most oily variety known, and it is said that if you set one on its head, and strike a light to its tail, it will burn like a candle until consumed."

"Oh, come, Will!" exclaimed Mr. Bradford. "Do you expect us to believe that?"

"Well," said his brother, "salt and fish generally go together, and in Alaska even a fish-*story* must sometimes be taken with a grain of salt."

"Evidently," said Mr. Bradford.

Exclamations from David and Coffee Jack, who sat facing the lake, now caused the others to look that way. The little stick was pointing up again.

Roly dropped everything, and ran out to the hole. Again he felt a heavy weight, and this time found a gamy customer enough, for the fish darted violently around as soon as it was conscious of the tug on the line. The young fisherman had his hands full, but hauled in as steadily as he could, and out came the fish at last, — a magnificent six-pound lake trout. The hook had caught so deeply that it had to be cut out, and the bait had mostly disappeared, so the line, hook, and fish were brought ashore together.

"Him good!" said Lucky, as pleased at this capture as he had been disappointed at the other.

"I should say so!" exclaimed Mr. Bradford. "We shall have a royal dinner at least, and by supper-time we ought to reach the cache."

"Yes," said Uncle Will; "and the sooner we get across this lake the better. It's coming on to rain and blow, and the ice may break up. We've not a minute to lose."

Mr. Bradford looked anxiously out over the storm-swept expanse. "It would be the height of folly," he declared, "to try to cross that rotten ice with packs strapped on our backs. We ought to be free to swim if worst comes to worst. I don't like the looks of things."

"Nor I either," Uncle Will agreed. "I think each of us had better cut two long poles, fasten his pack near one end of them, and drag it over the ice. Then, if any one breaks through, his load won't sink him, and the poles will be handy for his rescue."

This plan was approved by all. Small poplar trees were quickly felled in the neighboring forest, and their branches lopped off. Two of these poles being laid flat on the ice about a foot apart, the load was made fast near one end, and the owner, stepping between them at the other end, grasped them with his hands. A rope passing loosely across his shoulders from one pole to the other took a part of the weight. It was also found advantageous to trim the ends of the poles where they came in contact with the ice.

All being ready, they started, but progress was slow, both for caution's sake, and because in the absence of ice-creepers their feet could obtain little hold upon the slippery surface. Not far out lay a chain of small islands, around which were stretches of open water, now lashed into foam by the wind, and lapping hungrily at the weakening edges of the ice. It was necessary to go between two of these islands where the ice was not to be depended on, but this dangerous passage was made in safety, and all breathed more easily when they reached the firmer ice of the broad, open lake. The rain now fell, or rather drove, in torrents, and the travellers were wet to the skin. Four miles away lay the shore they sought, at the southern base of the dark mountain slopes. At the head of the company went Lucky, his black, narrow eyes, almost Mongolian in shape, keenly fixed on the ice, and the rude drag scraping along behind him. Then came Coffee Jack, then Uncle Will with the lake trout slipping after his load, and finally Roly, David, and Mr. Bradford. It was hard work, — hard upon hands and arms, — though the lame backs and shoulders were somewhat relieved by the new mode of travel.

After an hour and a half, the party approached the southwest shore. Here the ice became more treacherous.

Sometimes they could feel it settle beneath their feet, as if an upper layer had been pressed down upon an underlying one. There were many little cavities a few inches deep and filled with water, at the bottom of which were slender green plants like seaweed, which seemed to possess the power of melting the ice immediately around them. Strict orders were given that no one should approach within thirty feet of another, lest their combined weight should prove disastrous. And now Lucky stopped and pointed toward the shore.

"Water!" he exclaimed.

Consternation was depicted on every face.

"It's too true," said Uncle Will, as he made out the dark line all along the beach. "Looks as if we couldn't get off the ice now we're on it."

"We've got to get off," declared Mr. Bradford, decisively. "There's nothing else to do. We can't go back. Very likely the ice-bridge is gone by this time."

"Can't we chop out an ice-raft?" suggested David, who recalled certain youthful adventures upon the millpond at home.

Uncle Will nodded. "We'll do that very thing," said he, "if we can't find a crossing. First, however, let us explore a little."

Contrary to all expectation, as they rounded a rocky point, they discovered beyond it a narrow ice-strip not more than fifty feet wide, similar to the one they had crossed that morning, but much weaker, spanning the hundred feet to the beach. One at a time they passed across in safety and stood at last, with a great sense of thankfulness and relief, upon the solid ground. And now the rain ceased, and the cheerful sun broke through the masses of clouds.

## CHAPTER XXIV

### DAVID GETS HIS BEAR-SKIN

THE cache was reached after a half-hour's walk along the pebbly beach, and as provisions were now plentiful once more, the lake trout was served for dinner in bountiful style with apple-sauce, desiccated potato, and bannocks, — the latter baked in tin plates before an open fire. The remainder of the day and the night were spent at the cache, since all were in need of rest, and some changes would have to be made in the packs before proceeding to Alder Creek.

Not far away two men were encamped with a large outfit. They said they had come in with sleds and had taken claims on the Kah Sha River; but by the time they were ready to continue toward Dawson City, the ice of the lake was too treacherous for heavy sledding, so they had decided to build a boat. This boat was now finished and lay bottom up on the beach.

It was constructed of spruce boards whip-sawn with great labor from dry tree-trunks, and was tightly calked with oakum and putty, but lacked paint because the builders had brought none. They were confident, however, that the craft would prove water-tight and seaworthy. It was to carry one mast, and they were making a sail out of the fly of their tent. It was also provided with seats, rowlocks, and a rudder. By the time the ice broke up, the two voyagers would be ready to begin their cruise of over fifty miles by lake and river, to the point where they must take the trail.

One of the men asked David if he had any map of the region, and David hunted up a railroad folder which contained a map of Alaska. But on examining it in the light of his own experience he found many serious errors. Klukshu Lake, for instance, had been confused with some lake farther to the east, and appeared under the name of Lake Maud. Its outlet, instead of flowing from the south end and emptying into the Alsek just above Dalton's Post, was represented as flowing from the north end and reaching the Alsek thirty miles below. Then instead of lying within four miles of Lake Dasar-dee-ash, as he knew to be the fact, it was placed at least twenty-five miles to the east. Lake Dasar-dee-ash appeared of a decidedly wrong shape, and its outlet was made to flow almost directly west, instead of northward, as it did for many miles. As for all the smaller lakes he had seen, the large stream flowing into Dasar-dee-ash from the east, which they had crossed on the jam of logs, and the

Kah Sha River and its tributaries, they were nowhere to be found, — all of which went to show how little was known in the outside world of the region into which they had penetrated.

David therefore drew a rude but reliable map of the trail, to which he added from time to time as his travels warranted.

Toward the middle of the afternoon, when the boys had finished cleaning the rifle and shot-gun, Coffee Jack, who had been roaming through the woods for no apparent purpose, came running breathlessly into camp, shouting, "Beer! beer!" and pointing straight behind him.

"Beer?" said Roly, with a laugh. "What in the world does he mean? There can't be any beer in this neighborhood."

"I'm sure I don't know," said David, much puzzled. "Come here, Coffee. What have you found?"

"Beer!" repeated the Indian boy, excitedly. Then, seeing that he was not understood, he gave a low growl and dropped on all fours.

"Bear!" exclaimed the Bradford boys, in one breath, as they jumped to their feet.

"Yes, beer, beer!" insisted Coffee Jack, unable to improve on his first pronunciation, but delighted to perceive that they understood him at last.

David and Roly were in a flurry at once. They felt

that not a moment must be lost or the prey would escape. It is not unlikely they had a vague idea that their elders would veto a bear-hunt if they knew of it; at any rate they did not stop to summon their father and uncle from the beach, but hastily snatched up the guns and some cartridges and set off through the woods, Coffee Jack leading, armed only with a hunting-knife. Lucky was absent, having gone with a load of provisions to Alder Creek.

It must not be supposed that the boys were entirely foolhardy in thus setting off alone. The Indian knew from experience, and the white boys from previous inquiry, that the grizzly, the fiercest of bears, which will attack human beings without provocation, was not known in this part of the country. What Coffee Jack had seen must have been a black bear or a cinnamon, the latter being considered by some authorities as nearly identical with the former. Such a bear, they had heard, always preferred to run away, and was not much to be dreaded unless cornered or wounded. With a rifle and a shot-gun they were sure they could defend themselves effectively.

After forcing their way through thick willow bushes, they came into an open patch of woods, where Coffee Jack motioned that they were to make no noise. They were now in view of a bare spur or ridge jutting out along the lake from the lofty mountains behind. Coffee

## DAVID GETS HIS BEAR-SKIN

Jack paused in the shadow of a tree and examined the open ground ahead with extreme care, but seeing no sign of the bear he looked up on the ridge. The others followed his motions, and now at the same instant they all saw a large dark animal and two smaller ones scrambling up the steep slope. The old she-bear was cuffing first one cub, then the other, with her great paws to make them move faster, and butting them along with her head in a comical manner. The boys noticed that one of the cubs was dark brown like the mother, while the other was a cinnamon cub.

Coffee Jack rushed across the open space with David and Roly at his heels, and did not pause until he reached the foot of the slope, from which point the bears were in range of both guns.

"Shoot little beer," said he, breathlessly, "then ol' beer stop."

"You take the cinnamon, Roly," directed David.

"All right," said Roly. "Blaze away."

The two reports rang out together, and as the smoke rose, the boys' faces grew very long. All three bears were still going and apparently untouched. And every moment they were increasing the distance between themselves and their pursuers.

"We must get closer," cried David, as he charged up the hill, followed by the others. "Did you take buckshot cartridges, Roly?"

Flashes of recollection, enlightenment, and dismay succeeded one another in Roly's face.

"No," he admitted in a doleful tone, "I never thought of it at all in the hurry. I'm afraid I've got nothing but bird-shot." And such proved to be the case.

"Well, then," said David between breaths, as he struggled over rocks and logs, "there's no use in your firing except at the very shortest range, and then only at the cubs. I'm going to try again now."

So saying, he stopped, took careful aim at the brown cub, of which he had a clear view at that instant, and dropped it in its tracks. The old bear thereupon turned to see what was the matter with her offspring, and it was some time before she concluded that the cub could go no farther. Meanwhile the boys had closed up a part of the distance.

"Here, Roly," said David, taking pity on his younger brother, and handing him the rifle, "perhaps you'd like a shot at the cinnamon."

But Roly was not accustomed to the rifle, and though the cinnamon, which had advanced but slowly since the old bear stopped, was not far distant, he only succeeded in breaking its leg. David supplied another cartridge, and at the second shot Roly brought down the game.

The old bear now displayed anger and defiance, and

sat up on her haunches with a growl that made the boys look instinctively around for cover. There was none to be had, however, — not a tree or large rock to which they could escape. They had but one effective weapon. Furthermore, they now realized their inexperience as never before, and almost wished themselves well out of the scrape. It was evident that the old bear had made up her mind to defend herself and the cubs to the last extremity. She would be still more dangerous if wounded.

All this passed in an instant through David's mind. As the oldest of the three, he felt responsible for the safety of his companions. The battle could not now be avoided. He had no doubt that to retreat would only bring the enemy upon them at once. In spite of himself, he trembled with the excitement and danger of the situation. However, his mind was quickly made up. He remembered a little friend back in Seattle to whom he had promised a bear-skin. It had seemed easy enough to make the promise. To fulfil it, now that he was facing the bear, did not seem quite so simple. But he was no coward.

"Roly," said he, quickly, as he took the rifle, "you and Coffee Jack go back. You can't help me. Shout as soon as you reach the woods, and I'll take care of the bear."

"Not much!" declared Roly, promptly and decisively.

He had also been considering the situation, was likewise trembling with nervous excitement, but had resolved that, come what would, he would stand by his brother.

David looked at the lad's sturdy figure and saw in his face, usually so round and smiling, a look of resoluteness which he could not but admire.

"You're the right stuff," said he, quietly. "Here goes."

He raised the rifle to his shoulder just as the bear sat up again, and aimed at her breast. Unfortunately in his excitement he jerked the rifle when he pulled the trigger. The ball just grazed the bear's side.

With an angry growl of pain the great beast came down upon all fours and charged the little group.

"Kneel, Dave!" cried Roly. "It'll steady you."

David dropped on one knee as the bear came on, while Coffee Jack clutched his knife convulsively.

"Bang!" went the rifle the next instant. Through the smoke they saw the bear plunge to the earth within a dozen yards of them with a bullet through her head. The battle was won.

"Well, well, what's all this?" they heard shouted in Mr. Bradford's voice from the foot of the hill. Presently he and Uncle Will appeared breathless upon the scene.

"You can see for yourself, sir," said David, pointing to the fallen game.

"A bear and two cubs, as I'm alive!" exclaimed Uncle Will. "You've done a good piece of work, boys."

"At close quarters, too!" observed Mr. Bradford. "They must have stood their ground like Spartans." And nothing would do, after the game was skinned and the supper of tender bear-cub meat eaten that evening, but the boys must tell, to the least detail, how the bears were killed.

"All I have to say," said Uncle Will, as he re-lighted his pipe when they had finished, "is that you deserve great credit for pluck, but very little for prudence. Next time, my lads, just let us know when you start out after bears."

## CHAPTER XXV

### MORAN'S CAMP

IT required a week of hard work to transport the contents of the cache at the lake by frequent trips to the claims ten miles away. The tents were pitched on the grassy top of the bank from which Uncle Will had panned the gold in April. In the Kah Sha gorge there yet remained a few old drifts of snow which dwindled day by day, but under the influence of the almost incessant sunlight, vegetation was everywhere springing fresh and green.

There were now seven members of the Thirty-six — no longer mysterious — encamped in the gorge hardly a mile above its entrance, under the leadership of Moran, a gray-haired veteran of the Civil War, who was the only practical miner among them. The rest, like the majority of men who entered Alaska and the Northwest in the great rush of 1898, were drawn from other walks of life. One had been a railroad brakeman, another a railroad clerk, a third an ice-man, a fourth a travelling salesman, a fifth a farmer, and the sixth a steamboat man. The occupations represented were still more numerous when Pennock's men arrived several days behind the Bradfords, Pennock himself having gone out to the coast. One of these had been a grocer, another a foreman employed by a gas company, and another a journalist.

Still further accessions were made from time to time, as men were sent back from the camps beyond Pennock's, till Moran's Camp became a bustling and populous place. A log cabin was built for a kitchen, dining-room, and storehouse, and half a dozen tents were set up for sleeping quarters. This little settlement was situated in a wild and rugged spot, bounded in front and at the sides by the roaring, foaming torrent of the Kah Sha River. Directly at the rear rose foot-hills, and beyond them a high mountain, while from the water's edge across the stream frowned an enormous perpendicular cliff of dark rock three hundred feet high, from which not infrequently a mass of crumbling débris came crashing down. The sun now rose over the mountain to the east at about nine o'clock and set behind this cliff at four, after which the gorge was always chill and damp.

The Thirty-six had located their claims along the river and on Alder Creek. They had found numerous colors of gold in the gravel of the hillside which they had levelled for the cabin, and operations for taking out the gold were actively begun. As soon as the cabin was finished, the men turned to whip-sawing boards from spruce logs, nailing the boards together in the form of sluice-boxes, and digging prospect-holes here and there along the streams to find the most promising spot.

They were still hampered by an insufficiency of food, but as the captain had sent word that he had bought supplies from several discouraged prospectors at Dalton's Post, a party of six was detailed to go to the Post with an Indian guide and bring back as much as they could carry. They returned six days later, footsore and lame, with loads of from fifty to eighty pounds. There was no late news of the war at Dalton's, they said. The Alsek was very high and running at least ten miles an hour. Ike Martin, the storekeeper, had onions already sprouted in his little garden-patch, and he had sown some barley. One of the men told with much relish how he had found enough dandelions for a "mess o' greens."

This meagre batch of news was eagerly seized upon, the least item possessing no little interest to men so long shut away from all the world beyond their own camps. The Bradfords, having heard it all as they passed the cabin, imparted every scrap faithfully to Moore and King and the latter's partner Baldwin, who had recently returned, and so every one in the district soon had the latest information from the Post.

Early in June the gorge became almost impassable by reason of the rising waters. The snow in the mountains was melting rapidly, and every brooklet grew into a flood. To ford the main river was no longer possible, for the heaviest man would have been swept off his feet in an instant. All but three of the dozen trees which had been felled across it at various points were carried away like straws.

One of those which remained was an enormous spruce about ninety feet long, spanning the stream directly against Moran's Camp. This tree had been raised at the farther and lighter end, so that it barely touched the water in midstream, and was braced with rocks and logs. At its heavier end it lay firmly against its own stump. Every precaution had been taken to insure its safety, for at no point was a bridge more necessary. Furthermore, it would be no easy matter to find and drag to the spot another tree so tall. Owing to its great length, this rude bridge swayed dizzily in the centre, hence a rope was stretched tightly above it as a hand-rail.

It was with no small dismay that the campers, late one afternoon, saw a giant tree-trunk as solid as a battering-ram come thumping down the swollen river. It crunched along over the rocky bed of the stream and showed no sign of stopping until within a hundred and fifty feet of the bridge, where it lodged rather insecurely against a shallow. As it was the habit of this glacial river to rise during the afternoon and evening with the accumulation of the day's meltings and fall more or less through the morning, it was tolerably certain that if the big log stuck through the night it would come no farther. The Thirty-six watched and waited, and speculated upon the threatened disaster.

About the middle of the evening, when it was still broad daylight and the mountain summits were yet flushed with the lingering sunbeams, the log betrayed symptoms of restlessness. It began to roll a little in the violent current, which steadily rose around it. Then one end swung out, and at last the great mass was free, launched full tilt against the very centre of the bridge, which at that point dipped slightly into the water.

Was there room for it between the bridge and the river-bottom? Could the long tree-trunk withstand the shock? Were the braces firm on the opposite shore? These were the questions Moran and his companions asked themselves, for there could be no doubt that the bridge would be struck. It was an exciting moment as that great bulk came on, its tons of sodden wood backed by the impetuous forces of the torrent.

There was a tremendous thump as the opposing masses met. The bridge log trembled from end to end and all but gave way; but it stood the strain. The battering-ram had met its match, and seemed to appreciate the fact as, with a sort of bow to its sturdy antagonist, it ducked beneath, and after much scraping and bumping swung clear and headed down the stream, while the bridge-builders drew a deep breath of relief and turned away to their tents.

The Bradfords had by this time finished the transportation of their goods from the lake, and fortunately, for there was no passing through the gorge. When the water was at its normal height there was a passage on one side or the other, and the stream had to be frequently crossed by ford or log; but now that the river in many places filled all the space between its rocky walls, the traveller must needs scale treacherous slopes of loose gravel where a slip would carry him over the cliffs and into a river whose waters were icy and whose bed was not composed of feathers. Sometimes he must toil to the very top of the precipices to avoid the more dangerous spots. So for some days the party on Alder Creek lived in seclusion, seeing no one but King, Moore, and Baldwin, whose tents were well above the worst portions of the river. They busied themselves by constructing a saw-pit where lumber could be turned out for sluice-boxes and a rocker, not deeming it practicable to build a cabin where available trees were so few.

## CHAPTER XXVI

#### HOW THE GREAT NUGGET NEARLY COST THE BRADFORDS DEAR

THE lump of gold which Lucky had declared was as big as his head had not yet been secured, and the likelihood that many prospectors would come in as soon as the rivers were fordable caused Uncle Will to undertake this excursion at an early day. The Stik indicated that the treasure lay in the valley of the Kah Sha River above its junction with Alder Creek. As the creek was the principal stream above that point, just as the Missouri River carries far more water than the upper Mississippi, it seemed probable that there would be little difficulty, even at this season of flood, in ascending the upper river-valley.

It was a cool, invigorating morning on which the Bradfords began their quest. The mountains about them wore below the snow-line the soft green of spring vegetation, while round their summits a few fleecy clouds vied with the snow in brightness. The Indian boy was left in charge of the camp, — an arrangement which he accepted without visible disappointment, — and the gold-hunters proceeded down the brawling creek, walking with difficulty over loose pebbles of quartz, granite, and slate. Occasionally Uncle Will picked up a stone and examined it through a magnifying-glass for traces of the precious metals.

Having reached the river after walking nearly a mile, they turned to the left up its valley, and soon, owing to the boulders below, were obliged to clamber along the hillsides. Few trees were to be seen, but there was a profusion of low bushes and plants on every sunny slope. Often in shaded places they crossed old snow-drifts which promised to last the summer through. Lucky led the way, picking the best path by a sort of instinct.

The hills became more and more precipitous. Great bluffs of gravel alternated with rocky walls, and often it was difficult to maintain a foothold. While crossing the face of one of the bluffs, Mr. Bradford met with an adventure which, as he afterwards declared, almost turned his hair white. The rest of the party had passed the declivity near its top by digging their feet and sticks into the soft gravel, while he had lingered to secure a blue forget-me-not which grew below him.

When he turned to follow the others, they were out of sight around the shoulder of the hill, and he could see nothing to mark their path across the bluff. He had descended fifty feet or more, and since there appeared no reason for scrambling up again, he began to advance at that level. Perhaps a third of the bluff had been crossed slowly and carefully when, without warning, he encountered a gravel of different character. Instead of being soft and loose, it was now compact, firmly bedded, and so steeply inclined that it offered not the slightest foothold. The moment Mr. Bradford's foot struck this hard gravel he slipped and fell, but as he did so he drove his staff firmly into the slope. By this means he was able to stay himself temporarily.

He now felt carefully about for a support for his feet, but the crumbling pebbles rolled away with every movement. However, he discovered a projecting stone which seemed able to bear some weight, and this relieved the strain upon his hands and arms. And now he shouted as loudly as possible, hoping that his friends would hear.

It was a perilous situation. Below him for a hundred and fifty feet the gravel was of the same hard, deceptive consistency. He could see that it ended abruptly at least fifty feet above the little stream, and rightly conjectured that this interval was occupied by a perpendicular precipice of rock. What lay at the bottom he shuddered to imagine, — boulders, sharp rocks, at best a rough gravel-bed! And he could move neither hand nor foot; while, as if in mockery of his plight, the pebbles kept bounding and rattling merrily down the terrible slope below him, leaping out into space at last as if it were a pleasant pastime.

Again and again he shouted, and now he was gladdened by an answering shout, and saw his brother hastening along the bluff above, followed by Lucky, David, and Roly.

"Quick, Will," he cried; "I can't hold out much longer."

Uncle Will grasped the situation in a twinkling. "Has any one some twine?" he asked.

"I have," answered David, quickly producing a small ball of it from his pocket.

"Tie the walking-sticks together, then, and don't lose an instant. Roly, run to the top of the bluff and see if you can cut a tall poplar." With these words Uncle Will hastened to work his way down the face of the bluff toward his brother, while Lucky ran down to the point where Mr. Bradford had found the flower, and thence followed his course as far as he could out across the bare gravel. He was able to approach much nearer the imperilled man than was Uncle Will, who came upon the hard surface before he had covered half the distance, and could go no farther.

Indeed, the Indian was within a yard of Mr. Bradford and kicking one last foothold in the treacherous bank preparatory to reaching out for him when, to the horror of all, the stone upon which the white man stood gave way. The sudden wrench tore the stick also from its place. Having thus lost all support, the unfortunate man at once slipped and slid and rolled toward the brink of the precipice. He was beyond human aid. Another moment, and, in spite of his frantic efforts to clutch at the shelving bank, he dashed over the edge of the rock and passed out of sight amid a shower of small stones dislodged by his fall.

There is something indescribably frightful in the sight of a strong man thus powerless to avert his own destruction, and when the victim is a father or brother the horror is intensified a hundred-fold. Uncle Will groaned and shut his eyes.

But he was a man of action, and quickly recovering himself he ran back along the hill with Lucky and David until they could descend to the stream, up which they made their way with reckless haste. Lucky was the most nimble; and as he scrambled to the top of a boulder which had obstructed his view ahead, his usual stolidity gave way to a glad cry. Mr. Bradford lay at the foot of the cliff upon a great bank of snow.

But he lay there so still and lifeless that the rescuers anxiously hastened to his side. They were immediately joined by Roly, whose face was pale with dread. Mr. Bradford had either struck the cliff in his descent, or had been struck by one of the stones which fell with him, for blood was flowing from a cut in the forehead, and he was unconscious. Uncle Will washed the blood from the wound, and wetting his handkerchief in the cold water of the stream, soon coaxed back the life.

"Well, Charley," said he, in a tone of intense satisfaction as he saw his eyes open, "that was the closest call you ever had, but you're coming through all right." And Mr. Bradford did. He had been stunned and shaken, but not seriously injured, and after an hour's rest was able to proceed.

They had not much farther to go. Lucky, who had keenly observed all landmarks, soon halted in the rocky river-bottom and began to search carefully among the boulders. A few minutes later he called out, "Big nuggit here!" and pointed to a sort of knob projecting from a large rock in the stream. Uncle Will hastened to the spot and saw at a glance that this knob was an almost solid mass of yellow metal. But he was too careful a man to accept first appearances, and brought the microscope to bear.

"Ah!" said he, and his face grew long, "it's fool's gold, after all,— just a big chunk of iron pyrites."

"Why, it looks just like gold!" declared Roly, coming up. "I never saw iron of that color."

"Very likely not," said his uncle. "This is n't iron in its pure state, but combined with sulphur. Look through the microscope and you'll see that the metal is crystallized. You won't find gold in that shape."

Lucky did not comprehend this explanation, but he

read the disappointment in the faces of the others. To make him understand, Uncle Will tapped the blade of his knife and said, "Iron — no good," — a simple form of expression which the Indian easily interpreted. He too showed genuine disappointment, for he had intended to do a kindness to Uncle Will.

"Well," said David, with at least a show of resignation, "I suppose there's nothing to do but retrace our steps."

"I don't care to retrace all of mine," said Mr. Bradford, whose pale face wore a smile beneath its bandage.

"Oh!" exclaimed his brother, "but those weren't steps! You didn't take a single step in the whole two hundred feet! The first fifty you slid, the next hundred you rolled, and the last fifty you flew, and we won't ask you to do it over again."

Indeed, they were all so thankful at Mr. Bradford's escape that the nugget was hardly given a thought, and on the whole it was a happy party which returned to Alder Creek that evening.

## CHAPTER XXVII

### AN INDIAN CREMATION

"WE 'RE nearly out of sugar and salt," Uncle Will announced a day or two later. "The water spoiled a good part of what we had when my sled went through the ice. Do you feel like taking a walk down to Dalton's, Charles, while I finish up these sluice-boxes?"

"Yes," replied Mr. Bradford, "and I might take along one of the boys."

So it was decided that Roly and his father should go to the trading-post with Coffee Jack for guide.

They set out early in the morning to take advantage of the lowest stage of the river, which, owing to the coolness of the last few days, had fallen considerably. They were thus enabled to make the fordings without undue danger, and found themselves in about three hours at the mouth of the gorge, having stopped but a moment at each of the camps.

Directly opposite them across the valley, which extended, with a uniform width of about four miles, from Lake Dasar-dee-ash on the east toward a range of lofty peaks far to the west, loomed a fine cluster of mountains ribbed with melting snow. By skirting the eastern slopes of these mountains over a new trail made by prospectors, they would come upon the Dalton trail at Klukshu Lake, and this was the route Mr. Bradford preferred, but Coffee Jack was not familiar with it and desired to follow the old Indian trail to the west of the mountains. Accordingly, they passed out of the gorge along the great dry gravel deposit, which they followed in its turn to the right, having first exchanged their rubber boots, with which they could now dispense, for the stout shoes which they had slung across their shoulders. The boots were hung in the forks of a clump of willows, where they could easily be found on their return.

Mr. Bradford called Roly's attention to the long stretch of treeless gravel curving to the west.

"It is evident," said he, "that the Kah Sha River once flowed in this westerly course, but having choked itself up by successive accumulations of gravel and boulders ejected from the gorge in its spring floods, it now takes the opposite direction and empties into Lake Dasar-dee-ash."

"That's something I never should have thought of," said Roly, with interest, "and it's plain enough, too."

"You can read a good deal of geological history," observed his father, "by keeping your eyes open and noticing simple things. Every boulder, cliff, and sand-

## AN INDIAN CREMATION

bank has a story to tell of the forces of ice, flood, or fire."

At length Coffee Jack left the low ground, which had become swampy, and followed a line of foot-hills, where the trail could sometimes be discerned by Mr. Bradford and Roly, but more often not. The young guide walked silently, with his head bent and his eyes fixed upon the ground.

"No white man would be content with a trail like this," Mr. Bradford remarked. "The white man blazes the trees and looks up for his signs, while the Indian relies upon footprints, faint though they may be, and looks down. I imagine that by their manner of following a trail you may gain an insight into the characteristics of the two races, — the one alert, hopeful, business-like, brainy; the other keen of instinct, easy-going, stealthy, and moody."

"But what signs does Coffee Jack see?" inquired Roly. "There are plenty of places where I can't see any path, but he goes right along."

"The marks are various," said his father. "It may be that the grass is matted or less vigorous or of an altered hue where it has been trodden, or a twig may be broken, or a mouldering tree-trunk rubbed a little, but I presume that in such a place as this the boy is guided partly by his knowledge that the trail follows the side of these hills at about this height."

Coffee Jack discovered footprints of the moose and the caribou in several places, and took delight in pointing them out to his companions, whose powers of observation he evidently did not rate very high. He gave them, too, a glimpse of a large lake to the northwest which was not on the map

Late the second afternoon they circled a small lake, swung around the southern slopes of the mountains on their left, and entered the main trail on the summit of the great hill above the Stik village. How changed was the valley of the Alsek since last they looked upon it! Where before were snow and ice now smiled a landscape of rich green. Below them clustered the Indian houses in a grassy clearing by the river. The sound of voices and the barking of dogs came plainly up. It was difficult to realize that they were not looking on a white man's village, yet not until they reached the trading-post, now surrounded with the white tents of incoming prospectors, would they see any members of their own race.

Ike Martin received them cordially, and after the sugar and salt had been weighed out he suddenly exclaimed, "By the way, here's something more for you!" and took from the drawer of an old desk a batch of letters, which he handed to Mr. Bradford, remarking that an Indian had brought them in with mail for the Thirty-six.

## AN INDIAN CREMATION

To say that these were received with delight would be putting it mildly. The wanderers repaired in haste to their tent, where the missives from home were eagerly read; and although the latest letter was just a month old, yet so long had they been exiled that all this news seemed fresh and recent. At home all were well and in good spirits. Knowing how anxious her husband and sons would be for accounts of the war, Mrs. Bradford had sent many clippings from newspapers, which Mr. Bradford and Roly devoured with hungry eyes, reading and re-reading them far into the night.

Early next morning, before his father was awake, Roly, acting on a hint from Ike, stole over to the Klukshu River where it joins the Alsek, and with red salmon-roe supplied by the obliging storekeeper coaxed forth half a dozen handsome brook trout. These he supplemented with some of the fresh dandelion leaves which grew abundantly near the storehouse, and the three had a most enjoyable breakfast.

"Better stop at the Stik village," advised Ike, as they were preparing to return. "There's going to be a cremation, and it'll be worth seeing."

So Mr. Bradford, Roly, and Coffee Jack, with their light packs on their backs, walked leisurely down the trail in company with several prospectors. Among their companions were the two nephews of Mrs. Shirley, whom they had assisted at the fords in March.

"So the ladies gave it up, did they?" said Mr. Bradford, in the course of the conversation.

"Yes," answered one of the young men. "They came as far as Pleasant Camp, but found it best to stop there while we two went in and located claims. We've just been out to the coast with them, and now we're going back to work the claims."

At the village Ike joined them, and others came at intervals until the entire white population of the trading-post was present. The body to be burned was that of a young Indian who had died of consumption. Before the house in which he lay, the natives and the white men assembled and awaited the appearance of the family, while dogs of all ages, sizes, and degrees, attracted by the concourse, ran restlessly about the place, barking or quarrelling as their dispositions prompted.

At length the door opened, and the female relatives of the deceased issued, both young and old, all bareheaded, and attired in their best, though faded, calico dresses. They grouped themselves before the door, and were followed by the men, also evidently dressed in their best. Some of them had wound bright blue or red ribbons around their dark felt hats.

The body was borne out of the house on a rude litter covered with a blanket, and its appearance was the signal for an unearthly chorus of wails and lamentations from the women, who continued to howl until the procession was well on its way to the graveyard, the men, meanwhile, preserving countenances of the most unruffled indifference.

The graveyard was a grassy level containing a row of miniature wooden houses with glass windows and sloping roofs, which looked for all the world like children's playhouses. They were raised about three feet above the ground on stout wooden supports. The storekeeper informed Mr. Bradford and Roly that the ashes of the dead were deposited in boxes in these houses.

As the procession reached the cemetery, four rifle-shots were fired into the air by those about the corpse, which was then placed within a pyre of dry spruce logs, made ready to receive it. Fire was applied to the pile, and soon the logs were blazing fiercely.

And now into the midst of the flames, to Roly's great surprise, was thrown all the property of the dead Indian, including a good rifle and a watch. However wasteful this custom might appear to the white men, they could not but respect the feelings which led these poor children of the wilderness to part with treasures to them so valuable. The dead man would need his blankets, his rifle, and his watch in the happy hunting-grounds, and some morsels of food for the journey were not forgotten.

Meanwhile the women wailed and moaned with the

tears streaming down their dark faces, as they sat upon the turf and watched the curling smoke and leaping flames. When Mr. Bradford turned away toward the hill, it was with a feeling that grief is very much the same thing all the world over.

## CHAPTER XXVIII

### THE PLAGUE OF MOSQUITOES

HAVING learned that he would find upon a tree near Klukshu Lake directions for following the new trail to Shorty Creek, as the district was popularly called, Mr. Bradford determined to return by the Dalton trail to the lake, as the relief party of the Thirty-six had done. Here and there along the way they saw traces of the winter's travel. Broken sleds and gee-poles, stumps of trees, and the ashes of camp-fires recalled the memory of labors amid the ice and snow which now, in the heat of summer, seemed like a dream.

Up to this time the mosquitoes had been rather large, but neither numerous nor aggressive. But now on a sudden came myriads of small ones, evidently a new crop, voracious, persistent, overwhelming. They swarmed up from every marsh until their combined singing made a continuous murmur in the trees, and the travellers, who were without head-nets, were forced to protect their necks with handkerchiefs, and their faces with small branches, which they must needs wave to and fro incessantly.

Camp was pitched near the Klukshu River, where two ancient and abandoned Indian houses stood, in a level valley mostly free from trees. The low bushes in the neighborhood allowed the breeze free play, and it was hoped that here the mosquitoes would be less numerous. There was no getting away from them entirely, however, and a fire was speedily built in order that the smoke might aid in discouraging the pests.

The two houses, which they had noticed as they passed in April, were constructed of hewn boards gray with age. Such a wealth of ready fuel in a spot so poor in timber had proved irresistible alike to prospectors and Indians, and the entire roof of one hut and much of the roof of the other had gone up in camp-fire smoke. Mr. Bradford was averse, however, to further despoiling either structure, and directed Roly and Coffee Jack to gather up only such loose boards and odd pieces as were lying about on the ground.

While roasting several red squirrels brought down with a revolver, they were startled by a sudden snort in the bushes near by, followed by a crackling of twigs as some heavy animal made off precipitately. The three jumped to their feet and searched through the thicket in that direction, but could see nothing of the beast which had caused the alarm. There could be little doubt, however, that it was a bear.

"If we're going to have visitors of that kind," said

Mr. Bradford, as he returned his revolver to his belt, "we'll pitch the tent in one of the houses. I don't anticipate any trouble, but bears are brimful of curiosity, and it's just as well to put ourselves and our belongings out of their reach."

This suggestion pleased Roly, whose imagination, boylike, seized eagerly upon the idea of converting the better of the two houses into a fort and barricading it against the enemy. He collected an abundance of soft shrubbery and spread it upon the floor of the hut, while Mr. Bradford, keeping a sharp lookout for the unwelcome prowler, cut some tent-poles on a distant hillside.

When all was ready, the tent was set up within the hut, and, being mosquito-proof, it promised a complete refuge from at least one foe. A sufficient number of boards was now appropriated from the other cabin to cover the portion of the roof above the tent. Then the packs were brought in, and finally Roly arranged a door of boards. This done, the fort was declared impregnable, and the tired travellers turned in, well assured of complete security.

Coffee Jack had brought no tent, and as there was no extra space in that of his companions, he rolled himself in his blanket, head and all, till he seemed to invite suffocation, and lay down on a bed of leaves in a corner of the cabin, where he slept comfortably enough, except that his breathing was heavy and labored for lack of air.

The mosquitoes were even more numerous next day, and the travellers were obliged to keep in motion. Flowers were springing up on every side. There were strawberry blossoms, which awakened great hopes. There were violets and forget-me-nots and yarrow, and almost touching elbows with the flowers of spring flamed the autumnal golden-rod, so brief in that high latitude was the season of warmth.

The Indian boy pointed out with delight a large-leaved plant with a hollow, juicy stalk, which grew abundantly in shady places, exclaiming, "Muck-muck! Good! Make strong!" Seeing him eagerly stripping the stringy fibres from the stalks and eating the soft inner part, Mr. Bradford and Roly followed his example, and found that the flavor was of a medicinal sort, but sweet and not unpleasant. The leaves were shaped somewhat like those of a maple tree, but were of lighter green. Coffee Jack could give no name to the plant.

"Its flavor reminds me a little of celery," said Roly.

"Yes," said Mr. Bradford; "but in some respects the plant more resembles rhubarb, and as that is, I believe, a native of Asia, this may be a variety which has crossed Behring Strait. If the taste were sour, I should be pretty certain of it."

## THE PLAGUE OF MOSQUITOES

Camped at the foot of Klukshu Lake on a pleasant knoll east of the river, they found Reitz and Johnson, two of their friends of Pennock's Post. Reitz said they were stationed there to catch salmon for the main party on the Kah Sha River, and from what they could learn from the natives the fish ought to come up-stream very soon.

A family of Indians were quartered on the low ground west of the river near the cabin in which the wounded Lucky had been left in the winter. They also were awaiting the salmon, which constitutes the chief food of the Alaskan tribes.

"How would you like to spend a week with us, Roly?" asked Reitz, as the three were about to continue their journey. "You enjoy fishing, don't you?"

Roly answered that he would like to stay very well, and his father readily consented. "You can take this tent," said the latter. "It's only ten miles to Moran's Camp, and I guess you can find your way there when the week's up."

"Oh, yes!" declared Roly, without hesitation. "I'll get along all right." He added, as he counted a score of mosquitoes killed at one slap, "If you get a chance to send my head-net down, I guess I can use it."

"We'll try to," said Mr. Bradford, as he and the Indian boy re-crossed the river on a mass of débris.

No sooner had Coffee Jack exchanged a few words

with the Indian family than he fell into a fit of the sulks. He cast more than one fond glance at a little Indian girl of about his own age, and Mr. Bradford heard the father of the family repeat the word "potlash" several times. As this term signifies a feast, it was clear that Coffee Jack had been invited to dine.

Mr. Bradford had determined to push on a few miles in order to reach the Kah Sha gorge early next morning before the time of high water. But when he undertook to find the trail, which was here invisible across a level deposit of small stones, he found himself baffled.

"Where's the Shorty Creek trail, Coffee Jack?" he asked.

"Shorty Kick t'ail?" said Coffee, with well-feigned innocence. "I dunno."

Now, Coffee Jack had been uniformly treated with kindness, and was certain to be so long as he deserved it, but when he said, "I dunno," Mr. Bradford had every reason to think he was stretching the truth and presuming upon his own good-nature. In view of the falsehood he resolved to teach the boy his duty. It would never do to let him override the will of his employer.

"You don't know?" repeated Mr. Bradford, with the frown and voice of a thunder-cloud. "Tell me where that trail is, quick!"

As he said this, he raised his stick so threateningly over Coffee Jack's head that the boy, fearing instant annihilation, produced the information with incredible speed.

"Shorty Kick t'ail there," said he, pointing to the edge of a grove of great balm-of-Gilead trees, to which he led the way without another word.

At the first stream, perhaps two miles beyond, Coffee Jack declared that there was no more water for five miles. He had evidently obtained information regarding the new trail from the Indian at the foot of the lake, and as Mr. Bradford did not believe the lad would lie again, he halted for the night. The white man all the while had a tender place in his heart for the young Indian lover, and when the boy asked permission to go back, he readily gave it. So Coffee Jack, delighted, ran swiftly down the trail toward the dusky little maiden and the "potlash."

## CHAPTER XXIX

### LOST IN THE MOUNTAINS

FOR several days after Roly's arrival at Klukshu Lake all efforts to catch fish were unavailing. The weather was now warm and dry, and the thick, smoky atmosphere indicated an extensive forest fire at no great distance. The salmon had not appeared, and there was no sign of brook trout in this part of the Klukshu River, consequently the energies of the campers were directed toward the lake. A raft was built, by the aid of which lines were set in deep water near the outlet, the hooks baited with raw bacon, — but not a fish was caught.

A small party of Canadian mounted police — fine, stalwart fellows — appeared at this time on their way to Five Finger Rapids, and the hearts of the exiled fishermen were rejoiced. Their arrival meant that horses could now come in from the coast, and Reitz and Johnson began to look eagerly for the first instalment of supplies for the Thirty-six. Several prospectors with small pack trains followed the police, and invariably camped on a dry meadow at the foot of the lake. The tinkle of the bell of the leading horse sometimes floated up to the knoll where the tents of Roly and his companions stood, and conjured up memories of pastures far away. Had the prospectors only known it and cared to take the trouble, they would have found far better pasturage on the hillsides above the timber line, where the grasses grew tall and luxuriant.

A happy thought on the part of Roly was the means of solving the fishing problem. Bacon was evidently worthless as bait, there was not an angle-worm in the country so far as he knew, and grasshoppers were seldom seen; but he had noticed shoals of young fish like minnows in the outlet, and thought that if they could be caught they would make excellent bait. The others thought so too, and Reitz contrived an ingenious scoop-net out of a willow branch and some mosquito netting, which proved very effective.

Roly's week would be up on the following day. It was agreed that in the morning a supreme effort should be made by the three, and as Moran's Camp lay directly in his path, Roly volunteered to carry the fish if they should be successful.

At an early hour he rolled his tent and blankets into a pack and set off with his friends, who had provided a luncheon and a plentiful supply of minnows. The main trail followed the east shore, but there was another along the western which connected about halfway up the lake with the new trail to Shorty Creek.

At the junction of the two was the tree upon which the directions had been written.

The party passed this tree and continued along the lake, their objective point being a certain rocky shore where they hoped to find deep water. Having reached this spot, they lost no time in cutting slender poles of poplar and attaching the lines. Floats, or bobs, were made from bits of wood, and the baited hook was allowed to sink ten or twelve feet.

It was some time before the finny inhabitants of the depths discovered the tempting morsels thrown out to them, but at last Roly's float began to tremble in a way that could not be attributed to the wavelets, and the next instant down it went under the clear water. Now was the time to strike, and the boy raised his pole with a quick firm jerk.

The fish was securely hooked, and proved both strong and gamy; but as soon as it tired, it was drawn gradually toward the shore and up near the surface of the water. It was a four-pound lake trout and a beauty. Roly landed the prize with the assistance of his friends, and stowed it safely away in the shade of the rocks in an empty flour sack.

At the very next nibble, however, fortune turned against him. The fish broke the line and carried away his only hook; and as his companions had but one hook apiece, he was forced to abandon the sport. Before the fish stopped biting, the two men had caught four trout, all of about the same size.

Having lunched, and dressed the fish, the three agreed about two o'clock that Roly ought to start, especially as the first thunder-storm of the season was growling and threatening in the mountains to the east. With fish, tent, and blankets, and David's camera, which he had carried upon this excursion, he had a load of about thirty pounds, which Reitz carried for him as far as the guide-tree.

The inscription on the tree was written in pencil on a space freed from bark, and stated that by holding a course two points north of west for a mile a clear trail would be found.

"Have you a compass, Roly?" asked Johnson.

"Yes."

"Well, then, strike off here and keep the direction carefully, and you won't have any trouble. There's a stretch of burnt and fallen timber where the trail has been wiped out, but beyond that it's a plain path."

"And remember to keep the trout you caught," added Reitz, as he said good-by.

Roly started off in good spirits. He had his uncle's revolver with him, but there was little reason to apprehend danger from wild beasts. If he let them alone, they would be pretty certain to return the favor. As to finding the way, he knew the general direction in which the Kah Sha gorge lay, for he could occasionally catch a glimpse of the Dasar-dee-ash Mountains eight miles to the northwest. Nearer, not more than two miles away, loomed the familiar Conical Mountain, and to the right of it another summit, the two forming the northernmost elevations of an extensive mountain system running far back toward Dalton's Post.

From the directions on the tree the boy conceived the idea that his route lay between Conical Mountain and its right-hand neighbor, in a narrow pass which he could see very distinctly. So, without depending longer on the compass, he fixed his course at once toward this gap, struggling through a new growth of bushes and stepping over or crawling under the fallen trees as best he could. A fresh breeze along the lake had kept away the mosquitoes while he had been on the rocks; but here it was more sheltered, and the little pests, attracted by the smell of the fish, swarmed about him and nearly drove him frantic, for he was still without a head-net and gloves.

An hour of this slow and difficult travel brought him into the growing forest, and he kept his eyes open for the path. Denser and denser the woods became until it was hardly possible to force a passage. In a little swampy glen he found the prints of a bear's great paw on the moss, but what caused him much more anxiety was the sight, welcome as it was, of a little brook. Reitz had told him that for nearly five miles from the guide-tree there was no water on the trail. Yet here was water! Plainly, then, he had made some error and had lost his way.

Roly was not easily frightened, but the thought of wandering through that lonely forest longer than was absolutely necessary was anything but pleasing. To be sure, he would not starve, for he had the fish, but it was disquieting to be off the trail. He would have liked to sit down a few minutes to consider the situation, but the mosquitoes would not let him rest. He could only pause long enough to take a deep draught from the brook, then on he must go again, and do his reflecting as he walked.

He now came upon a path fairly well defined, which led, without a doubt, straight into the pass before him. This was probably the trail he sought. At any rate, its general direction was assuring, and he reasoned that it must bring him out on the other side of the mountains in plain view of the Kah Sha gorge, which he could then reach by crossing four miles of valley. So he followed the path, which appeared little used, and presently came to the brow of a high, shelving bank.

The steep side of Conical Mountain, patched with old snow-banks, towered on his left, while the end mountain of the chain rose to the right. Before him in the hollow was a level, grassy amphitheatre, on the farther side of which opened out a narrow passage, also grassy and treeless. The absolute seclusion of the place made it an admirable retreat for wild game and, indeed, for robbers, and the imaginative Roly looked carefully around before he ventured to descend into it. There was not a living creature to be seen. The path crossed the circular meadow and followed the narrow pass beyond, and as it was level, firm, and unobstructed, the boy walked rapidly.

He had proceeded in this way nearly a mile between the slopes of the two mountains, when he came upon a beautiful lakelet whose placid waters filled the valley — now somewhat wider — from side to side. In the shallow water near the shore he could see several small fish basking just below the surface. As for the trail, it had disappeared, and there was no trace of it along either side of the water. Indeed, the steep ridges looked quite impassable, from which he concluded that the path had been made by Indians or wild game, or both, whose objective point was the lake. There could be little doubt that he was the first white person who had penetrated here, — a thought which quite tickled his fancy, so he photographed the lake in proof of this bit of original exploration.

He was now obliged to return through the defile, fully convinced that the new trail passed around the outer mountain. Goaded on by swarms of mosquitoes and compelled to wave a leafy branch continually across his heated face, he struck the trail at last, and soon afterward found a sparkling brook at the foot of a high hill. If this was the water mentioned by Reitz, he had come only half the direct distance, in spite of his long, tiresome tramp. He drank, then pressed forward through a region of bogs and woods, crossed a muddy stream on a log, and set off across the four miles of valley. Here the walking was good. The gorge was now plainly in view, and he thought his labors nearly at an end.

Unfortunately, it was the wrong time of day to ford the Kah Sha. It had been warm for a week, and the water was high again. Besides, the stream was now swollen with the meltings of the day. Roly could hear an ominous roar long before he could see the river.

He encountered it first in the woods, where it spread out into so many channels that each was comparatively shallow. Some of these he crossed on logs, and others he waded without getting very wet, but when he came out upon the open stretch of gravel the outlook was far from encouraging. Compressed into one or two principal channels and filling its banks to the brim, the river was thundering madly down from the gorge. Not a log was in sight, and yet the stream must be crossed three or four times to reach Moran's Camp.

Roly's heart sank as he gazed on the hurrying torrent, but he resolved to make the attempt. He therefore returned to the edge of the woods and cut a stout pole with which to try the depth of the water and brace himself against the current. His rubber boots, if his father had left them in the willows, were on the other side of the stream, so it was useless to think of keeping dry.

Carefully selecting a point where the stream ran in two channels, the boy waded into the first and smaller of the two. The water came to his knees, but with the assistance of the pole he crossed in safety. On trying the other, however, he found the volume of water much greater. The current almost whirled his feet from beneath him at every step. The icy water surged higher and higher till it was far above his knees, and now it was wellnigh impossible to hold the pole firmly down to the bottom. He felt the stones roll against his feet as the flood swept them along, and, worst of all, the deepest part was not yet passed. The bed of the stream shelved plainly down. To go on would be folly. It was nearly as difficult to go back, but he managed to turn slowly and dizzily and reach the shore he had just left. Tired and wet, he longed to rest, but even here his insect tormentors had followed.

There was but one thing to do. He must climb the hills on the side of the gorge and work his way along at a height of three or four hundred feet until he could scramble down to the camp. It was a rough ascent through bushes and over fallen timber, and the boy was utterly spent when at last he caught a glimpse of the little cabin and the white tents of the Thirty-six far below.

He had been steadily tramping from two o'clock in the afternoon, and it was now nine in the evening. But he had obstinately clung to the fish with which he had been intrusted, knowing how welcome they would be to the dwellers by the river. It is needless to say that Roly was received with open arms by Moran and his men, who gave him dry clothes and a hearty supper, and many compliments on his pluck and perseverance. A place was cleared for his blanket-bed in one of the tents, and nothing would do next morning but he must share with his friends a delicious breakfast of fried trout before setting out for Alder Creek.

## CHAPTER XXX

### WASHING OUT THE GOLD

"HELLO! you've brought us a trout, have you?" cried Uncle Will, cheerily, as he untied Roly's pack. The boy had succeeded in reaching Alder Creek during the morning period of low water.

"Yes," said Roly, and related his experiences to the interested group.

"You got along better at this end of the journey than I feared you would," said his father. "I expected you yesterday, and when I saw how high the water would be, I went down to the mouth of the gorge to help you, but there were no signs of you at seven o'clock."

"You must come and see the rocker and sluice-boxes as soon as you're rested," said David. "We've not been idle here since you went away, I can tell you."

Accordingly, after dinner Roly, armored at last with head-net and gloves, went out with David and Uncle Will to inspect the mining operations at the foot of the bank beside the creek.

We have already described panning, the crudest manner of separating gold from gravel. The appliances

WASHING OUT THE GOLD 249

which Uncle Will and his helpers had now constructed were capable of doing much more work than the pan in a given time, yet required the expenditure of comparatively little labor. Uncle Will first called Roly's attention to the rocker, which at that moment was standing idle at the side of the stream.

"The rocker, or cradle," he explained, "consists of a deep box set upon rounded rockers so that it can be swayed from side to side. Within the box are several inclined planes at different heights, covered with canvas and so arranged that water and gravel flowing down the upper one will pass from its lower edge through an aperture to the top of the one below, and from that to the next, until finally the stream issues near the bottom of the machine. Across these planes at intervals are nailed small strips of wood called riffles. A sieve is fitted to the top of the box, its bottom being made of a sheet of tin punched with numerous holes half an inch in diameter. Now let us see it work."

So saying, he placed the rocker under the end of a wooden trough set in the bank at a height of three feet. A ditch had been hollowed along the bank to this trough from a point higher up the stream, and David now lowered a similar trough into the water at the upper end. This allowed a stream to come into the ditch from the creek. As soon as the water began to pour into the sieve of the rocker, Coffee Jack, whom Uncle Will had summoned, threw into it a shovelful of gravel from the bottom of the bank.

"Now you see," said Uncle Will, as he gently rocked the machine from side to side, "the water carries the sand and smaller pebbles, including the particles of gold, down through those holes and over the riffles on the inclined planes. The gold is so heavy that it lodges against the riffles, but the water, swashing from side to side as it flows down, carries most of the sand and gravel over the riffles and out at the bottom. The operation is almost instantaneous in the rocker, and gravel can be shovelled in quite rapidly, whereas it would take perhaps ten minutes to wash out a very little in a pan. When the sieve becomes choked, it is lifted up and the stones thrown out."

Coffee Jack shovelled mechanically, as if all this fuss about the yellow metal were quite beyond his appreciation. In a few minutes Uncle Will released him and sent him back to help Lucky at the sluice.

"Now we'll take a look at the results," said Uncle Will, as he removed the sieve, picked out the riffles, which were loosely nailed, and carefully took up the canvas which covered the inclined planes. All the sand and gravel which remained upon the canvas he rinsed off into a pan and proceeded to wash it out at the stream after the usual method of panning. Roly was delighted to see two little yellow nuggets appear, besides many small flakes and grains.

"There," said Uncle Will, as he finished, "you see we have here the yield of several panfuls, and it has taken but a few minutes to secure it. The rocker is a handy machine to carry from place to place wherever, by panning, we find the gold most abundant."

"But what would you do without the ditch?"

"We should pour in water from a pail. Now let us examine the sluice-boxes."

Uncle Will led the way down the stream to the point where Lucky and Coffee Jack were at work. A second ditch, similar to the first, had been prepared for the sluicing; and the boxes, three in number, were set in the lower end of it, each consisting of a bottom board about twelve feet long and a foot wide, and two side boards of the same dimensions. The lower end of the first or upper box was reduced in width sufficiently to allow it to fit into the upper end of the second box, the latter fitting in like manner into the third, which extended slightly over the creek. All the boxes were inclined enough so that the water from the ditch would flow through them quite rapidly. Instead of transverse riffles, two sets of poles were laid lengthwise in the bottom of each box, each set having a length of about five and a half feet and consisting of three poles held an inch apart by pieces of wood nailed across their ends.

Into the upper end of the upper box Lucky was shovelling gravel, which was immediately swept through the three boxes by the strong current of water. Coffee Jack, shovel in hand, kept the larger stones moving when they threatened to choke up the boxes. At the lower end a stream of muddy water and gravel was constantly discharged into the creek, the impetuous current of which bore it instantly away.

"Sluicing," said Uncle Will, "is another step forward in placer — or gravel — mining, since the sluice will handle more material than even the rocker. It is the favorite method on a claim of this character."

"And how is the gold caught here?" asked Roly.

"It falls down between the poles, and is held there by its own weight and the cross-pieces."

"You must have had to do a lot of whip-sawing to make so many boards," observed the boy.

"Indeed we did," replied his uncle. "That was the hardest part of the work. We built a saw-pit — that raised log platform over yonder — and there we did the sawing, Lucky standing on top of the log and holding the saw from above, while I was under the platform to guide it on the down stroke. I rather had the worst of it, for the sawdust came into my eyes. When your father returned from Dalton's, he took a turn at it, which gave me time to make the rocker."

## WASHING OUT THE GOLD

"How often do you take the gold out of the sluice-boxes?" asked Roly.

"We may as well clear the boxes now," answered his uncle. "It's three days since we began operations."

Accordingly, the two Indians were sent off to cut firewood, and Uncle Will and Mr. Bradford, having despatched David to the head of the ditch to shut off the water, shovelled out of the boxes the stones and gravel which had lodged above the poles. Then, removing the poles, they scraped and washed into a pan at the lower end all which remained. There was a heaping panful.

Uncle Will washed it out at a quiet eddy of the creek, while the others gathered around with suppressed excitement, for estimates of the value of this claim could be based upon the results. Little by little the gravel was reduced until the black sand and yellow particles alone remained. A portion of the sand Uncle Will was able to wash away by careful manipulating, but when he could safely continue the operation no longer, he brought a magnet into use, which quickly gathered up all the remaining specks of iron. A goodly mass of yellow metal shone in the bottom of the pan, which, when weighed, was found to be worth about sixty dollars. Among the little gold nuggets were discovered two larger ones of pure native copper. On the surface they were of a greenish hue, but when whittled with a knife their true character appeared.

"That isn't exactly Klondike richness," said Uncle Will, as he held up to view the pan and its contents, "but I doubt if we've found the richest part of this claim. We've been working in what is called bench gravel on the rim-rock. I wish we could get down to the low bed-rock near the present channel of the stream. We might find a first-rate pay-streak there."

"Can't we do it?" asked Roly.

"I fear not. We've tried it, and the Thirty-six have tried it; but the minute you go below the level of the stream, the water comes through the loose gravel faster than you can throw it out. For this reason the Thirty-six are working almost entirely in the gravel along the hillsides in former channels of the river. They've begun two tunnels through the gravel on the rim-rock about fifty feet above the present stream."

"Well," remarked Mr. Bradford, cheerfully, "even if we can't make more than twenty dollars a day, we can pay a good part of the expenses of our trip before the end of the season."

"That's true," said his brother. "And, besides, we've only to make another set of sluice-boxes to double our income. Lucky and Coffee Jack can work this one profitably, and you and I can take care of another, while the boys can work with the rocker almost anywhere. I haven't a doubt that we shall do far better than thousands who are now crowding over the White and Chilkoot passes. Why, I feel amply repaid for all my labors by just looking at you, Charles. I never saw you in better health."

Mr. Bradford laughed and rubbed his arm doubtfully. "Maybe I *look* well," said he, "but what a place this is for rheumatism! Evenings and mornings when the air is chill I can hardly move."

"Yes," said Uncle Will, "I can sympathize with you there. I feel it more or less myself, and I understand that two or three of the big party are fairly laid up with it. But I don't think we shall carry it home."

## CHAPTER XXXI

### DAVID MAKES A BOAT-JOURNEY

LATE in June, when the leaves were full-grown and the grass and flowers luxuriant, there came a storm of rain which turned into a damp snow. About two inches fell, and remained on the ground several hours. The hardy vegetation seemed to suffer no injury, and indeed the storm proved quite a godsend, for it discouraged the mosquitoes, and they were unable to rally again in such numbers and with such vigor as before.

By the middle of July the Bradfords had two sluices in operation, and were taking out from thirty to fifty dollars a day. The Thirty-six were working with varying success on the hillsides. Their first supply train of horses had arrived with provisions and the mail, including a few Seattle newspapers only three weeks old.

About this time the leader of the Thirty-six invited David to join a small party which he was going to take north on an exploring trip. He needed a young fellow, he said, to take charge of a cabin at Champlain's Landing, twenty-five miles north of Pennock's Post, for a week or two, until one of Moran's men could be spared.

David begged to be allowed to go, since he was not imperatively needed at Alder Creek, and his father consented, believing that the experience would be valuable as a training in self-reliance. He warned his son, however, that he might be very homesick and lonely. As David had never been homesick in his life, that malady had no terrors for him, and he declared that he was quite willing to take the risk.

Thus it happened that he found himself one afternoon starting down the gorge from Moran's Camp in company with the captain, a civil engineer named Dunn, who had recently arrived, and Greenwood, who had been a cook in the army. Three others had already set out with horses to make the journey overland, while the captain's party was to proceed by boat down Lake Dasardee-ash and its outlet river to the Landing. There the parties would unite and continue the journey by land, leaving David at the cabin.

At the shore of the lake Paul Champlain was encamped. He was that member of the Thirty-six who had selected on the north branch of the Alsek the landing place called by his name, and had built the storehouse there, while Pennock's party and the Bradfords, on the same stream, were building Pennock's Post. He was a Michigan man of French descent, possessing a thorough knowledge of woodcraft and a magnificent physique. By the captain's directions he had hired and brought up the boat which had been built near this point earlier in the season.

Hardly had the tents been pitched on a gravelly open space overlooking the water, when a cold and drenching rainstorm came on. A fire was kindled with difficulty, around which the shivering party gathered to cook and eat their evening meal. Rubber blankets and oiled canvas were pressed into service to protect them from the storm, but there was no keeping entirely dry in such a downpour. Around the small tent which had been assigned to David, the ground was so level that the water was presently standing an inch deep, and only by hastily digging a ditch was he able to prevent it from being flooded. As it was, he found a comparatively dry spot along the centre of his blanket-bed when he crawled in out of the rain, and having rolled up his damp coat for a pillow, he went to sleep in a twinkling in spite of all discomforts.

By morning the sky cleared, tents were struck, provisions and goods of all kinds were put aboard the little craft, and soon they were sailing merrily northward before the wind, the captain at the helm, Champlain holding the sheet in his hand that he might let it go instantly in case of a squall, Mr. Dunn on the centre seat, and Greenwood and David sitting forward near the slender mast. Occasionally they were obliged to bail, but considering the fact that there was not a drop of paint on the boat, she was remarkably seaworthy.

It was a glorious morning. A fresh, bracing wind blew from the south. The cloud-flecked mountains loomed sharp and blue around the lake, and the great range on the western shore was especially grand and imposing. David discovered beneath one of its glaciers, several thousand feet above the lake, what appeared to be a yawning cave as big as a house, and the captain's glass brought it out more distinctly. Here was a natural wonder fairly begging to be visited, and right well would David have liked to explore its mysteries; but time was precious to the voyagers, and they held their course steadily to the north, crossing the mouth of a great bay which extended several miles eastward. There was a similar bay to the west, but the lake narrowed again as they approached the outlet. At noon they landed for dinner in a little cove, which they named Shelter Bay, and there, the wind deserting them, they had recourse to the oars and rowed the short distance to the river, after which the current assisted them. The water was here so clear that they could see the fish as they darted away from the shadow of the oars. Several yellow-legged plover were shot along the banks, but no attempt was made to bag ducks, as it was their breeding season.

Early in the evening they reached the sandy bluff near Pennock's cabin and moored the boat to a tree.

The cabin was now deserted by human beings, but when David opened the door a fat ground-squirrel scurried across the floor and ran out through a hole under the side log. It seemed too bad that such a stanch dwelling should be given over to neglect, but such is often the case in a new country. The travellers did not sleep in it, for the mosquitoes were in possession. They pitched their insect-proof tents by the side of the river and passed the night in comfort.

But before they turned in, Champlain and David took trout flies and lines and sauntered down the stream to try to discover what kind of fish they had seen. They cut rude willow poles and fished carefully but in vain until they came to the mouth of Frying-Pan Creek. Here the current of the brook cleared for a space the now muddy river water, and Champlain had a rise almost immediately. A few seconds later he landed a delicately spotted, gamy fish about eight inches long, which he recognized as a grayling. The sport became exciting at once, and David soon had half a dozen catches to his credit. When the anglers could no longer induce a rise, they marched back to camp in triumph with a handsome string.

The voyage was continued next day. Champlain entertained his companions with an account of his successful moose-hunt a few weeks previous, which had relieved the hunger of the northernmost party of the

Thirty-six. Then he told of the difficulties he and others had overcome in rafting the goods from their great cache and Pennock's Post down to the Landing. He had shot an otter on one of his journeys along the stream, but said he had seen hardly a trace of beavers.

The river now became extremely tortuous. Greenwood wondered how it could make so many loops without tying itself into a knot, and expressed a decided preference for walking as a means of getting to the Landing. As he was taking his turn at rowing at that moment, it was easy to account for his sudden feeling in the matter.

By skilful use of helm and paddle Champlain guided the boat through a number of rocky stretches in safety, but he was not to be invariably so successful. David, who had been intently gazing forward, suddenly shouted a warning. Five or six boulders lay in the stream so nearly submerged that they could hardly be discerned from a distance, while others just below the surface betrayed their position only by eddies. Champlain put all his strength into the paddle, but in that current the heavy boat could be swerved but little. A dangerous eddy was barely avoided, but beyond and directly in their path a ragged rock appeared. How the paddle flashed! And how the rowers struggled! But in a moment it was evident that the boat must strike.

Crunch! went her side against the rock. She careened as she stopped, and the current piled up against her, while her passengers fully expected shipwreck and instinctively measured the distance to the shore. But the force of the stream, instead of swamping the stout little craft, swept her past the obstruction, and all breathed freely once more. By great good fortune not the least damage had been sustained.

Early in the afternoon they passed between Father and Son, otherwise known as Mount Champlain and Mount Bratnober respectively. The pass was about a mile wide, with perpendicular cliffs several thousand feet high on either side. In this wild place they found the forest recently burned, and in one spot near the base of Mount Bratnober smoke was still rising. It was this great conflagration, covering thousands of acres, which had filled the atmosphere with smoke a few weeks before and caused the sun to look like a blood-red ball as it sank in the west. Champlain related how, in company with a Canadian government surveyor, he had climbed the mountain which had received his name. He was sure they could have seen Mount St. Elias in the west had not clouds obscured the view. They noticed a flock of mountain sheep, but did not get near enough for a shot.

The voyage was presently enlivened by a race with a brood of little ducks which Mother Mallard had taken out for an airing, — or "watering," as David put it. There were a dozen of the little fellows not two weeks out of the shell, and what a splashing they set up when they saw the strange, oared craft bearing down upon them! The mother duck quacked anxiously from the rear of her flotilla and urged the youngsters forward at the top of their speed, which proved just about equal to that of the boat.

The little ducks could not fly, and the river was so narrow that at first they dared not swerve toward either shore, but flapped and paddled and splashed straight down the river. Not until they became utterly exhausted did they seek the bank. Then one by one, as a convenient log or hole appeared, they dropped away from the others and hid themselves while the terrible monster went by. The old duck paid not the slightest attention to these stragglers, but continued with that part of her brood which was still in danger, turning her head from side to side and talking vigorously in duck language to her terrified children.

Finally only one duckling remained in the middle of the river, probably at once the strongest and most foolish of the brood. He did not know enough to follow the example of his brothers and sisters, but kept splashing along until he could flee no longer. Then he too sought the friendly bank. And now, having seen all her brood safely disposed, the brave mother-bird made use of her wings, rising in a graceful sweep and turning back up-stream to gather her scattered family.

## CHAPTER XXXII

### CHAMPLAIN'S LANDING

IT was well into the evening, though before sunset, when Champlain assured his fellow-voyagers that the Landing was near. Soon afterward, they saw two men appear on the brow of a sandy bluff ahead. These proved to be Hovey and Herrick, who were in charge of the camp. They had heard voices and the plash of oars, and had hurried out to see who was approaching, waving their hats and shouting a welcome as soon as they recognized their friends. The boat was brought close to the narrow beach, and the captain, Dunn, and Greenwood disembarked, leaving Champlain and David to row around to the other side of the bluff, where the craft could be more securely moored.

David was now accustomed to the interminable windings of the river, and took it quite as a matter of course that the stream, after flowing a quarter of a mile to the left or southwest from the bluff, turned capriciously back to within fifty yards of the spot where the three had landed. The bluff itself was thus a narrow, high neck of land connecting a low, wooded point with what we may call the mainland east of the river.

RAFTING DOWN THE NORTH ALSEK

With oars and paddle, the crew of two soon rounded the point, and approached the bluff once more. Here the river turned abruptly northwest, and in the bay formed by its curve lay a flotilla of log rafts. To one of these the boat was made fast, and the occupants sprang ashore and made their way up the slope.

David looked with interest at the place which for a fortnight was to be his home. The top of the bluff was about thirty feet wide, and covered with short grass. It was as level as a floor, except along its southeastern edge, where a ridge of sand six or eight feet high, and fringed with spruces, offered a natural protection for a cook-tent and a sleeping-tent. Champlain, who had discovered this spot, took pride in pointing out to David its advantages.

"It's the finest place in this valley for a camp or a fort," he declared, with a Frenchman's enthusiasm. "Every time I look at it, I almost wish there was an Indian war, and I had a good garrison here. You see, it's defended on three sides by the river, which is too deep for fording, and can only be crossed with canoes or logs, or by swimming. From the top of the bluff we have a clear view for an eighth of a mile both up and down the stream. If the enemy came down the river, the ridge of sand behind the tents is a natural breastwork for riflemen; while if they approached from the other direction, the defenders would simply lie down a little back from the edge of the bluff on that side, and give them a good peppering."

"And what if they came from the land side?" asked David, who began to wonder if an attack were within the bounds of possibility.

"We should put a stockade of logs across the neck of land on that side," answered Champlain. "Already I have built a strong log house. Come and see it."

He led the way landward from the narrow part of the bluff to a point about a hundred yards up-stream, where David now beheld the neat little cabin in which the supplies were stored. It had a door of boards, evidently constructed from the material of a coffee-box, but there was no window, either because no more boards were to be had, or because the cabin was less vulnerable with but a single opening in its heavy walls. The door was fitted with good hinges and a padlock. Forest enclosed the cabin, except on the side from which they had come, and toward the river; and off among the trees wound a path which joined the main trail about fifty rods away.

"You won't have to fight Indians, my lad," said Champlain, who was aware that his imaginative talk might cause David some uneasiness; "and as for bears, you don't seem to mind them much, judging from what I've heard."

"I think I can take care of the bears," said David.

Champlain eyed the lad with evident approval. "I

A Herd of Cattle.—Yukon Divide in the Distance

like your pluck," said he; "but let an old hunter advise you to leave such beasts alone, when you're not in reach of help. You see, we should never know where to look for you if you should meet with an accident off in these woods. Better stick pretty close to the cabin."

On their way back to the cook-tent Champlain pointed out a pile of saddles and blankets near the embers of a fire.

"Must be a pack train somewhere about," he observed. "I wonder where the men and horses are. It's too early for ours to be here."

The explanation was quickly forthcoming. A large herd of cattle, convoyed by five or six horsemen, had arrived on the previous day on their way to Dawson, and had been halted for a day's rest at the Landing. The men were now rounding up their charges into an open meadow half a mile distant, preparatory to an early start in the morning.

"And you'll be very glad they came when you know what you're to have for supper," added Hovey, with a twinkle in his eye, as he bustled about the sheet-iron stove in the cook-tent.

"Oh, we live high at this hotel!" Herrick chimed in. "How would fried liver strike you, — and hot biscuits and butter, — and tea with cream and sugar, — and a custard by way of dessert?"

"What's this you're talking about?" cried the captain, who had overheard the last few words. "Cream and custards? I'll believe when I see and taste!"

"All right, my sceptical friend! Come in. Supper's ready. Muck-muck!"

No second call was needed, for the travellers were ravenous. They entered the cook-tent at once, and took their places on empty boxes around a small improvised table.

"Now then," said Hovey, who, with Herrick, had finished supper some three hours before, and now presided gracefully over the cook-stove in the interest of the guests, "pass the plates."

These much battered articles of aluminum were promptly presented, and as promptly filled with the savory contents of the frying-pan, which proved to be real liver, after all. Herrick meanwhile told how they had secured it.

It appeared by his narrative that one of the steers had driven a sharp stick into its foot in such a way as to lame it badly. On noticing this, he had strongly represented to the cattlemen that it would be cruel to drive the animal farther, and that they ought to kill it then and there. Aided by several expressive winks, the cattlemen had seen the point of his remarks, and having found the two campers pleasant, sociable fellows, they killed the steer, and made them a present of a considerable portion of the carcass. The cream and custard were accounted for by the presence of a milch cow in the herd.

"To-morrow," said Herrick, as he finished his tale, "we shall have roast beef with brown gravy; and if they can catch the cow, we may get a drink of milk all around."

"What would the boys at Shorty Creek say, if they heard that?" asked Greenwood, smacking his lips.

"They'd mutiny," replied Dunn. "But is this the only cattle train that has come along?"

"No," answered Hovey. "This is the third big one within a couple of weeks, and they all belong to one man. There have been some smaller herds, too. Over a thousand head must have gone over this trail this season, and they're in prime condition. They ought to sell high in Dawson, for the Yukon steamers can't carry cattle to any great extent, and there must be thousands of people there by this time."

Next morning, previous to their departure, the cattlemen made an attempt to milk their solitary cow. Obviously the first thing to do was to catch the animal, but for some reason she was particularly contrary, and refused to be either coaxed or coerced. At last one of the men mounted his horse, and set out with his lariat to lasso the refractory beast in true cow-boy style. The poor cow, frightened out of her wits by the shouts and the turmoil, rushed frantically through thickets and over sand-banks, closely followed by the horseman, who, after several throws, succeeded in roping her and checking her wild career.

It now looked as if the drink of milk might materialize, but alas for human expectations! The cow had been wrought up to such a pitch of excitement by the events of the morning that she could not be made to stand still, and it was with great difficulty that the milking could be commenced. The man who essayed this task had all he could attend to with her kicking and plunging, and finally, losing all patience, he threw pail, milk, and all at her head, accompanied by something very like an oath. So faded the dream of the drink of milk.

Hovey and Herrick, who had been informed that they were to take the boat and a moderate cargo and start for Moran's Camp, where they were to sign certain papers connected with their claims, now made ready to depart. They appeared to relish the idea of joining their comrades on the Kah Sha River, but David thought, as he watched them pull away against the current, that long before they could hoist their sail on Lake Dasar-dee-ash, they would wish themselves back at the Landing. The cattle train started toward Dawson about the same time, and Champlain's Landing was left to the captain's party.

The following morning he, too, made ready to leave. The horses, which had now arrived, were loaded with the necessary provisions from the cache in the cabin, and David was given final directions about the camp.

"Shep," an Indian dog which had accompanied the horses, was left with him as his sole companion, and then the captain, Champlain, Dunn, Greenwood, and the three packers bade him good-by and disappeared in the woods.

## CHAPTER XXXIII

### ALONE IN THE WILDERNESS

DAVID had not realized what it meant to be alone in the wilderness. When he had agreed, back in the camp on Alder Creek, to take charge of a cabin for a fortnight, he had looked upon it as rather a novel and pleasant undertaking, in spite of his father's warning. Now, as he watched his friends ride away, and whistled back the dog, who showed a desire to follow them, it must be confessed that he felt quite differently about it. But he was a stout-hearted lad, and sensibly decided that the best way to forget his loneliness was to keep busy.

Fortunately work lay ready to his hand. His predecessors had carried away their sleeping-tent, but they had shown him in the cabin some large pieces of canvas which, with a little ingenuity, could be transformed into quite a comfortable shelter. They had built a raised bedstead of poles inside their tent, and this structure remained in place. Above it was a sort of ridge-pole, which had supported the tent. With some difficulty David flung an end of the largest piece of canvas over this pole, and found, on drawing it into position, that it would quite reach the ground on both sides and completely cover the bedstead. Having made the corners fast to small spruces, he set the other pieces of canvas in place across the rear of the tent; and though they could not be made to fill the whole space, they contributed materially to the shelter. Besides, that end was protected by the ridge of sand with its fringe of trees. The front of the tent was entirely open and faced northwest upon the beautiful stretch of the river where it flowed away from the bluff. Beyond, and perhaps ten miles distant, was a long range of mountains bounding the valley on the north, which Champlain had said was the Yukon Divide. The waters on its farther slope flowed into a tributary of the Yukon, while those on the nearer side reached the Pacific much more directly.

When the tent had been made as snug as possible, David brought heavy blankets from the cabin and spread them upon the poles of the bedstead. So interested did he become in arranging his quarters that he quite forgot that he must get his own supper; and when hunger at length compelled him to think of the matter, his watch informed him that it was after six o'clock. By good luck, he found, on examining the larder, that there were odds and ends of one kind and another sufficient for a meal.

After supper he cut dry wood for the little stove and

piled it in the cook-tent. Hardly was this done when a thunder-storm, which had been brewing in the north, drove him into the new tent. The sky grew dark, the lightning flashed over the northern mountains, the wind arose and howled in the forest, and the rain beat down on the frail canvas roof. David lay on his rude couch, with Shep curled up on the ground at his feet, and watched the storm, and thought, with a longing he had never known before, of his far-away home in New England, — of his father and brother and uncle in their camp on Alder Creek, — and more than once, it is certain, of the fair-haired little girl at Seattle. But at last, in spite of his loneliness, having carefully arranged his head-net over his face and settled down among the blankets, he dropped off into oblivion, and only awakened when the morning sun was smiling warmly down on the valley.

It was indeed a fine morning. A few gray clouds curled about Mount Bratnober and Mount Champlain and an unnamed peak to the west. Red squirrels were scampering and chattering in the trees, a fat ground-squirrel was sitting up demurely on the point of the bluff like a small brown statue, birds were singing in all directions, and the feeling of isolation which had oppressed the solitary youth in the evening vanished like magic under the bright influence of day.

Having fetched a pail of water from the river, David

performed his toilet, and then set about getting breakfast. He had helped his uncle more or less and could fry bacon to a turn; but he was rather tired of bacon, and cast about for some more appetizing dish. Picking up a can of baking-powder, he read the recipes printed thereon, but without finding just what he wanted. Then he bethought himself of a rule for johnny-cakes which Hovey had written out for him. Johnny-cakes would be an excellent breakfast dish, he said to himself. With the aid of a few dry twigs a fire was quickly kindled in the little stove, and a kettle of water set on to heat for coffee and for dish-washing, while the young cook measured out the flour, corn-meal, crystallized egg, baking-powder, and salt which were to compose the cakes. When he had stirred sufficient water into this mixture to moisten it thoroughly, he greased the frying-pan with a bacon rind, and as soon as it was hot he ladled out the batter.

How deliciously it sizzled in the pan! He could hardly wait for the cooking to be done; but at length there were nine nicely browned johnny-cakes begging to be eaten. A little sugar and water heated on the stove served for syrup, and canned butter was also at hand. David found not the slightest difficulty in disposing of the nine cakes, and thought them by far the best he had ever eaten. They were much too good for Shep, who was offered some canned corned beef instead; but to

David's surprise, the dog refused to eat the meat and declined all invitations to join his master at breakfast. Indeed, for nearly a week Shep would eat nothing; but as he seemed in good condition, David came to the conclusion that he had found the carcass of the steer which the cattlemen had killed, and was living by preference on that.

But if the dog would not partake, at least the birds would. They fluttered fearlessly about the tent — magpies, butcher-birds, and others — and carried off every stray scrap; while two tiny song-sparrows, most fearless and friendly of all, actually hopped into the tent and over his feet and upon the table while he was at meals, and picked up the crumbs as fast as they fell.

With a little practice David became a competent cook. His johnny-cakes had turned out so well that he made them every morning. He also had biscuits, omelets, baked beans, rice, dried fruits and vegetables, bacon, squirrels, and grayling to choose from, and lived very comfortably. The biscuits were as successful as the johnny-cakes, with one notable exception, — that was when he conceived the idea of adding a pinch of nutmeg spice. All might have gone well had not the cover come off unexpectedly and allowed half the contents of the can to go into the batter. When he had removed all the spice he could with a spoon, there still remained so much that the biscuits turned out a dark pink color;

## ALONE IN THE WILDERNESS

and as for eating them, it required a pretty strong stomach.

The grayling could sometimes be caught quite plentifully from the rafts or from the sandy curve on the other side of the bluff. As for the squirrels, he could not find it in his heart to kill those which chattered so sociably around his dwelling; so when he needed fresh meat, he strolled down the trail with Shep and shot squirrels with which he was in no wise acquainted.

One evening he shot an animal which was swimming in the river. It proved to be a musk-rat. He remembered reading that some Indian tribes relish the flesh of this rodent, and, having cooked it experimentally, he found the meat both wholesome and palatable.

He early set himself to the task of bringing order out of chaos in the cabin, where boxes and cans of provisions were indiscriminately mixed with clothing bags and snow-shoes. Cutting down two straight young trees, he contrived a shelf across the rear of the building upon which a portion of the goods could be disposed, thus leaving much more room upon the floor. After the first two or three nights he slept in the cabin, because the mosquitoes were less troublesome in the comparative darkness of the building, and also because he felt more secure there against the larger inhabitants of the forest. Presently he found himself almost reconciled to this mode of life. He was his own master. He could go or come with absolute freedom. In the intervals of his work he could hunt or fish, read or dream, or study nature in the animal and plant life about him. There was a sort of charm in it, after all. But as often as evening came around, he heartily wished he might have some one besides the dog to talk to.

Day after day he saw no human face and heard no voice but his own. If a regiment had passed on the main trail he might never have known it, had they gone quietly. How many pack trains actually went by in that lonely week he never knew. Once he heard a rifle-shot and the bark of a dog, and running down his own path to the trail, he found fresh hoof-prints, but the travellers were out of sight. He happened to meet no one on any of his hunting excursions, nor did any Indian visit him. For seven long days he was alone.

## CHAPTER XXXIV

### RAIDED BY A WOLF

THE third evening after the departure of the captain's party David was sitting in the cook-tent watching the last embers of the sunset and the varying lights and shadows on the river. Shep stood near the edge of the bluff.

Suddenly the dog's ears pointed forward attentively and his whole body quivered. It was clear that something unusual had come in sight. No sooner had David reached the brow of the bluff than he saw the cause of Shep's excitement. A black animal was lapping the water where the river curved to the northwest, about three hundred feet distant.

The semi-darkness and the heavy mosquito net over his face prevented David from seeing clearly, but he instantly formed the conclusion that it was a dog belonging to some pack train on the neighboring trail, and whistled to see what it would do.

On hearing the whistle the animal raised its head, gazed a moment at the two figures on the bluff, resumed its drinking, and then, having satisfied its thirst, turned and started up the slope. As it did so, David was conscious that it had a slinking gait unlike that of a dog, and for the first time he thought how queer it was that Shep had not offered to run down and make friends with the stranger.

"It's a small black bear," flashed into his mind. Instantly he ran with all speed to the cabin for the shotgun, which he kept loaded with buck-shot. The captain's party had carried off the only rifle, and David was now sorry he had not brought his own. He caught up the shot-gun, however, and slipping a few extra cartridges into his pocket, ran back to the bluff where Shep stood guard.

The strange animal had disappeared.

For a moment David was disconcerted. He had not thought the bear could get away so quickly, nor could he be sure whether it had gone into the fringe of trees and bushes along the river-bank or continued up the slope. He hesitated, too, before setting out to attack such an animal with only a shot-gun for a weapon and a dog of doubtful courage as an ally. The next instant, however, he had decided to track and kill the beast if possible, and calling Shep to follow, he hurried down to the river's sandy brink to examine the tracks by the waning light. He was quite puzzled at finding that they were almost identical in appearance with those made by Shep, but at length the truth dawned upon him. He had to deal, not with a young bear, but with a full-grown wolf!

## RAIDED BY A WOLF

He now endeavored to make Shep take the scent, but Shep was not trained to such work and sniffed around indiscriminately without attempting to follow the animal's trail. There was nothing for it but to track the wolf himself. He accordingly traced every track as far as it would lead him. One proceeded from the fringe of bushes to the point where the animal drank, while another led straight up the face of the bluff. The latter he followed as far as the sand continued; but the top of the elevation was grassy, and in the growing darkness the trail was quickly lost. Keeping his eyes and ears alert for the slightest sound, David penetrated some distance into the open woods, but without discovering further signs of the animal. Satisfied that nothing more could be done, he returned to camp, and took unusual pains to fasten the frail cabin door securely when he turned in for the night.

Nor was he destined to sleep without an alarm. A noise of rattling tin awoke him with a start. The interior of the cabin was quite dark, since, as we have said, there were no windows; but the nights were not yet without some light, and feeble rays outlined every chink as David sat up, threw off his mosquito net, and looked around. Again came the rattle of tin. It evidently proceeded from a pile of empty cans just outside the cabin. He brought himself to a kneeling posture and pressed his face close to one of the widest chinks. Presently he distinguished an animal nosing among the cans and making the noise which had awakened him. It was Shep. David spoke to the dog, and having seen him walk away with a somewhat shamefaced air, he settled himself once more among the blankets and was soon asleep again.

Seven days had passed when the monotony of his existence was broken by the arrival of strangers. It was in the afternoon that he heard voices and the sound of horses from the direction of the trail, and a minute later saw two young fellows ride up, followed by a dozen pack animals.

"Hello!" exclaimed the foremost rider as he saw David, "this place has changed hands, I guess, since we was here last. How d' you do? Hovey and Herrick gone away?"

"Yes," answered David. "They left for the Kah Sha River a week ago. You 've been here before?"

"Oh, yes! We 're packing back and forth between Pyramid Harbor and Five Finger Rapids for the owner of these horses. We always like to put up here for the night, for it 's pretty lonesome on this trail."

"That 's so," said David, feelingly. He, too, was not a little pleased at the thought of company, and the more so in the present instance, because the new-comers were near his own age. The elder was slender, with dark hair and a rather sparse growth of beard, and might have been twenty-two or three, while the other was a ruddy, plump lad of about seventeen.

"My name's Close," said the dark-haired one, as he dismounted and proceeded to unsaddle his horse. "We're from Wisconsin."

In return for this information David gave his own name and residence.

The Wisconsin boys took the packs from their horses and turned them loose to graze.

"Now for supper," said Close.

"You'll find a stove and dishes and a table, such as it is, in the cook-tent yonder," said David, hospitably. "I guess you know your way around. Just make yourselves at home, and I'll have the fire going in a jiffy."

It took the strangers but a short time to cook their evening meal, and as soon as they had finished with the stove David prepared his own supper, and the three sat down together.

"Can you spare us enough butter for our bread?" asked Close. "We're all out."

"Yes," said David, passing it over, "help yourself." He knew there were but two more cans in the cache under his charge, but he felt certain the captain would wish him to extend such hospitalities as lay in his power; and he would much rather have gone without butter himself for a time than deny it to his guests.

They, however, had no intention of trenching on David's slender stock without returning an equivalent.

"You don't seem to have any condensed milk," observed the younger of the two.

"No," said David. "There isn't a drop. I've looked the whole cache over for it."

"Well, here! You just take what you want out of our can. We've got milk if we haven't got butter. Try some of that dried fruit, too."

Having thanked his friends, David inquired if the trail was in good shape. He was thinking that before long he would be tramping back over it.

"Yes," answered Close, "most of it's good; but there's some bad bogs where the horses get mired. Those cattle herds have cut it all to pieces where the ground is soft. We haven't had much trouble, though."

"No," put in his companion, "when we get started we can go along well enough. The worst of this packing business is ketching the horses in the morning. The critters are as sly as foxes. They'll stand so still in the thickets when they hear you coming that you can go within ten feet of 'em and never know they're there."

"They keep pretty well together, though," said the other, "and the tracks are generally plain. Besides, there's a bell on one of them."

"If they were my horses," declared David, "I would bell them all."

## RAIDED BY A WOLF

"And it wouldn't be a bad idea," said Close, with a laugh.

By David's invitation the Wisconsin boys slept that night on the bedstead in the tent. They breakfasted early and then set out to round up their horses, which they accomplished in a couple of hours after a long tramp through the woods. Having loaded the animals, they bade David good-by and rode away toward the trail, presently shouting back, "Better call the dog; he's following the horses."

David whistled Shep back and ordered him to lie down. It was no wonder he thought every one his master, he had changed owners so often. He now lay down quietly enough on the ground before the cook-tent and appeared to have forgotten all about the pack train.

An hour later David finished his wood-chopping and suddenly noticed that Shep was gone. At first he thought little of the matter, supposing him to be somewhere in the neighborhood, but when another hour passed without him, he feared Shep had followed the horses, after all. He whistled again and again, but no dog came; and now he was perplexed to know what to do. By this time the pack train was six or eight miles away. The dog would overtake it easily, but *he* could not hope to do so before it halted for the night; and he did not like to leave so long the property of which he was in charge. The Wisconsin boys might send the dog back, or, failing in that, they would doubtless deliver him up to the captain, whom they would probably see before many days. So, however much he regretted the loss of his only companion, he concluded to let the matter drop.

A little later, from the sand-ridge back of the tents, he perceived a column of white smoke above the trees near the river, a quarter of a mile to the southeast. It indicated the presence of either white men or Indians on the trail, and Shep might be with them. David lost no time in locking the cabin door and setting out rapidly in the direction of the smoke.

On his hunting excursions he had noticed an Indian canoe bottom-up near that spot, and naturally supposed that the dusky owners had now arrived. He found, however, that two white men had kindled a fire against a fallen tree for the purpose of cooking their midday meal. Their two horses were grazing near by. The strangers were men of middle age, with thick, grizzled beards and sunbrowned faces. They seemed surprised to see David, but greeted him pleasantly.

"Camping near here?" they asked.

"Yes," answered David, seating himself sociably; "at Champlain's Landing."

"Oh, yes!" exclaimed one of the men, "I saw the signboard on the tree where your path turns off, but I didn't know any one was there."

"Have you come from Dawson?" asked David.

"Yes; we left there nine days ago."

"Any new strikes?"

"No, none recently; but the people keep swarming in over the other trails."

"What are they paying in wages?"

"Seven to ten dollars a day."

"I've heard it was very unhealthy there."

"Yes, there's a good deal of scurvy and pneumonia."

"Any starvation last winter?"

"No, but it was a tight squeeze for some of them."

"Does a man stand much chance of a fortune who goes there now?"

"Not if he expects to dig gold. The paying ground is all taken up and a good deal more. There's a better chance now in trading. In fact, that's what my partner and I are going into. We've discovered that some things are mighty scarce in Dawson, and people will pay almost anything for them, so we're going out to the coast to bring in a stock of goods. We shall try to be back before cold weather."

David had kept his eyes open for Shep, but seeing nothing of him, he asked if they had met two young fellows that morning and had noticed a black and white dog. The men remembered the pack train well enough, but neither had any recollection of seeing the dog. So David went back to the Landing more mystified than ever.

With Shep away, he felt instinctively that the wolf would pay him another visit; nor was he mistaken. That night he slept deeply and heard no sound, but when he arose and went out to the cook-tent, he rubbed his eyes in astonishment. Wolf-tracks were everywhere, dishes were scattered about, a five-pound piece of bacon had disappeared, and the butter can, which had stood in a pail of water on the top of the rude sideboard five feet above the ground now lay on the grass, where the wolf had ineffectually tried to get at the contents. Strange to say, the pail from which the can had been abstracted stood unmoved in its accustomed place.

David picked up the scattered utensils and smiled rather grimly to think how he had slept for two nights in the open, unprotected tent, exposed to this midnight prowler.

## CHAPTER XXXV

A LONG MARCH, WITH A SURPRISE AT THE END OF IT

AS the time approached for David to be relieved from duty, he began to watch for the expected traveller and to conjecture as to who would be sent. Two weeks had passed since he had left the camp on Alder Creek. It was now near the end of July.

About noon of the day following the departure of Shep and the midnight visit of the wolf, as he was cooking his dinner, he saw Davidson, a young Bostonian, swinging rapidly up the path. The two exchanged cordial greetings, and David immediately prepared to give his friend a hearty meal.

"How did you leave the people in the Shorty Creek district?" asked the young cook when the new-comer had removed his light pack and seated himself in one of Hovey's rustic chairs.

"Everybody was well when I left," answered Davidson, "except old Tom Moore, the recorder. He's down with scurvy, but I guess our doctor will fix him up. They've sent him a lot of dried fruit and vegetables, and that diet ought to help him. I don't believe he had eaten much but bacon for a month, and he hardly ever stirred out of his tent. It's no wonder the scurvy caught him."

"I should think so," said David. And then he asked abruptly, "How long did it take you to get here, Davidson?"

"Two days and a half from Reitz's tent on Klukshu Lake," was the reply.

"That's quick time. You must be a good walker. I just wish my legs were as long as yours. How far do you think it is?"

"About sixty-five miles by the trail. You'd better allow three days if you carry anything."

"I shall have about forty pounds," said David. "The men at Moran's gave me a list of things they wanted out of their clothing bags, and I sent all I could by the boat; but in the hurry I couldn't find everything. Is Reitz catching any salmon yet?"

"Oh, yes; plenty of them. Humphrey is with him now, and they're having all they can do."

Next morning David gave his friend such directions regarding the cache as had been given to himself, and surrendered the key of the padlock on the cabin door. Then he cooked three days' rations of bacon, biscuits, and rice, to which he added some pieces of jerked beef which Davidson had brought and kindly offered him. Finally he made up his pack, and an hour before noon was ready to start on the long, solitary tramp. If he had stopped to think much about it he might well have shrunk from so lonely a journey through the wilderness, for he was armed only with hunting-knife and hatchet, but the thought of getting back to his friends was uppermost and made him light-hearted; and, besides, if Davidson had made the journey, he was sure *he* could.

"Hold on!" exclaimed Davidson, suddenly, as he saw the lad taking up his pack. "I'm going with you a few miles. I'll carry the pack."

"Oh, no indeed!" said David, whose pride was touched. It seemed almost effeminate to surrender his burden to one who had hardly yet rested after a long journey. "I'm perfectly fresh, and you must be tired. It's mighty kind of you, but I can't let you."

"You don't feel the need of a lift now," said Davidson, kindly, "but you may at the other end of the day's march. And it's only at this end that I can help you."

"But surely I can carry that load all day. It isn't heavy, — and it really belongs to me to take it."

"Then I won't go with you, Dave."

David instantly perceived that if he refused the generous offer of his friend he would hurt his feelings, and that he ought to yield. "Well, then," said he, "rather than lose your company, I accept your conditions, and please don't think me ungrateful."

So Davidson fastened the pack upon his own shoulders, and having locked the cabin, the two set off down the path to the trail, which they followed till they had covered about five miles and were near the entrance to the pass between Mount Bratnober and Mount Champlain. They now sat down beside a brook, and David proceeded to eat his dinner, which he insisted his companion should share. This Davidson was reluctant to do, since he knew the lad would have to calculate closely to make his food last. He was finally prevailed upon to accept a piece of bacon and half a biscuit, but would take no more.

"If I were you," said Davidson, "I should divide the journey into three parts as nearly equal as possible. From the Landing to Pennock's Post is about twenty-five miles. You'd better try to reach there to-night. Then it's twenty miles to the river that flows into Dasar-dee-ash from the east. You'll have to wade it, unless there's somebody there with a horse. I was lucky enough to find a pack train at the ford. The water won't come much above your waist."

"H-m!" said David, laconically. "Ice-water, I suppose."

"Very likely. Then on the third day you can make the remaining twenty miles to Reitz's camp, and go over to Moran's any time you like."

"Thank you, Davidson," said his young friend. "That's just the way I'll plan to do it."

They parted with mutual good-will, and David, with

## A LONG MARCH, WITH A SURPRISE

the pack now on his own back, soon found himself traversing the recently burned district within the pass. The mighty cliff of Mount Champlain towered on his left, while across the river rose the hardly less stupendous crags of Mount Bratnober. On every side the country was bright with the purple fireweed, which had sprung up from the ashes as if by magic.

There were scattered patches of forest which the great conflagration had spared, and in the midst of one of these David was suddenly aware of a crackling sound ahead. The next instant he caught a whiff of smoke and saw it rising in a dense cloud through the trees. A few steps more and he found himself in a shower of sparks which a sudden gust blew toward him. Forced to beat a precipitate retreat, he made a détour to the windward of the burning area, from which side he was able to make a closer examination.

Plainly some careless traveller had allowed his campfire to get beyond his control, or else had neglected to extinguish it when he moved on. The flames had crept through the moss and communicated with several dry spruces, which were now blazing fiercely. It was utterly beyond David's power to check the spread of the flames, but he reflected that the whole country around had been burned over, and the fire could not extend past the limits of the oasis-like grove in which it had originated, so he continued on his journey.

In an open stretch of meadow he came upon a white horse and a mule grazing contentedly. The animals raised their heads in mute inquiry, and then resumed their feeding. David looked about for the owners, but seeing no one, came to the conclusion that these were waifs from some pack train, and might now be appropriated by any one who could catch them. It was a great temptation to try. Riding was certainly an improvement on walking; and if he could not do that without a bridle, he could at least lead the horse with a bit of rope and make him carry his pack. On second thought, however, he abandoned the idea. Perhaps the animals were not lost. The owners might be somewhere in the neighborhood. If this were the case, and he were seen leading the horse away, he might be accused of horse-stealing, — a very serious charge on the trail. It was better to let them alone, and he plodded on.

A little later he caught sight of a black animal among the trees ahead, and it must be confessed that a lonely, creepy sensation ran up his back at that moment. He loosened the hatchet in its leather case as he walked, but soon saw that the beast was not a bear, but a large black dog which, having even more respect for him than he had felt for it, turned out of the trail and gave him a wide berth. A few minutes afterward he met two men with a small pack train, and concluded that the dog was theirs. The men nodded pleasantly as they passed; they were the only persons he saw on the trail that day.

By mid-afternoon he found himself getting tired. A great many trees had fallen across the path, and the labor of stepping over them contributed materially to his fatigue. There were bogs, too, so cut up by the passage of horses and cattle that it was difficult for a pedestrian to cross without becoming stuck fast. Usually, however, a sapling had been cut down and laid over the ooze, and David crossed all but one of these rude bridges successfully.

The one exception nearly cost him dear. He made a misstep, and his right foot slipped into the mud beside the log. The mud and water offered no support, and the sudden lurch having thrown the weight of his pack to that side, his foot sank deeper and deeper without reaching solid ground. By good fortune his other foot was still on the log, and, better still, there were stout bushes on the other side. These he grasped desperately as he sank, and by a violent effort restored his balance and drew himself back upon the log.

In the early evening he waded Frying-Pan Creek and caught the first welcome glimpse of Pennock's Post. "Now," thought he, "I shall have a good night's rest in my own bunk," — for he had brought no tent; so with a light heart in spite of his weariness, he turned toward the cabin.

But he was doomed to disappointment. What was his astonishment at finding an enormous padlock and a heavy chain upon the door! And hardly had he touched the contrivance to determine whether it was locked, when there was an angry growl and the rattle of a chain within the building, and he knew by the sound that a fierce dog had sprung toward the door to oppose his entrance.

If he had been surprised at seeing the padlock, it was nothing to the burning indignation which now possessed him. He passed around to the north window. Some-one, probably an Indian, had loosened one of the wooden bars and torn a hole in the cheese-cloth in order to look into the interior. He took advantage of the rent to do likewise. In the southeast corner of the cabin he could see a great pile of goods. The dog, a huge and savage-looking beast, was chained to the corner post of Pennock's bunk, and there was a dish of water and another of meat on the floor. David was locked out of his own house, and it was garrisoned against him.

## CHAPTER XXXVI

### HOW DAVID MET THE OFFENDER AND WAS PREVENTED FROM SPEAKING HIS MIND

HAVING satisfied himself that the owner of the cache was not about, David threw off his pack, and sat down upon it with his back against the log wall to consider what he would do; and the more he thought about it, the more his anger rose.

It was the custom on the trail to cache provisions anywhere. Both Indians and white men respected the unwritten law which held the theft of food in such a region to be worthy of death. No one but a starving man or a desperado would violate that law, and there were few such. Indeed, David had never seen any indication that this chance of loss was being reckoned with. But here was a man who apparently distrusted all his fellow-men, — who suspected every traveller on the trail, — who not only confiscated a cabin for the storage of his goods, but took contemptible measures to protect his property. David felt instinctively that he had to deal with as mean, sour, and selfish a person as it had ever been his lot to meet, and had not the slightest doubt that the character of the master, as is often the case, could be accurately surmised from the temper of his dog. The latter still growled and barked viciously at every sound.

At last he rose and went to the rear of the cabin, thinking to enter by way of the fireplace. He knew he could easily loosen and remove two or three of the stakes which had surrounded the stove, and once inside the cabin, he could sleep in his own bunk, which was situated diagonally opposite the corner where the dog was chained. But no sooner had he begun to carry out this plan than the savage animal became furious, and it was perfectly evident that he would have no rest in the company of such a brute.

"If I only had my rifle," he groaned.

It is entirely safe to say that with it he would have made an end of the animal without a moment's hesitation, flung its body into the creek, and taken possession of the cabin, which his own hands had helped to build. To be sure, he might kill the dog with the hatchet, but such butchery was repugnant to him, and he quickly dismissed the idea. On the whole, it would be best, he decided, to spend the night under the open sky, where there would be no distractions other than the wind in the trees and the continual singing of the mosquitoes. So he picked up his pack, trudged off into the grove of spruces to the south, and selected a dry, level, sandy spot near the edge of the bluff which fronted the river. Here he ate a frugal supper, then spread his blankets on the

## HOW DAVID MET THE OFFENDER. 299

ground, and so passed the night, though the assiduous musical insects which swarmed upon his head-net robbed him of nearly all sleep. After an early breakfast, he resumed his march, fully resolved, in the event of their meeting, to tell the owner of the cache exactly what he thought of him.

This part of the trail was familiar, and he walked briskly, only pausing at the foot of the first small lake to catch two or three grayling, with which to eke out his scanty rations. These he roasted before a fire at noon, and, rudely cooked as they were, they proved very palatable, accompanied by small berries of a bluish color and black moss-berries, which grew there in abundance.

He had passed the point where in May the Bradfords had left the main trail to turn toward the lake, when he descried a pack train approaching across an open meadow. As the caravan came nearer, David was convinced that he saw before him the owner of the cache and the canine. At the head of the procession leaped five or six dogs of fierce aspect. Following them came a round-shouldered old Irishman, riding on a big gray mule, and behind him was a string of mules loaded with sacks and boxes.

The dogs set off toward David with a rush, as soon as they saw him, and it was all their master could do to check them. As it was, David made sure that his hatchet was free before he encountered the pack, and even had he brought that weapon into play, he would have been overwhelmed in a twinkling had not the dogs been in evident fear of the old man. Having jumped about David noisily, but without offering violence, they passed on in obedience to a gruff command. The rider of the mule now drew up and eyed David in silence a moment.

"Where 'd ye come from?" he asked, in a rather impertinent tone, as David thought.

"Champlain's Landing," said David, shortly. He was not in a mood to be trifled with.

"How far may it be to Pennock's Post?" asked the stranger, still eying him suspiciously.

"All of fifteen miles," said David.

"Fifteen miles!" exclaimed the man, in anything but a pleasant voice. "I would n't have said 't was that far, — an' it 's there I must be to-night." Suddenly he glared again at David. "An' where 'd ye stay last night?"

"At Pennock's Post," said David.

"Stayed at Pennock's, did ye?" snarled the old fellow. "Did n't ye find something there, hey?"

This was just what David had been waiting for. Another moment, and he would have uncorked the explosive phials of wrath, but hearing a light footstep he turned, and the next instant, without a single angry word, set his lips hard.

It was neither fear nor irresolution which occasioned this remarkable change on David's part, but a delicate, chivalrous sense of the consideration a man always owes to the gentler sex. On turning his head, he became aware, for the first time, of the presence of a woman.

She was slender, gray-haired, and gentle-faced. She was neatly dressed in black, and had been walking behind the pack train. It flashed through David's mind instantly that this was the old man's wife, and he was conscious of a feeling of pity. Furthermore, she was the first white woman he had seen for many months. It was a delight just to look at her. Quarrel in her presence he could not, nor add one jot to the burden which he felt sure she must bear as the consort of such a man.

It was the sight of this elderly woman which had sealed his lips, and now, to the astonishment of her husband, David turned and walked away without a reply. The woman spoke to him kindly as he passed, and he touched his cap respectfully. Hardly had he cleared the pack train before he heard the old man belaboring the mule on which he rode, and swearing roundly at the other animals. He wondered if the poor wife would have to walk those fifteen long miles while her husband rode.

Not long afterward he met a second section of the train, in charge of a tall, broad-shouldered fellow, who evidently preferred not to overtake his employer.

David pressed on with all possible speed, but since noon his left foot had been giving him pain, and he now became more crippled with every step. Whether it was rheumatism or a bruise or strain he did not know, but by the time he reached the river he was ready to drop.

To his delight, a large tent on the hither bank indicated the presence of some one at the ford, and he had no doubt he could cross dry-shod on the morrow. On reaching this tent he was surprised to find no one within, but, confident that the owner was near, he threw off his pack with a sigh of relief, and stretched himself wearily on a pile of canvas coverings.

An hour or more had dragged by when David saw a slender young man, with a bushy brown beard, leading a bony horse toward the opposite bank of the river. He mounted at the ford, and, having crossed, took off the saddle and turned the steed loose.

"How are you?" said the stranger cordially, as he noticed David. "Been here long?"

"About an hour," answered David. "I thought you would n't mind my resting here."

"Not at all. Make yourself at home. Did n't see anything of a stray mule round here, did you? I've been hunting that mule all the afternoon, but I can't find the critter."

"No, I did n't see it."

"I s'pose you met the old man? He owns this outfit here."

"Oh, ho!" exclaimed David. "Is that so?" A sudden light came into his eyes, and traces of a smile appeared at the corners of his mouth. "What sort of a man is he?" he asked.

"Well," replied Smith, — he had informed David that such was his name, and Yonkers, New York, his home, — "he's different from any Irishman I ever saw. Has n't any more sense of humor than a cow, and he's the worst-tempered man in this whole country. Look at that sick horse and you'll see how he treats his animals, and he don't treat his wife and us men much better. He's going to winter on a claim of his near Dawson, and wants me to work for him up there, but I don't know about it. I'd never have started with him if I'd known him. He has n't paid me a cent of wages yet, and I don't believe he intends to."

David saw that he had a friend and sympathizer in Smith.

"I'll tell you what I'm going to do," said he, "provided you're willing. I'm going to sleep in the tent to-night. If a man ever owed me a night's lodging, he's the man." And David told how he had been locked out of his own house, and cheated out of his rest.

"Well, well!" exclaimed Smith, when he heard the tale. "I just wish you could have put some lead into that dog. You'd have been perfectly justified. I guess you're entitled to rather more than a night's lodging. If the miserly old fellow had left me anything to eat, I'd see that you had a good supper and breakfast, but he took every scrap of bacon with him, and I've only flour and coffee to live on till he gets back."

"I've a pretty good chunk of bacon, but no flour," said David. "We'd better join forces. I'll contribute the bacon if you'll make some flapjacks."

Smith gladly assented, so it was not long before David was eating a supper partly at his own, but largely also at the disagreeable packer's expense. Doubtless because it is human nature to enjoy levying a just tax on a mean man, he swallowed those flapjacks and drank that coffee with peculiar zest.

The meal was no sooner finished than Smith caught sight of the truant mule on a distant hillside and set off to capture it, while David spread his blankets within the tent and presently turned in. He slept soundly till broad daylight, when he awoke with a start and found a fat ground-squirrel sitting comfortably on his breast, and eying him complacently. It ran out as soon as he stirred, and then amused itself by running up the roof of the tent on one side, and sliding down the other. Altogether it was the most lively ground-squirrel he had seen.

This day was Sunday, and aside from the principle of the thing, David would have liked to rest on account of his lameness, but circumstances were against him. It was clearly necessary that he should make an exception to the usual rule of the Bradfords, and travel throughout

## HOW DAVID MET THE OFFENDER

this Sabbath. Smith's stock of food was running as low as his own. Breakfast over, he himself had only a piece of jerked beef and two biscuits for a luncheon. His only course was to proceed.

Smith caught and saddled the poor horse, which had been a fine animal, but was now so weak with overwork, starvation, and sickness that it could hardly stand. David mounted with misgivings as to whether the tottering beast had strength to carry him, but they crossed the ford in safety. Dismounting on the farther bank, he turned the horse back into the water, and headed him for the point where Smith was standing; then shouting his thanks and a good-by, he limped off along the trail.

Twenty miles on a foot which could scarcely bear the touch of the ground! He set his teeth hard and plodded on until the pain compelled him to sit down for a brief rest. Every mile was earned with suffering. All day long the struggle continued, and it required all the grit he possessed to keep him going. Not a person did he see, though he caught sight of several horses grazing, and heard distant shouts of men who were probably searching for them. At seven in the evening he threw himself into Reitz's camp utterly spent.

## CHAPTER XXXVII

#### HOMEWARD BOUND

THE condition of David's foot obliged him to remain two days at the fishing-camp with Reitz and Humphrey, who feasted him royally on fresh-caught salmon.

Under the teaching of Reitz he soon acquired the knack of using the long gaff, tipped with an iron hook, with which the fish were caught. Standing on the bank beside one of the deeper pools of the Klukshu River, which here was little more than a brook, he would poke about the bottom with the gaff until it struck against a salmon, when by a quick and dexterous jerk the fish would be hooked and drawn up out of the water. Often the salmon were so heavy that they had to be dragged out rather than lifted, for fear of breaking the pole.

The finest variety was the king salmon, very large and with flesh of a deep pink tint. Then there was a smaller kind whose flesh was red. Not infrequently a fish was caught which, in its long journey from the sea, had been bruised and gashed on the sharp rocks. Such were unfit for food, but the healthy salmon were split and dressed and hung upon a frame of poles to dry, a smoky fire being built underneath to promote the curing and keep the flies from laying their eggs in the meat.

The Stik Indians across the stream caught the salmon not only with the gaff, but also by a weir of poles which they constructed in the brook. In this trap hundreds were ensnared, and the natives were able to take a sufficient number to supply them with food throughout the winter and spring. One of the Indian women in this family was noticeable for a spike of wood or bone set in the flesh of her chin by way of ornament.

On the third day David proceeded to Moran's Camp, accompanied by Humphrey, who carried a load of fresh salmon. Almost the first question asked of him there was, "Where are Hovey and Herrick?"

"Why," replied David, in astonishment, "I supposed they were here long ago. It's a little over two weeks since they left Champlain's Landing in the boat."

This intelligence caused a flutter of alarm in the camp of the Thirty-six, and a searching party would undoubtedly have been despatched on the following day had not the missing men turned up that evening, weather-browned and hungry, with a remarkable tale of obstacles encountered and overcome. They had been several days in forcing their heavy boat up the river to the lake, and there they had met with such continuous head-winds and rough water that progress had been difficult and dangerous, — often, indeed, impossible. They had camped for days upon the shore with little to eat, waiting for a chance to proceed, and were almost despairing when the wind providentially changed.

"Hurrah!" shouted Roly, when David appeared on Alder Creek. "You're just in time, Dave. Now we can go out with the next pack train."

David failed to grasp his enthusiastic brother's meaning until later, for he was immediately surrounded and made to sit down and relate all his adventures up to that moment. This done, he begged Roly for an explanation of his remark about going out.

"Why," said Roly, delightedly, "we're all ready to start for home. Father or Uncle Will can tell you more about the reasons." The boy seemed as eager to go out of the country as he had once been to come into it.

"Yes," said Mr. Bradford, corroboratively, "the leader of the Thirty-six wished to control the whole of the river and its tributary creeks, and instructed Mr. Scott, his second in command, to make us an offer for our claims. We thought the offer a fair one, and as we can not well winter here nor look after our claims another season, we have accepted his price."

"Good!" said David. "I'm glad to hear it."

Uncle Will added that they had made arrangements

to accompany the next pack train of the Thirty-six when it returned to the coast.

"Do you mean that we shall ride out on horses?" asked David, incredulously. The thought of such luxurious travelling after his recent hardships surpassed his wildest dreams.

"No," answered his uncle. "The horses will carry our loads, but it is n't likely we shall ride except in fording the rivers. I understand it's extremely perilous to try to cross the Alsek, the Klaheena, and the Salmon rivers without horses, and several men have been drowned this season in the attempt. Even horses are sometimes swept away. You must know that in summer these streams, fed by the melting ice and snow in the mountains, become swift, muddy torrents of far greater depth and force than in the winter. Streams which a boy could wade last March would now give an elephant a tussle. It's most fortunate that we can have the use of the pack train."

Two days later, on the fifth of August, word came that the horses had arrived at Moran's and would leave there the following evening on their return. Several of the animals were brought up to Alder Creek and loaded with the goods of the Bradfords, who of course had very little to carry out, compared with what they had brought in, since their provisions were nearly exhausted and they were to leave their tools and surplus goods of all kinds with the Thirty-six. Lucky and Coffee Jack were also to be left behind in the employment of the larger party.

On their way down the river the Bradfords paused at the tent of the scurvy-stricken Tom Moore to leave him some delicacies and wish him a speedy recovery. Here also they exchanged farewells with King and Baldwin.

Not far above Moran's Camp David discovered a gray boulder thickly studded with fossil trilobites, which he would have liked to present to the museum at home, but its great weight made its removal impossible.

Having taken leave of the Thirty-six, and of Lucky and Coffee Jack, who had served them so long and faithfully, the Bradfords followed the horses to the valley below, where they were to spend the night.

The pack train was in charge of a tall, lean, brown-whiskered man known as Bud Beagle, and two assistant packers, one of whom, a big, thick-set, good-natured Missourian, went by the name of Phil. The other, a gray-haired man named Joyce, had once kept a bookstore in one of the Eastern States, and now, after a life of varied fortunes, found himself a packer and cook on the Dalton trail.

Phil made an important find soon after the camping-place was reached. He came upon some bushes loaded with ripe red currants not far below the mouth of the gorge, and, having gathered a heaping panful, brought them to Joyce, who gladly set about making some currant preserve in the most approved style. He boiled the currants over a hot fire, added an extravagant amount of sugar, and at length produced the most delicious mixture imaginable.

As the night was fair, no tents were pitched. The blankets were spread on the grass under the open sky, and the party would have spent a comfortable night had not the weather turned frosty. So cold was it that a skim of ice formed in a pail of water which was left uncovered.

"Gentlemen," said Bud, addressing the elder Bradfords at breakfast, "if you take my advice, you'll start right away as soon as you've finished. It'll take us an hour or two to round up and load the horses, but there's no need for you to wait. It's close on to thirty mile to Dalton's, and it would be late afore you got there if you was to start right now."

Accordingly, the Bradfords were on the march before eight o'clock. They paused for a salmon dinner at Reitz's camp, where the pack train overtook and passed them, then plodded on again. It was the longest day's march in their experience, and without special incident save the meeting with a large herd of cattle and a flock of sheep bound for Dawson.

Near the trading-post a party of mounted police were

building a cabin. They hospitably invited the tired four in to supper, treating them to roast mutton, for which the recently passing flock had evidently been laid under contribution. During the meal Mr. Bratnober strolled in and entertained them with an account of a long journey to the headwaters of White River, from which he had just returned. He had been accompanied by Jack Dalton and a tall native called Indian Jack. Their object had been to find copper, and they had been successful. Mr. Bratnober exhibited several rough slabs of the pure metal as big as a man's hand, and said that he had brought back about thirty pounds of it, and could have picked up tons if there had been means to carry it. He naturally would not tell the exact locality where these riches were discovered, but said it was in a region never before explored by white men. They had not remained in the copper district as long as they had wished to do, because of a band of Indians, armed only with bows and arrows, who had made hostile demonstrations.

From the police the Bradfords learned that Dalton's store had been robbed of several thousand dollars a few days before, while Ike Martin was temporarily absent, and that about the same time two prospectors had been held up by highwaymen on the trail and relieved of considerable gold dust. Search was being made for the robbers, who were supposed to be two tough-looking characters who had been seen around the premises, and Ike Martin had started for Pyramid Harbor to put the authorities there on the watch. Ike, imprudently, as the police thought, had taken quite a sum of his own money with him, which he purposed to send to a Seattle bank.

"Have you any idea who the robbers are?" asked Uncle Will of the police captain.

"Yes," replied that officer; "we think they are two of 'Soapy' Smith's gang. The suspicious characters seen here answered the description of two of 'Soapy's' men.".

"And who is 'Soapy' Smith?" asked Mr. Bradford, who had heard the name, but could not recall in what connection.

"Why," explained the officer, "he's that chap who organized a gang of toughs at Skagway last winter and terrorized the place. Finally he insulted the wrong man, and received a quieting dose of lead; after which the citizens drove his followers out of town, and they scattered over the various trails."

Uncle Will said nothing, but the boys noticed that he puffed with unwonted vigor on his pipe and seemed to be thinking deeply. He was, indeed, thinking that it would be a serious matter to encounter those two desperadoes in a lonely part of the trail.

## CHAPTER XXXVIII

### A CARIBOU, AND HOW IT WAS KILLED

A DAY was spent at Dalton's, as it was found that several horses needed shoeing, but the following morning the pack train forded the Alsek and clattered off along the trail, while the Bradfords were ferried over the swift stream by a Stik Indian in a dug-out, — a canoe which consists of the trunk of a single large tree hollowed by fire and the axe.

The trail led through the woods, and Mr. Bradford and Uncle Will agreed that in such a region the little party of four should keep together, since the two robbers, if they were concealed anywhere in the neighborhood and still had lawless intentions, would hesitate to waylay and attack an armed party of twice their numbers. The three packers were also well armed.

The forest was left behind at noon, and they gladly ascended to the top of a range of treeless uplands where there was no cover for an enemy. Here a small pack train of oxen and horses, in charge of five or six New Englanders, was met. They had seen no suspicious persons since leaving Pyramid Harbor. When questioned about the fords of the Klaheena and Salmon

## A CARIBOU, AND HOW IT WAS KILLED

rivers, the travellers laughed and pointed to one of their number whom they called Mr. Green, as being most likely to have a vivid recollection of his experience.

"Yes," said Mr. Green, good-humoredly, "I shall not soon forget the ford of the Klaheena. You see, our pack animals are loaded down with about all they can carry, and I'm no feather-weight. Consequently, instead of mounting one of the already overburdened beasts, I crossed the two fords of the Salmon River by wading. The water was cold, but I didn't mind the wetting much, and took the precaution to hold fast to the tail of the largest ox. This plan succeeded so well at the first two fords that when we reached the Klaheena I felt no hesitancy about crossing in the same manner. I stripped off most of my clothing, took a firm hold of the tail of the big ox, and we started.

"Well, gentlemen, if you've ever seen a pickerel spoon whirl round and round when it's dragged behind a boat, you will have some idea of the motions I described when I struck that deep and rushing current. I was off my feet in a twinkling and thrashing about in the wildest manner imaginable; and if I hadn't gripped the tail of that ox with the strength of desperation, I shouldn't be here to tell about it. Even the ox was forced down the stream quite a distance, but his heavy load enabled him to keep his feet, and he hauled me out at last on the opposite bank, more scared than hurt. But next time, gentlemen, I'm going to ride."

Mr. Green's droll recital was listened to with much amusement. He now wiped from his brow the perspiration which his exciting reminiscences had induced, and added a last item of advice.

"My friends," said he, with a serio-comic expression on his round face, "don't you try swimming, either. We saw a young fellow do that, and — I swan! if he did n't go down-stream like a chip. He would reach the shore time and again and try to get hold of something, but there was nothing but loose gravel, and it gave way as soon as he touched it, and away the current would hustle him. It kept that fellow moving for a mile, and he might be going yet if he had n't been washed up on a gravel bar."

These tales of the dread Klaheena were anything but reassuring to the Bradfords; and in the imagination of the boys that river began to assume the form of a ravening monster. What with mountain torrents and highwaymen, they felt that they would be the most fortunate of mortals if they reached the coast in safety. They discovered, as many a brave man has done, that the terrors of anticipation are often far more unnerving than a real and present danger.

About the middle of the afternoon they crossed two

deep ravines, each the bed of a noisy brook, and soon afterward found themselves on the highest ridge of the bleak uplands. It was not thought necessary here to keep together, and Uncle Will and Roly were fully a quarter of a mile in advance of Mr. Bradford and David, who had paused to make pannings at the streams in the ravines.

"Keep a sharp lookout for our pack train," cautioned Uncle Will. "I think they've camped somewhere here, and we don't want to miss them."

As he spoke, he and Roly were approaching the crest of a low hill. Suddenly Uncle Will, who was leading, stopped, then threw himself at full length on the ground.

"Down, Roly, quick!" he whispered. "There's a caribou coming. Don't make a sound."

Roly dropped instantly, and the two lay there, quiet but excited, gazing at the crest of the hill not more than forty feet ahead, Uncle Will meantime drawing his revolver. Roly had no weapon but his knife, and the only kind of a shot he could take was a snap-shot, — for he happened to be carrying David's camera. Even that might not be possible, for the sun was almost in line with the game.

Fortunately the wind was blowing from the caribou's direction, and without scenting danger he trotted briskly along the trail. After a moment of thrilling suspense the two watchers saw first his antlers and then his head and body rise above the sky-line, until the magnificent animal stood full in view. He paused an instant as if to reconnoitre, which gave Uncle Will his opportunity. The report of the revolver rang out sharply.

The caribou started, looked about without seeming to discover the two crouching figures, then circled slowly off to the right as if to get the scent from the point of danger. Uncle Will fired again and with better effect, for the caribou stopped and wavered. Meanwhile Roly, camera in hand, was manœuvring for a position from which he could take a picture. Before he had succeeded, a third shot brought the caribou to his knees. He rose, struggled forward a step or two, then sank never to rise again. All three bullets had struck him, and it was found that the first, which appeared to have so little effect, had gone clear through his body, from front to rear.

"We've got him!" exclaimed Uncle Will, delightedly, as he ran toward the fallen game. "It's queer for an old hunter like me to have buck fever, but I had it that time. Did you see my hand tremble, Roly? Did n't think I could hit the side of a house. Did you get the picture?"

"No," said Roly, "not the one I wanted. The sun was right behind him."

Shouts were now heard, and three men and a horse were seen approaching, while some distance behind them in a cloud of dust galloped a party of mounted men. They all arrived on the scene together. The mounted men proved to be a squad of police in charge of a sergeant and accompanied by Jack Dalton and an Indian, all bound for Pleasant Camp; while the three men on foot were Mr. Bradford, David, and Phil. The new-comers gathered around the caribou and plied the successful hunters with questions.

"You went clean by our camp," said Phil. "Didn't you see the horses off to the left of the trail about half a mile back?"

"No," said Uncle Will, "and we looked out for them too."

"I saw you go by," continued Phil, "and shouted, and when you didn't seem to hear I started after you. Then I heard your shots and saw the caribou, and concluded you had gone ahead because you had seen the game, so I went back for a horse."

Uncle Will and Phil set to work to cut up the carcass, first removing the hide, which the former wished to preserve. A generous portion of the meat was given to Dalton and the police, who had always shown unfailing hospitality to the Bradfords; while the Indian received permission to take certain sinews and cords which are utilized in the manufacture of the native snow-shoes. The remainder of the dressed carcass was placed upon Phil's horse and taken back to the camp, where the cook took charge of it with much rejoicing.

"Venison!" exclaimed the old man, again and again, as if it were too good to be true. "No more bacon for the rest of this trip! Now we'll live like kings!"

## CHAPTER XXXIX

### DANGERS OF THE SUMMER FORDS

TWO more days were occupied in ascending the valley of the Alsek to its headwaters. The trail crossed many tributary streams, through which our pedestrians were obliged to wade, and twice it was necessary to cross the Alsek itself. Although the stream was here much narrower and shallower than at Dalton's Post, its current was still so turbulent that on each occasion the Bradfords took advantage of the pack train. Not infrequently they saw the bodies of horses and cattle which had either become hopelessly mired or had broken a leg among the rocks, and been shot and abandoned by their owners.

Beyond Rainy Hollow the summer trail was quite independent of the winter one, and led across a bleak summit now devoid of snow save the grimy remains of a few old drifts. Here they were startled by a sudden deep booming and thundering which seemed to proceed from nowhere in particular. The boys thought it an earthquake, but Uncle Will said he had no doubt the noise was similar to those they had heard in that vicinity in March, and was occasioned by a tremendous avalanche or the disintegration of a glacier on the lofty peaks across the Klaheena.

On the highest point of the pass they met an inbound pack train belonging to the Thirty-six, in charge of one Paddock.

"Is this the Bradford party?" asked Paddock, as he came up. On being assured that it was, he continued, "I was on the lookout for you. I met Bud Beagle's outfit about an hour ago, and he said you was close behind. I've got some mail for you."

He fumbled in an inner pocket of his coat, which was tied to the pommel of his saddle, and presently extracted a little bundle of letters, which he handed to Mr. Bradford.

"Mebbe there ought to be more," he said with a trace of embarrassment, "but the fact is, we lost a hoss in the Klaheena River. He carried one o' the mailbags, besides all our cooking outfit and consid'rable provisions."

"Lost the horse?" said Mr. Bradford. "How did that happen?"

"Well, you see, sir," explained Paddock, "that hoss got sep'rated from the others when we crossed the river, and he struck a deep hole. His load was jest heavy enough so he couldn't swim, and away he went. We follered along the bank for two good miles, but didn't find him."

After eagerly reading their letters, they descended the steep mountain-side and soon found themselves at Pleasant Camp, where they discovered that the mounted police had built two snug log cabins with real shingled roofs, and a corral for horses; and a roving sutler had set up a store-tent where one could buy almost anything, though the articles most in evidence were bad cigars and "tanglefoot" whiskey.

This being the boundary station of the police, they recorded the names of the Bradfords and the packers, the number of horses in the train, and various other items. Since the establishment of the station all incoming travellers had been obliged to pay customs duties at this point.

There was one person at Pleasant Camp whose arrival a few days before had awakened no little curiosity. This was a young woman introduced to the Bradfords by the police sergeant as Miss MacIntosh. She appeared to possess a fun-loving, yet quiet and ladylike disposition, while her flashing black eyes revealed unusual determination and spirit. She was travelling independently, with saddle horse and pack horse, with the object of reaching Dawson City; but her progress had been so slow and the season was so far advanced that she had abandoned her original idea, and was now intent only on reaching Dalton's Post. Owing to the difficulties and dangers of the way, she had found it advisable to travel in company with pack trains or the police, and intended to proceed with the next inbound party. She had many questions to ask about gold-mining and the Klondike, which gave Uncle Will the clue to the business upon which she was engaged.

"'I know the breed,' as Kipling says," declared Uncle Will. "I used to be a reporter myself, and I'll wager Miss MacIntosh is performing this feat in the interests of some newspaper. She's going to write all about it when she gets home."

"It's a foolhardy adventure, though," said Mr. Bradford. "I should have looked for more Scottish caution in the girl."

"On the contrary, Charles, I think she's to be admired for her pluck. She believes a self-respecting woman may go anywhere without fear, and if she travels with pack trains or the police, so as not to meet rascals like those robbers, I'm sure her confidence will be vindicated. Miners and soldiers and packers may be rough, but they all respect a lady."

The Bradfords began the descent of the Klaheena valley on the following morning, keeping to the hillsides on the left through forests far more varied than those of the interior. This part of the trail had been extensively improved by men in Dalton's employ, and in place of the narrow and uneven path over which they had picked their way, they now gloried in a smooth, hard trail al-

FORDING THE KLAHEENA

most wide enough for a wagon. Hills had been cut through, hollows filled in, small bridges thrown across several of the brooks, and corduroys of logs laid through every swamp.

At length they came down to the gravel flats and beheld, some distance below, Bud Beagle and Phil sitting on a log and evidently awaiting their appearance. Two saddle horses stood near. They had reached the dreaded ford of the Klaheena.

"We thought you wouldn't care to wade this here river," said Bud, with a twinkle in his eye, as the four approached.

"Right, Bud," responded Uncle Will; "your thinking apparatus is in perfect order. I trust you got the pack train over safely."

"Well," said Bud, slipping his quid into the other cheek, "I don't see no drownded horses anywhere."

With this reassuring remark he mounted, and invited David to climb up behind him and clasp him tightly about the body, — a performance which required some agility, owing to the restiveness of the horse. Meanwhile Roly had scrambled upon the other prancing steed behind Phil, and off they started, Mr. Bradford and Uncle Will watching their progress intently. Several side channels not more than a foot in depth were crossed before the main river was reached, but presently the horses stood at the edge of the mighty flood.

The stream was not more than two hundred feet wide, but it filled its gravelly banks to the very brim with an impetuous current so impregnated with glacial silt that it looked like a mixture of coffee and milk. It was impossible for the eye to penetrate much more than an inch beneath the surface, and as the horses stepped cautiously over the crumbling bank the boys had no idea how deep they would go.

The water proved to be shallow at first, rising only to the knees, but a moment later the bottom shelved abruptly down, the current surging higher and higher on the animals' sides till they began to yield before it, and it became necessary to head them up-stream a little. They stepped slowly and carefully, picking their footing, yet now and then stumbling on some unseen boulder. The nearness of the rushing water made the boys fairly dizzy. But just when it seemed as if they must be overwhelmed, the river grew shallower, and soon, with much scrambling, they mounted the bank.

"That was n't so bad, after all," said Roly, as he slipped to the ground.

"No," said David, "it's easy enough on horseback, but no wonder Mr. Green performed gymnastics!" And the nervous tension being now relaxed, they laughed heartily at the recollection.

Bud and Phil turned back and brought over Mr. Bradford and Uncle Will.

## DANGERS OF THE SUMMER FORDS

"The worst o' these fords," said Bud, as he landed his second passenger, "is that the river-beds are all the while changing. We may hit on a good place like this, one day, and the next time we try it we'll slump into a hole that'll raise the mischief. The bottom drops out in a single night."

In the next few miles the trail crossed the watershed separating the valley of the Klaheena from that of the Salmon River, and near the latter, camp was pitched for the night. On the march thither the horses were almost thrown into a panic by a bear which went crashing off into the bushes near the trail, but so precipitately that no one was able to take a shot.

The two fords of the Salmon River were essayed next morning. The first was for some distance of the same general character as that of the Klaheena, but it was necessary to ride with the stream a few hundred feet to round the base of a high cliff. Near these crags the water became so deep that it nearly covered the backs of the horses, but fortunately at that point the current slackened.

The second ford was reached soon afterward. This was not a crossing; the horses were forced to take to the river-bed because, for a quarter of a mile, no trail had yet been cut through the dense thickets of the shore. Here at last our travellers were destined to experience the treachery of an Alaskan river.

At Uncle Will's suggestion they did not mount behind the riders as before, but climbed upon the backs of those pack horses which carried the lightest loads. These horses had no bridles, but as they always willingly followed the packers, no trouble was anticipated. All being ready, Bud, Phil, and Joyce rode into the stream with the whole bunch close behind.

At first the river divided into so many channels that none were deep, and the cavalcade proceeded merrily down the valley, now high and dry upon the gravel, now wading a muddy runlet. The packers came at length to the point where they were to turn back toward the shore. There remained but one stream to cross, but it was a very considerable one, formed by the reunion of several channels. Beyond it rose the steep, curving bank, on which the trail was corduroyed to the water's edge.

As the packers had experienced no difficulty here on their previous passage, they rode confidently into the water, heading for the trail. Before they were halfway across they found that the stream had deepened; and as they neared the shore, first Joyce's little white mare and then both the other horses were carried off their feet and compelled to swim, while the rapid current hurried them all down-stream.

"Stop!" shouted Bud to the Bradfords, as soon as he realized the danger. "Don't try it there!"

But the warning came too late. The pack horses, with one impulse, had entered the water close behind their leaders, and among the rest those bearing the Bradfords, who had no effectual means of checking their steeds or guiding them. In two minutes every horse in the train had gone beyond his depth and was snorting and floundering in the current, or vainly trying to gain a foothold on the steep bank, while some of the more heavily laden ones, including those to which the Bradfords were clinging, borne down by their loads and the pressure of their neighbors, sank beneath the surface more than once. Several became entangled in submerged tree-roots, but cleared themselves. The whole mass of frightened, splashing, struggling animals was presently going down the stream as the steeds of the packers had done. In the midst of this confusion the Bradfords, drenched and helpless, could only hang desperately to ropes and packs, holding themselves ready, however, at a moment's notice, to abandon the horses and swim out independently.

In the mean time the packers by shouts and kicks had urged their animals close to the shore, where they succeeded in dismounting, and then pulled the exhausted beasts out of the water almost by main strength. This done, they turned their attention to the pack horses, grasping the heads of all which came near, and guiding them down to a point where the bank was lower. Some of them struggled out unaided, and all were at last brought safely to the solid ground. But blankets, packs, and men were thoroughly soaked.

"Speakin' of the bottom droppin' out," said Bud, with a dry smile, — the only dry thing which remained to him, — "this was one o' them cases."

## CHAPTER XL

### SUNDAY IN KLUKWAN

THE Salmon River was crossed on Sunday, the packers wishing to reach a good feeding-ground in the woods two miles below the Indian village of Klukwan, and not more than ten miles below their previous camping-place. This short march was accomplished before noon, and by dinner-time clothing and blankets had been dried before a huge fire.

The boys thought a visit to Klukwan that afternoon would pass the time agreeably, so having obtained permission they set off through the woods toward the gravel flats. They had some doubts as to how they should cross the Chilkat River, but upon reaching the first channel of that deep stream they found themselves within hailing distance of the town, and easily attracted the attention of the red-skinned inhabitants, who promptly despatched two canoes in their direction. One was manned by a thin old native whom they had never seen before, while the navigator of the other proved to be a short, thick-set young Indian known as Tom Williams, who had been a guide to the Mysterious Thirty-six. Tom recognized the two lads also and appeared glad to see them. He was a convert of Haines Mission, and could talk fair English.

"What will you charge to take us across and back?" asked David, presently.

In the native gutturals Tom consulted the old Indian, and then answered, "Fifty cents apiece."

This being a reasonable price, as prices run in that country, the bargain was closed. As the boys were without rubber boots and several small channels separated them from the canoes on the main stream, the Indians readily agreed to carry them on their backs to the point of embarkation.

Once in the village, David and Roly looked about them with interest. Most of the houses had been erected by the Russians and straggled in an irregular line along a narrow foot-path, facing the river. Tom Williams with his wife and family occupied one of the neatest of these dwellings, and his name appeared prominently painted near the door. Children and dogs swarmed everywhere.

"There's your African dodger, Roly," said David, as they approached the curious totem figure which had attracted their attention in March. "We must have a picture of that." The next instant the click of the shutter in the camera announced that the prize was secure.

A little farther on, an Indian whose black hair was sprinkled with gray was sitting on his doorstep. As they approached, he beckoned and made signs that they might enter the house, — an invitation which they gladly accepted, since they were curious to see something of the home life of these natives upon whom civilization had thrust at least its outward form.

The large living-room into which they were ushered had a bare wooden floor and contained several chairs, a good stove, a chest of drawers, and a table at which two women, dressed in gingham, were sewing. One was evidently the wife of the host, and the other, a plump girl of about fourteen, his daughter. They looked up as the boys entered, but said nothing, and indeed no member of the family seemed able to talk much English.

Ancient chromos of various subjects hung upon the walls, and David discovered a curious brass plate, about four inches square, bearing a figure of Saint Peter in relief with a large halo around his head. This would be an excellent memento of Klukwan, he thought, so turning to the Indian and pointing to Saint Peter he asked, "How much?"

The Indian understood this simple phrase, consulted his wife and daughter, and answered, "Four dollars."

This was more than David cared to pay; and as the owners did not seem very desirous of parting with their patron saint, he pressed the matter no further.

The incident appeared to remind the Indian that he had another interesting treasure. Going to the chest of drawers, he took out a large, time-stained document and spread it before them. It was printed in Russian, but David easily made out that it was a certificate of their host's membership in the Greek Church, — the national Church of Russia. It contained his name, which was utterly unpronounceable, and at the bottom appeared the signature of the Bishop at Sitka.

Only a brief call was made at the house of this kindly disposed man, for it was impossible to carry on any conversation. Continuing their walk, they came upon a group of young fellows seated on the ground around a checker-board and very much engrossed in that diversion, while just beyond was a similar group playing some card game which they had learned from the white men.

Near the end of the village the boys found several old iron cannon lying on the ground near the path. Evidently they had once been mounted there by the Russians for defence against the Chilkats. Stirring scenes no doubt these old pieces had witnessed, but however loudly they had spoken in times past, they were now mute, telling no tale of pioneer and savage, of stealthy attack and sturdy defence.

While they examined the cannon, a large sailing canoe had been slowly coming up the river against the strong current, and now made a landing near them. The occupants, men, women, and children, came up into the village, bearing cans full of berries, which seemed to constitute the cargo.

Perhaps it was the sight of the berries, which looked like New England huckleberries, or possibly it was the display of loaves of bread in a window, which aroused a sudden appetite in the boys, and they made inquiries by signs where they could obtain something to eat. Being directed to a neighboring house, they knocked on the door, made known their wants, and were ushered by a tall, bony native into the kitchen, where they were given seats at a table.

A fat Indian woman whom they took to be the tall man's wife set a tea-pot on the stove and brought out some old blue crockery, — the first they had seen in many months. All the while these preparations were making, a young man was sitting on the floor near the stove with his back against the wall and his hat down over his eyes, a picture of unambitious indifference. Whether he was a visitor or a member of the family, an invalid or only lazy, the boys could not determine.

The tall man and his round spouse now set forth the supper. There was real yeast bread which had a wonderfully pleasant home-like taste, there was prune pie, and cake, and tea with sugar and condensed milk, and canned butter for the bread. For this meal, which they thoroughly enjoyed and for which they would willingly have paid a larger sum, they were charged but twenty-five cents apiece.

It was now time to think of returning to camp, and, having hunted up Tom Williams and his companion, they were soon across the river, accompanied by a third native, who paddled over apparently out of curiosity and continued with them across the small channels. David and the old Indian were now considerably in advance of Roly and Tom, but when Roly had been carried over what he thought was the last channel, he paid Tom fifty cents, as he had agreed. No sooner had he done so than he beheld David being carried over another some distance in advance.

Tom was a Christian Indian, but he was no more averse to getting the best of a bargain than some Christian Yankees. He saw his advantage instantly and made a motion as if to return to his canoe. Roly scented trouble, but not having a mind to take a wetting when he had come so far dry-shod and paid for that comfort, he called Tom's attention to the channel ahead.

"Two bits," said Tom.

Now if there was anything the good-natured Roly hated, it was to wrangle over a paltry matter like that. He knew quite well that Tom was consciously taking advantage of the situation, but he preferred to act as if the Indian might really have misunderstood the original terms. He rather liked Tom on the whole, and even felt something like admiration of his shrewdness and unblushing nerve. Besides, he would never see him again, nor have any more dealings with him. The result was that Roly paid the twenty-five cents without so much as raising a question. No sooner, however, had the coin changed hands than the other Indian, who had been watching the course of events with simulated indifference, broke into a loud, triumphant laugh, — a laugh which grated harshly on Roly's ears, for it showed him that neither Indian had really expected success in so flagrant an extortion, and that instead of regarding him as a generous friend they doubtless thought him an easy victim. He heartily wished then that he had stood firmly for the agreement, or, failing to secure his rights, had taken the wetting.

The question of his proper course in the emergency was discussed pro and con around the camp-fire that evening, for Roly frankly told the story. There was very little pro and a great deal of con in the comments. The packers, who, on general principles, wasted no love on the Indians, were unanimously of the opinion that Roly should have gone through fire as well as water, rather than pay one extra penny. David was guarded in his opinion, since he had narrowly escaped falling into a similar trap. On the whole, however, he agreed with the packers. Mr. Bradford, whose sense of parental responsibility was aroused, emphatically declared that his son should have held strictly by the agreement. It would make the Indians tricky and overbearing, he said, if they thought they could outwit the whites so easily. Roly should have maintained his rights. As for Uncle Will, he seemed highly amused by the affair, but offered no views on the subject.

Poor Roly, seeing the weight of argument so heavily against him, cast about desperately for some ground of justification, and fell back at last upon the Scriptures.

"Does n't the Bible say," he asked, "'If any man will take away thy coat, let him have thy cloke also'?"

This defence hugely delighted Uncle Will. "There, Charles," said he, "you 're answered now."

Mr. Bradford laughed. "Well," he responded, "I 'll not only consider myself well answered, but I 'll give Roly a gold watch and chain if he thought of that verse when he paid that quarter."

Honest Roly sighed. "No," he said, "I did n't think of it until this minute."

## CHAPTER XLI

### THE ROBBERS AT LAST

BUD announced next morning that if two of the Bradfords would like to ride that day and were willing to help Phil with the pack train, he and Joyce would go down the river by canoe, as he had a mind to examine a likely ledge of rock on the other side of the stream. He had noticed its appearance, he said, from the trail on his journey in, and thought it might contain gold-bearing quartz.

This proposition was very welcome to the trampers, and they immediately drew lots, fortune favoring Mr. Bradford and Roly. Uncle Will and David accordingly set off on foot directly after breakfast, while Bud and Joyce departed toward Klukwan, and the other three went into the woods to find the horses, — a task which proved both long and tedious. Roly, who had taken an easterly direction, came out upon the open gravel, where he found plenty of hoofprints, but no horses. He looked carefully over the whole broad expanse and listened for the tinkle of the bell, but in vain, so he turned back into the woods toward the trail, encountering swamps and thickets which greatly impeded his progress. Mr. Bradford had no better luck, returning tired and alone. Phil, with a born packer's instinct, finally discovered the animals in a swamp in the densest part of the forest, and soon afterward brought them into camp.

Mr. Bradford and Roly, it must be confessed, were of nearly as little assistance in loading as they had been in rounding up. They knew absolutely nothing of the diamond hitch, which every up-to-date packer uses, and Phil would tolerate no other.

"You just bring up the horses and packs sep'rate," said the latter, good-naturedly, "and I'll put 'em together."

So one by one the horses were led up. The blankets and pack saddle were first placed in position, and the canvas band under the breast tightened until the animal fairly grunted. Then the packs were set in place on each side of the saddle and secured by many windings of the cinch-rope, all being finally made fast by the famous hitch, tightened by the united efforts of Phil and Mr. Bradford.

"There!" exclaimed Phil when the work was done, "now they'll pass muster.

"They may buck, they may roll, they may rub agin a tree,
But their loads will stick like — "

"Like your poet-ree," Roly suggested, after a pause.

"Haw! haw!" laughed the big Missourian. "Yes, that's it. I was going to say, 'like a bad reputation,' but that wouldn't rhyme. No matter how well I get started, I'm always floored by the second line."

The pack train was now put in motion, Phil directing his companions to ride in the rear and keep the animals from lagging. Their way lay through a wild, mountainous region. There were ascents and descents so steep that the riders were forced to dismount and lead their horses with the utmost caution, but wherever the nature of the trail permitted, the animals were urged to a gallop.

Roly and his father found it no easy matter to do rear-guard duty. There was a speckled horse called "Pinto" who made it his especial care to keep them busy. He had started in the van of the train, but, being a confirmed shirk, had gradually fallen back until there remained only a meek little white horse between him and the hindmost riders. Having gained this position, he dropped into a walk at every opportunity and was soon far behind the other horses, all efforts on the part of the amateur drivers to reach him with a switch or strap being futile. No sooner did he see them spurring up than he would jump ahead just out of reach, while the punishment intended for him — the clever rogue — fell upon the poor little white horse, whom he would not allow to pass him on the narrow trail. At the first wide clearing, however, Pinto got what he deserved, and, being thoroughly convinced that his new masters would have no trifling, he was as well behaved for the rest of the day as could be desired.

Now let us follow the fortunes of Uncle Will and David.

While the horses were being rounded up and loaded, the two pedestrians had obtained a good lead, walking as rapidly as the nature of the ground permitted, and pausing only to drink at a sparkling brook or to admire for a moment some scene of unusual beauty. They had covered several miles, and were ascending a wooded slope on the other side of which lay a deep and narrow ravine, when David broke a shoe-string and stopped to tie the ends, his uncle continuing over the crest and into the hollow beyond.

A moment later, hurrying to catch up, David also mounted the slope, and had almost reached the top when a gleam of light caught his eye, coming from the opposite edge of the ravine and a little to the right. Looking there to discover the cause, he halted abruptly. The sun had glinted on the barrel of a rifle in the hands of a man who, at that moment crouched beside a large rock, was facing away from him and motioning to some one in the woods beyond. The stranger wore fringed buckskin breeches and a red flannel shirt, and his broad-brimmed felt hat lay on the ground beside him.

There was something in the appearance and stealthy movements of this man which at once aroused David's suspicions. Instinctively he threw himself flat on the ground behind a young spruce which grew on the top of the bank, at the same time unslinging his rifle and laying it beside him. As he did so, he watched the gaudy stranger intently through the branches of the tree and tried to recall the description of the men who were suspected of robbing Dalton's Post. With every detail which he could remember, this man tallied exactly.

He glanced also to the bottom of the ravine, where he was amazed to see his uncle bending over what seemed to be a man's lifeless body. Startled and wondering, David dared not long avert his eyes from the opposite bank.

The stranger had turned, and now, kneeling behind the rock, raised his rifle to the shoulder, pointing it at the stooping figure of Uncle Will, who was all unconscious of his peril. He did this, however, with cool deliberation, since he had no idea he was watched.

There could no longer be the slightest doubt that murder had been done here, and that in another instant Uncle Will would be lying beside the first victim. David no sooner perceived the outlaw's cowardly intent than he aimed at the red shirt, and fired. At almost the same instant the other rifle was discharged, but its aim was spoiled. David had fired just in time.

Jumping to his feet with an involuntary yell, the lad saw the robber's rifle fall to the ground and the man sink backward. His confederate, hitherto unseen, immediately rushed forward, caught him, and dragged him back out of sight before David had collected himself sufficiently to fire again. Meantime Uncle Will, in the bottom of the ravine, startled by the sudden reports on each side of him, drew his revolver instantly, wondering how it happened that he could have been fired upon so closely without being even scratched. With the resolute look of a brave man at bay, he turned first toward one bank, then toward the other, not knowing how many his enemies were nor where they lurked. He caught only a glimpse of the robbers, but he saw David plainly enough as he shouted and leaped to his feet, smoking rifle in hand. The next moment Uncle Will was at his side.

"Shall we follow them?" cried David, excitedly.

"How many were there?"

"Only two, and I hit one."

But now they heard galloping hoofs, and conjectured that the uninjured man had lifted his wounded companion upon a horse and was hurrying him away to avoid capture.

"The birds have flown," said Uncle Will. Then with a quick impulse he added, "David, you have saved my life. Thanks seem very small at such a time, yet I must thank you with all my heart for a most prompt and courageous act. Give me your hand." And the two understood each other better by that silent, hearty hand-clasp than they could have done with any number of words.

They now crossed to the other bank, where David picked up the rifle as a prize of war, and the hat as an additional means of identifying the robber. Bloodspots showed that the wounded man had been dragged through the woods a distance of several hundred feet to the trail, where fresh hoof-marks confirmed the flight.

"Did you recognize that man in the ravine?" asked Uncle Will as they returned.

"No," answered David. "Do I know him?"

"It's Ike Martin, Dalton's storekeeper."

"Ike Martin!" exclaimed David, in an awe-struck voice. "Is he dead?"

"Yes, with a bullet through his brain."

It was true. They examined the body, and found that poor Ike must have been instantly killed. His money, watch, and revolver were missing. It was probable that the crime had been but just committed, the murderers not having had time to hide the body. Indeed, they both remembered hearing a distant shot.

Somewhat shaken in nerve, the two sat down to await the pack train. Upon its arrival a half-hour later, Mr. Bradford, Roly, and Phil were quickly made acquainted with the events we have narrated, and it was decided to carry the body of the storekeeper to Dalton's toll-tent a few miles beyond.

The two toll-gatherers had seen nothing of the robbers, who had doubtless taken refuge in some mountain fastness away from the trail. They were not a little alarmed to learn that they had such dangerous neighbors, and declared that but for David's wounding one of them, the toll-tent would almost certainly have been their next object of attack. As it was, there would be time to send the toll-money to Pyramid Harbor and take all proper precautions. They promised to see that Martin's body received decent burial.

By nightfall the pack train had clattered down from the mountain trail to the upper tide-flats, where camp was pitched within eight miles of the harbor. With his usual predilection for fruit, Phil went off and picked a quart of marsh-berries. They were of a yellowish-pink color, and contained a large pit which made the eating of them awkward, but when boiled with sugar they produced a sauce of very agreeable flavor.

Bud and Joyce had already arrived at the rendezvous. They had but little to say about the ledge, and the Bradfords could not make up their minds whether they had been disappointed, or had found good prospects and wished to keep the matter quiet, though the former supposition seemed the more probable. The canoeists had heard the rifle-shots, and the story of the adventure on the trail was related again for their benefit and discussed around the fire until late in the evening, David coming in for enough praise to have turned the head of a less sensible youth. All had a good word for poor Ike, too, for there was not one present for whom he had not done a good turn.

## CHAPTER XLII

PYRAMID, SKAGWAY, AND DYEA. — CONCLUSION

IN the morning, when the tide was out, the travellers crossed the long, level, sandy waste and rounded the northern point of the harbor. There lay the settlement on the farther shore at the foot of the mountains, but how changed! Where the Bradfords had pitched their first camp in March there was now an enormous tent with the word "Hotel" in large black letters on its roof, while just beyond stood a commodious frame structure which, upon closer scrutiny, proved to be a stable for Dalton's pack horses. The cannery was now in full blast, and the tall iron stacks belched forth columns of black smoke. A full-rigged ship lay at anchor in the bay. Beyond the Indian village stretched a row of frame buildings interspersed with tents, containing, as they soon discovered, a grocery, a storehouse, a post-office and store for general merchandise, and a saloon. The latter was already demoralizing the Indians, who in their cups had more than once threatened to exterminate the whole white population.

Thus, like a mushroom, had sprung into existence the nucleus of the future city of Pyramid, — for even

"Salmon by the thousand"

the name had undergone a change, growing shorter as the town grew longer.

At the cannery scores of Chinese laborers, brought from San Francisco and other coast cities, were busily cutting up and packing the salmon, which were collected by the thousand from the Indian villages of the neighborhood by the company's steamer.

A few days later the "Farallon" entered the harbor on her way north, and the Bradfords embarked, glad of the opportunity of seeing Skagway and Dyea, then only two years old, both of which were wonderful examples of American push and enterprise.

Skagway owed its size and importance largely to the fact that the White Pass trail, at the entrance to which it lay, had been completely blocked by the rush of Klondikers, who, with pack animals and hundreds of tons of supplies, had crowded upon it in the previous year without any knowledge of its difficulties. Balked in their purpose of taking up claims in the gold-fields, a great number of these people returned and staked out town lots instead, and built log cabins upon their claims. Then enterprising merchants of Seattle and Tacoma, hearing of Skagway's sudden boom, erected wooden storehouses and business buildings, and sent up complete stocks of merchandise of every description. Saloons, dance-halls, and theatres sprang up as by magic. Toughs and gamblers poured in, and United States troops were quartered there to keep the peace. So the town grew, and mainly for the reason that the original settlers could not get out of it. Finally, as if to hold their own against Dyea, whose Chilkoot trail, though rough, had remained all the while open, the Skagwayans projected and immediately commenced a railroad which should make their town, after all, the gateway to the Klondike.

Skagway was almost deserted when the Bradfords arrived, for gold had been discovered in the Atlin region, distant only a few days' journey, and a stampede had taken place. They walked through the gravelly business streets and out into the suburbs, where log cabins alternated with tents. Several streets, already lined with buildings, were thickly studded with stumps which the citizens had not yet found time to remove. Mr. Bradford bought a copy of the Skagway newspaper, in which he presently discovered among the advertisements an announcement that the Misses —— would give piano lessons at reasonable prices.

"Look at that!" he exclaimed. "Piano lessons in a place where a little more than a year ago there was nothing but a saw-mill and a few dirty Indians."

"Yes," said Uncle Will, "you can get anything here now from a first-class shave to a parlor stove. Just look in at that fruit-store window, — peaches and apples and plums, and even roasted peanuts! We're in civilization again, sure enough. Why, I even noticed a bicycle on the wharf!"

Dyea, which they visited next day, was similar in most respects to its sister town. It, too, lay in a narrow valley between rugged mountains at the head of a deep inlet. Its wharf had not been completed to the high-tide line, which, owing to the flatness of the ground, was half a mile or more inland. The town itself was about a mile back from the landing.

"We shall have to make a flying visit or the tide will cut us off," observed Mr. Bradford, as they left the steamer. "It has turned already."

The sight-seers accordingly made all haste, and, having tramped through the sandy streets, taken a few pictures, and found the town to be somewhat smaller than Skagway, they retraced their steps and none too soon. The water was already flowing around the uncompleted end of the wharf, but they jumped the rapidly widening stream. A young woman, a fellow-passenger on the "Farallon," arrived soon after. She was obliged to wade through, but escaped a serious wetting by walking on her heels. Ten minutes later the water-line was far up toward the town.

Of the voyage to Seattle, where they learned that Spain had sued for peace; of how David delighted Flora Kingsley with one of the cub bear-skins, reserving the large one for his mother and the other for Helen; of the homeward journey by way of Salt Lake City, where the boys and their elders — for Uncle Will accompanied them — saw the old Mormon tabernacle and the great new temple, and floated like corks in the buoyant brine of the lake, — space forbids an account.

Suffice it to say that all four, bronzed and healthy and happy, alighted from the train at their home city one beautiful afternoon in September, and were received with open arms and great rejoicing by Mrs. Bradford and Helen, who declared that they were bountifully rewarded for all their anxiety and loneliness by seeing their dear ones come back so strong and well.

"It has been a wonderful and profitable journey," said Mr. Bradford that evening, "in more ways than one. We are not millionaires, but we have gained in health and stored our memories with treasures."

"Yes," put in Uncle Will, "and we've turned out two as fine lads as there are in the country. If there comes another war, here are soldiers ready-made."

"Soldierly qualities," said Mrs. Bradford, with a pleased look in her eyes, "are useful also in peace."

THE END